Foreword

I first read Verne's Around the World in Eighty Days *in 1929. Between then and 1938 I reread it perhaps four or five times. I saw Todd's movie version and enjoyed it immensely, but about thirty-three years passed before I read the book again. I found it to be even more charming than I'd remembered and was amazed at how well it stood up. It's a true classic—of its own genre—though not in a class with* The Brothers Karamazov *or* Moby Dick, *of course. But I saw certain elements in it that had escaped me in my youthful reading days.*

After pondering on these elements for several months, I concluded that Around the World in Eighty Days *had two stories. One was the exterior, the easily observable, reported by Verne as an interesting but unsinister adventure tale. The other was esoteric, behind-the-scenes, and full of dangerous implications for humanity. There was a science fiction story in* Days *which Verne, the father of science fiction, had not told. He had not done so because, one, he did not know of it, or, two, he dared not reveal it, or, three, he suspected something was amiss but could only hint at it.*

Why were Fogg's origins so shrouded in mystery? Why was his life conducted as if he were a wound-up robot? Did he have a ~~_____~~ *e or a brain which c* ~~_____~~ *robability of future e* ~~_____~~ *hy did all the clocks o* ~~_____~~ *nine when Fogg got o* ~~_____~~ *?*

e Farmer

This is for the late Professor H. W. Starr, a brilliant Sherlogician who made Voyages Extraordinaries of the mind. It is also dedicated to the members of the Sherlock Holmes scion society of Peoria, The Hansoms of John Clayton.

ACKNOWLEDGMENTS

I thank Bill Starr for his permission to use some of the elements of his article, *A Submersible Subterfuge*, in this narrative-behind-the-narrative. I am also grateful to him and to the following for the permission to reprint the article as an addendum: Julian Wolff, M.D., commissionaire and editor of *The Baker Street Journal*, and Edgar P. Smith, president of *The Baker Street Irregulars, Inc.* I thank Jack Tracy, a regular Irregular, for his permission to use his dicovery of the identity of "a very tall dark man, with a heavy stoop" in his article, *Some Thoughts on the Suicide Club, The Baker Street Journal*, vol. 22 (New Series).

The Other Log of Phileas Fogg

PHILIP JOSÉ FARMER

TOR

A TOM DOHERTY ASSOCIATES BOOK

Distributed by Pinnacle Books, New York

Copyright© 1973 by Philip Jose Farmer

A Tor Book

First printing: January, 1982

ISBN: 0-523-48508-5

Cover Art by Vincent DiFate
Interior Illustrations by Rick J. Bryant

Printed in the United States of America

Distributed by
Pinnacle Books, Inc.
1430 Broadway
New York, N.Y. 10018

Introduction

How much did Jules Verne know of the real story behind *Around the World in Eighty Days?*

He could not have had all the facts. If he had, he would have been afraid to write the story in any form. Yet, he drops so many hints and ambiguities about Phileas Fogg that he must have suspected something. No other account of the famous global dash, and there were many of these, contain any such allusions or obliquities.

Did Verne get a glimpse into Fogg's secret note-book, the other log of his eighty-day voyage? It doesn't seem likely. He may have heard of it somehow and gotten from someone a few passages from it. But if he had, he would have been no more informed, though much more puzzled, than before. The secret log was written in the syllabary symbols of Eridanean A. Only one of the ancient blood, or an enemy Capellean, or a human foster-child, could read this. None of these would have imparted to a mere human the information in the strange writing.

There are always traitors, of course. Sentiency implies both loyalty and treachery.

Consider a few of Verne's hints about Phileas

Fogg. He might live a thousand years without
growing old. His admission to the exclusive
Reform Club was mysterious. The bankers Baring
had recommended him, but why did they do so?
No one knew where Fogg or his money came from.
Yet the reluctance of the upper-class mid-
Victorian Englishman to accept anyone without a
"good" family background or money is well-
known. He seemed to be a creature of absolutely
undeviating habits. Not only could the neighbors
set their clocks by his routine, they must have
wondered if he were truly human and not a clockwork robot. Certainly, he seemed either inhuman
or unhuman.

Yet he had a heart. He himself admitted that he
had one, when he could afford it. He could sit unmoving for hour after hour as if he were a big frog
watching unblinkingly for the juicy flies of time.

And had he traveled, this man who confined his
activities to a very small area of the world? He
seems to have known most of the world, even the
far-off places.

"The unforeseen does not exist," he was heard
to say more than once. Does this mean he had
clairvoyance? Or does it indicate something more
credible but far more sinister? Why did this
Englishman, fixed on a track like a locomotive of
the Great Western, suddenly jump the track and
take off across the horizon?

Why? There are many whys which Verne does
not answer.

The existence of Mr. Fogg's other log was not
known until 1947 when the house at No. 7 Savile
Row, Burlington Gardens, London, was

undergoing some repairs. This house, as everybody knows, was once occupied by the famous and witty but penniless playwright and Member of Parliament, Richard Brinsley Sheridan. He died in distressing circumstances in 1816, not in 1814, as Verne says. During the tearing down of a wardrobe wall, a small diary was found in a hollow space between two walls. This seems to have been in good condition until a hole in the roof permitted water to flow over it. Some of the pages were entirely-ruined and parts of others were illegible. Enough of the unknown writing was left to become a *cause cèlébre* among cryptographers and linguists the world over.

In 1962, the writing was recognized as neither a code or cipher but a hitherto unknown language. This would still be untranslatable if it had not been for the discovery of some notebooks in a house in rural Derbyshire. This was in the manor once owned by a Sir Heraclitus Fogg, baronet. These consisted of notes written to help an English-speaking child learn the language. With these referents, a noted linguist of the University of Oxford, Sir Beowulf William Clayton, fourth baronet, tackled the material found in No. 7, Savile Row. He managed to translate at least a third of what was left.

I was the first to hear about the translation because it was my researches* into the life of General Sir William Clayton, first baronet, father of Phileas Fogg, which enabled Fogg's childhood

* *Tarzan Alive,* A Definitive Biography of Lord Greystoke, Playboy Press, 1980.

home to be located and, hence, the illuminating notebooks.

The long-abandoned Fogg Hall was searched by my English colleague, the aforementioned linguist, a great-grandson of Sir William Clayton by his tenth wife, Margaret Shaw. Sir Beowulf's investigation resulted in the finding of the child's parallel texts and the consequent partial translations. From the notes furnished me by Sir Beowulf I have reconstructed the story behind Verne's story: *The Other Log of Phileas Fogg.*

CHAPTER 1

Phileas Fogg was said by Verne to be a bearded Byron, one who was so tranquil that he might live a thousand years without getting old. Was this statement about his possible longevity just a coincidence, a flying thought which chance happened to fit with the wings of truth?

A millennium of life was exactly what Fogg had been promised. In 1872 he was said to be about forty years of age, and so he was. But the Eridanean elixir does not effect its work until the body is about forty years old, and then it rapidly takes hold. Today, Fogg would look as if he had aged perhaps a year or two, if he is still alive. The chances are that he is alive and well somewhere in England. Can anyone point to a gravestone on which is carved his name, the date of his birth, 1832, followed by the date of his death? They cannot.

Mr. Fogg was tall and well-shaped and had a handsome face, which is to be expected from one who so closely resembles Byron. His hair and whiskers were light, which may mean in

Vernese that he was blond or had light brown hair. The color of his eyes is not mentioned by Verne. A Scotland Yard report, however, still available to the researcher who is diligent enough to dig for it, gives them as dark gray. This is to be expected in a member of a family noted for its gray eyes.

His face was pale, a natural consequence of exposure to the sun for only once a day during the time it takes to step off one thousand and one hundred and fifty-one consecutive paces. His teeth, unlike the typical Englishman's of that day, were magnificent. He had lost none to the dental decay which afflicted the people of Albion in the mid-nineteenth century. This quality, like the gray eyes, seems to have been a genetic factor. On the other hand, since he was given a number of elixirs during his child-hood, the dental health may have resulted from a drug which originated light-years and millennia away.

At the time this story opens, Wednesday, 2 October, 1872, Mr. Fogg seemed to have no relatives. He lived at No. 7, Savile Row, where the only other occupant was his valet. He had acquaintances but no close friends. His sole recreations were the walk from his house to the Reform Club, reading the newspapers, and playing whist. According to Verne, he had been living like a pendulum on a clock for many years. Actually, the "many years" were only four, from 1868 to 1872. But his presence was so full of "thereness" that people thought of him as an old fixture, like the milk wagon or even a house.

Fogg demanded that his shaving water be exactly at 86° Fahrenheit. On this morning, his man, James Forster, appeared at the right time with the water, at thirty-seven minutes past nine. He set the bowl down by the basin, and Mr. Fogg removed the thermometer from its water. It registered 84° F. There was no excuse for this deficiency. Few though his duties were, they must be performed precisely at the precise time. He was to awake his master exactly at eight in the morning. Twenty-three minutes later, he was to appear with a tray on which were tea and toast. Verne does not say that these had to be at a certain temperature, but we may assume that they had to be. Ten minutes later, Forster would remove these. There remained for him only the shaving water at 9:37 A.M. and the dressing of his master at twenty minutes to nine.

At 11:30 A.M., no few seconds given or taken, Mr. Fogg would go out the front door, and he would come back through it as the clocks of London struck midnight. Between his departure and arrival, his servant had little to do. He did have to clean up a little, arrange for a cleaning woman to come in once a week, ensure that his master's clothes were cleaned and pressed, the beds made, pay a few bills, and so on. Except for the unhuman require-ments of the schedule, James Forster was his own master.

Or was he?

Why, for instance, did Forster deliver the shaving water at two degrees less than that required? All he had to do was to check the thermometer. Why didn't he, when he knew it was so important?

The answer is that he *did* check it. Mr. Forster had waited until the temperature of the water had dropped to 86° before carrying it out of the kitchen. He knew very well that by the time he reached the bathroom on the third floor, the water would be below the desired temperature. Nor did he look perturbed when informed by Fogg that he was dismissed.

Fogg should have looked upset, since the metronome of his life had been checked. All was out of order, and while it is true that not many people would be disturbed by a mere two degree difference in their shaving water, Mr. Fogg regarded such as serious. But his serene expression changed only slightly. His eyebrows raised as if they were a pair of wings reluctantly flapped by a bird accustomed to gliding all its life. Then the eyebrows came down, and Fogg said, in a voice which was cold but not outraged, "You will leave as soon as I have acquired a new valet. You will inquire at some suitable agency for your successor, and I will interview the applicants. I will be here for that purpose until eleven-twenty-five."

Forster said, "Yes, sir. Very good, sir. And may I ask about my recommendation?"

"You have been satisfactory up to this

moment," Mr. Fogg said. "I will state that in
unmistakable terms for any would-be
employers. But I must also state exactly why I
was forced to dismiss you."

Mr. Forster did not reply, but he surely
must have been thinking that very few
employers would regard two degrees of
Fahrenheit as anything serious or even worth
commenting on.

Neither man smiled at the end of this
conversation, though it's difficult to understand how they could refrain. Though there
were no witnesses and no one could possibly
have seen or overheard them, neither let
down his guard. If there had been a hidden
camera or electronic ears, nothing untoward
would have been recorded. Of course, in 1872,
neither of these devices existed.

Or did they?

What about the very slight whirring that
could be heard in this house when neither
man was speaking? To what could that be
attributed? And what about the large mirror
in Mr. Fogg's bedroom? Could this possibly
be a one-way piece of glass, and could there be
equipment behind it, equipment which even
1972 A.D. might find very advanced indeed?

Whether or not the house was bugged, it
was certain that Fogg and Forster never said
a word or made a gesture which was not
expected from people of their class and in this
situation. There was nothing to indicate that
2°F. could be a signal for the dismissal of one
servant and the hiring of another. Or that the

famous bet made in the Reform Club was also the result of this signal.

This may be an excellent reason for Mr. Fogg's eccentricity of undeviatingness. To fire a man because he offers water two degrees off the standard is to be eccentric. Such behavior in a "normal" man would at once attract attention. But such behavior was to be expected from Mr. Fogg. Indeed, if he had not reacted as he did, he would have been regarded suspiciously by any hypothetical hidden observer.

At twenty minutes before ten, Forster assisted Fogg to dress. Fifteen minutes later, Forster left the house and took a cab to the employment agency specializing in valets, footmen, maids, and cooks for the well-to-do.

Phileas Fogg sat down in his armchair and assumed his habitual posture. His spine was straight; his shoulder blades were firmly pressed against the back of the chair. His feet were close together. His hands were placed palm down on his knees. His eyes were fixed upon a large clock across the room. This instrument indicated not only the customary seconds, minutes, and hours, but the day, month, and year. He did not move except for the rise and fall of chest associated with every living mammal, even Mr. Fogg, when he is breathing normally, and for the blinking of the eyelids. Despite what is said about the unblinking gaze of villains in the penny dreadfuls of 1872 or 1972, no one with eyesight can do without blinking. The results are too painful. And so Mr. Fogg blinked, as he would have voluntarily done even if he had not been naturally required to do so.

He doubted that there were any concealed spies, human or mechanical, in the house, but it was possible. He lived as if he were an automaton—almost like Mr. Poe's mechanical chess player—for two reasons. One, he had been taught to do so by his foster-father. Two, though he lived quietly, he did so conspicuously. There were few aware of his existence, but these few were very aware. His very standingoutness, however, was the quality to allay the suspicions of the enemy. They would believe that their enemies would be doing all they could to appear normal, to merge into the human herd. Therefore, Mr. Fogg, by his behavior, would convince them that he could not possibly be hiding from them.

Despite this theory, there was some evidence that Fogg was under surveillance. And so Fogg, whether in company or alone, always acted as Fogg should. He had done so for such a long time that he would have found it unnatural to do otherwise.

The image was he, and he was the image.

But this was to change very soon. It may be that the premonition of this, indeed, the certainty, made his heart beat faster.

Perhaps.

But was it not this man who said, "The unforeseen does not exist?" Was he, as he sat unmoving in the chair, using his brain as a computer to extrapolate the most likely of the

futures? Did his usual training as a child
enable him to switch certain neural circuits
and stimulate certain patterns in his brain
into computing unconsciously and with all
the speed of modern electronic brains? Could
he visualize the statistical chances of an
occurrence *in potentia?* Fogg never says so in
his log, but there are some statements that
sound as if he were referring indirectly to
such a talent. If he could do this, then he must
have known that he could not be sure that
such and such a thing would be inevitable.
And so, though in a sense the future contains
no unforeseens, it holds no inevitabilities. If it
did, and these could be anticipated, one side
or the other in this secret war would long ago
have acknowledged defeat. In fact, the war
might have been over before it began, since
computation would show both sides who
eventually win.

There was a rap on the door—foreseen?
James Forster opened the door and said, "The
new servant."

Why did Forster thus announce the appli-
cant? The new man had not yet been inter-
viewed, let alone hired. Why would Forster
speak as if the matter were settled? Was it a
slip on his part, and the matter had indeed
been predetermined?

If so, Fogg's expression did not change, and
Verne says nothing of Forster's. Why should
he? Verne knew nothing of what was taking
place behind the scenes.

A man entered and bowed. He was short

and stockily built; had a pleasant face with red cheeks and bright blue eyes; his hair was brown and always looked windblown.

Mr. Fogg said, "You are a Frenchman, I believe, and your name is John?"

"Jean, if monsieur pleases. Jean Passepartout . . . . "

Fogg had given the first code of inquiry when he had asked him if his name were John. And the Parisian had replied with the password when he said his name was Passepartout. Just as the name of Fogg indicated a certain role in the organization, by a happy coincidence, so Passepartout indicated his role. But the Frenchman's name was not the one with which he had been born. He had been dubbed Passepartout—"Passes everywhere"—for a good reason. It indicated more than the Frenchman's wanderlust and instability.

Passepartout, at Fogg's request, gave his background. He had been a wandering minstrel, though not necessarily of rags and tatters. He had also ridden horses in circuses, and he had danced on the high wire, like the famous Blondin. If Passepartout could emulate the feats of this fellow Gaul, as he hinted he could, then he should have stuck to the tightrope. It was Blondin who first crossed above Niagara Falls on a wire 160 feet above the water and 1100 feet long. This he did many times, blindfolded, on stilts, carrying a man on his back, sitting down on a chair and eating a meal, and so on. Only eleven years ago he had appeared at the Crystal Palace in London and there, wearing stilts, had somersaulted on a rope 170 feet above the ground.

It was not to be supposed that Passepartout was the equal of Blondin, but he may not have been far behind in skill. In any event, he had quit the high wire to teach gymnastics for a while. Then he became a fireman in Paris, but he had quit that five years before to take up valeting in England.

Surely this was a strange switch of professions, but he explained that he was tired of the dangerous and the unsettling. He desired the quiet life. He was now out of a position, but, hearing of Mr. Fogg, than whom no one led a more strictly scheduled and peaceful life, he had presented himself as a desirable valet. He did not even want to use the name of Passepartout anymore.

Mr. Fogg said, "Passepartout suits me. You are well recommended to me. I hear a good report of you."

This was strange, because from whom and when would Mr. Fogg have heard about Passepartout? Until a few hours ago, he had not even thought about getting a new servant. Since he had fired Forster and sent him out to get another servant, he had communicated with no one. He had neither inserted an ad in the papers, written a letter and received a reply, nor used the telephone. The latter he did not have, since Mr. Alexander Graham Bell was only twenty-six years old and a little less than four years from filing his patent on the electric speaking telephone.

Mr. Fogg could have sent Forster out to the nearest telegraph office, but Verne says nothing of this. No, just as Forster's introduction of Passepartout was a slip on his part, so Fogg's comment on the recommendation was his slip. The question is, were these slips intentionally made to affect the hypothetical hidden observer in a certain fashion? If the unforeseen truly did not exist for Fogg, would he have slipped? And if Fogg made a mistake on purpose, then it's safe to presume that Forster did so, too. This means that all three, Fogg, Passepartout, and Forster, were cognizant of a certain plan.

"You know my conditions?" Fogg said.

The Frenchman's answer indicated that Forster had filled him in on the way from the agency.

Fogg then asked Passepartout what time it was. The Frenchman drew an enormous silver watch from his vest pocket, looked at it, and said, "Twenty-two minutes after eleven."

"You are too slow," Mr. Fogg said.

Passepartout replied that that was impossible.

Fogg said, coldly, "You are four minutes too slow. No matter. It's enough to mention this error. Now from this moment, twenty-six minutes after eleven o'clock, this Wednesday, the second of October, you are in my service."

Phileas Fogg rose, took his hat in his left hand, put it on his head, and walked out.

Mr. Fogg was thoroughly satisfied that Passepartout was the man sent to help him in his new venture, whatever that was to be. Forster had checked him with certain pass-phrases at the agency. The bit about Passepartout's watch being slow had been another method of identification. In addition, the Frenchman's name had indicated his function, and the "enormous" watch was so large because it contained more than a time-piece. Mr. Fogg's taking his hat with his left hand had been the final signal, since he was right-handed. If he were left-handed, he would have used the right. Passepartout had observed his last confirmation and so was also pleased.

After Fogg left the room, he stood listening for a moment. The door to the street shut. That would be his ally and master leaving at exactly 11:30 A.M. A few seconds later, the door closed again. That would be James Forster going to wherever the plan dictated. There Forster would make another move in the secret and martial chess game that had been going on for two hundred years between the Eridaneans and the Capelleans.

CHAPTER 2

The Reform Club toward which Mr. Fogg proceeded at an exact velocity was only one thousand and one hundred and fifty-one paces from Mr. Fogg's house on Savile Row. Verne does not say what transpired during Fogg's walk. For him, the ordinary would not have been worth describing, and the extraordinary was not reported to him. However, the ordinary of our day and Fogg's may be contrasted for the benefit of the reader. The Londoner of 1872 had his own brand of smog. Indeed, the word, formed from smoke and fog, is of London origin. The smoke of hundreds of thousands of industrial and domestic furnaces and stoves burning soft coal often darkened the skies and laid a sooty film over everything. It also gave the London air a rather acrid odor and doubtless contributed to the generation of tuberculosis and other diseases of the lung.

Another odor, not unpleasant under certain conditions and when in not too great quantities, emanated from the horse droppings. These littered the streets from West End to East End. During the dry periods, clouds of manure rose to mingle with coal dust and dirt dust as the wheels of carriages struck the piles. Mingled with these were the huge and pestiferous horseflies that were once a familiar and seemingly permanent part of the civilized world. This, however, was October, and the chilly nights of the past few weeks had considerably discouraged the activities of these insects.

Mr. Fogg walked on the sidewalk from No. 7, Savile Row, turned left onto Vigo Street, after a few paces crossed Vigo to Sackville Street, and proceeded along it until he came to Piccadilly. Having traversed this with no apparent attention to the hansoms and vans which filled this main thoroughfare (London traffic was a nuisance and a danger a century ago), he walked eastward until he reached the narrow Church Street. Here he turned right and, coming to Jermyn Street, turned right again, walked a few paces, and then went across Jermyn to enter the Duke of York's. This led him to St. James Square. Having passed along this, he crossed Pall Mall to the Reform Club. This imposing and famed edifice is neighbor to the Traveler's Club, which admits no one as a member who has not journeyed at least five hundred miles in a straight line from London. Although Mr. Fogg could easily have joined this club both before and after his dash around the globe, he was never a member.

Across Pall Mall at an angle was the Athenaeum Club, devoted to bringing together the practitioners of the fine arts and sciences and their eminent patrons. This is the institution called the Diogenes Club in the Sherlock Holmes stories. However, at this time, Mycroft Holmes, its future member, was only twenty-six years old and his brother Sherlock was a mere eighteen. Yet, the paths of the younger Holmes and of one of the many pedestrians on Pall Mall that day were to cross many years later.

Although Fogg seemed to look neither to left nor to right, as if he were riding a rail and did not have to steer himself, he was missing little. Thus, he saw a tall, broadshouldered gentleman of about forty years of age standing in a doorway and lighting up a cheroot. Only the keenest of observers could have noted that Fogg's stride checked ever so slightly. And only a nearby and very perceptive person would have detected a minute paling of Mr. Fogg's skin.

His lips opened a tiny bit, and a name breathed out.

He did not otherwise betray himself. He walked on steadily as if he were a planet in its orbit and could be perturbed by nothing less than the sun going nova.

But behind that serene face millions of microscopic novas were exploding as neuron after neuron and neural circuit after circuit lit up. Could it indeed be *he?* Or had he been mistaken? After all, the man had been across

the street and in the shadow of a deep
doorway. The features had been
indistinguishable. The physique certainly
resembled the man whose name Fogg had
exhaled. The safety match with which he lit
his cigar could have illuminated his features
in the shadow of the doorway, but the hand
which held it shielded them. Nor could Fogg
determine if the fellow had an unusual
distance between his eyes.

Moreover, Fogg's glance had been too brief
to allow him any rechecking of his first
impression. And, the further he got from the
man, the less he thought that it could be he.
Why would he stand where he might be seen?
What purpose could he have in letting Fogg
know that he was alive and shadowing him?
Was it bravado? Or was he trying to stampede
the unstampedeable?

And how could he be alive? How had he
escaped? As far as Fogg knew, he and three
others were the only survivors. Still, at one
time he had thought he was the only one not
drowned, but he had found out later that
others had had good fortune, too. The other
survivors were French and Canadian and
there was not much chance that they would
ever see him again. To make sure that they did
not recognize him if they did encounter him,
he had grown his beard.

Despite an intensive investigation, no
evidence had been found that anybody else
had gotten away alive from the maelstrom.
However, that could mean that the Capelleans

had kept their secret a secret. They were very good at that.

Perhaps, Fogg thought, this was why everything was so suddenly upset, Forster ordered to an unknown destination, and Passepartout appearing with his distorter, the only one in the possession of the Eridaneans.

He walked on up the steps of the Reform Club. It was true that he had foreseen this possibility of other survivors, but he had calculated that the odds against this were so high as to make the event extremely unlikely.

But if anyone could survive, that fellow would be the one. He, Fogg, might have allowed his wishes to interfere with his mathematics.

CHAPTER 3

The Reform Club was political in origin, being founded by the Liberals of both houses of Parliament to help push through the Reform Bill, 1830-32. This was not what we of today would regard as a democratic measure. It redistributed the seats in Parliament, giving the new middle classes of the industrial cities the representation they had lacked, and getting rid of the "rotten boroughs." It failed to satisfy the radicals (whom we should regard as very conservative indeed by modern standards), but it was a step closer to true representative government. Why Fogg chose this club rather than another is not known. He seemed to have no interest at all in politics. At least, Verne records no opinions of his, and a diligent search has failed to find his name on any registry of voters.

The club itself was housed in a magnificent structure, the architectural style of which was pure Italian, supposedly based on the famous Farnese Palace at Rome, designed by Michelangelo. It contained six floors and one hundred and thirty-four apartments. In the center was a great hall fifty-six feet by fifty feet, as high as the building itself. Adjoining the drawing room are a library and a cardroom. It was the latter that Fogg intended as his final destination.

In the meantime, he made a scheduled stop at the dining room, the nine windows of which opened onto a garden. He sat at the table which had been laid out for him, and he ate his breakfast, for which he had to give no order since it never varied.

At thirteen minutes to one, he rose and walked to the large hall. He sat down there and a servant handed him the *Times*. Fogg cut the pages open with a small sharp folding knife and read the paper until fifteen minutes to four o'clock. Without Fogg's requesting it, he was handed the *Standard*. He then ate a dinner the menu for which deviated no more than that of his breakfast. Mr. Fogg then repaired to the washroom, an event which Verne discreetly omits to mention. Since his internal actions were as well-governed as his outer, Mr. Fogg reappeared in the reading room at the scheduled time: twenty minutes before six. He sat down to read the *Pall Mall*, and continued to do so until half an hour had passed. An acute observer, however, would have noticed that he raised his eyes from the paper more times than usual, and he might have deduced that Mr. Fogg was looking for someone. This someone, if he appeared, caused no visible reaction in Mr. Fogg.

Apparently, whatever the signal of the 2° F.

meant, events were proceeding slowly. If there was frenzy or desperation behind the plan, it was not obvious. Mr. Fogg read every word of the three publications with a remarkable swiftness. This was even more remarkable considering the lack of practice at other kinds of literature. Nobody at the club had ever seen Fogg read anything but the journals, and he certainly did not read at home since No. 7, Savile Row lacked books of any kind. And yet, he seemed to have been everywhere and to know everything about the most remote of places. From where had he gotten his knowledge?

He did not seem to be looking for anything in particular in his perusal of the papers. Yet his eyes did slow down sometimes and retrack. The delays were caused by certain items, accounts of strange happenings in every niche of the globe. They were the sort of thing put in to fill space, though certainly calculated to interest most human beings. Fogg was putting them together with other accounts in today's papers and also with those he had read in the past. He was trying to construct a coherent picture from them. He was especially interested in the stories of weird or unusual marine phenomena. Stories about sea serpents or missing or overdue ships caught his attention. Nor did he neglect the terrestrial, especially unmotivated murders or disappearances.

At ten minutes after six, five members stopped to talk before the fireplace and rid themselves of the chilliness of the autumn evening. These were Andrew Stuart, an engineer; two bankers, Sullivan and Fallentin; a brewer, Flanagan; and a director of the Bank of England, Gautheir Ralph. Mr. Fogg was aware of their presence, but, since he was not finished reading, he did not address them.

Mr. Flanagan asked Mr. Ralph what he thought about the robbery.

Stuart answered for Ralph, stating that the Bank of England would lose its money.

Ralph replied that the bank expected to get the robber. The best of detectives had been sent to all the large ports of America and Europe, and the robber would have to be very slippery indeed to elude the hawks of the law.

Stuart said, "But do you have a description?"

Ralph said, "In the first place, he is no robber."

Stuart was astounded. "What! A chap who makes off with fifty-five thousand pounds is no robber?"

"No."

"Perhaps, then, he is a manufacturer?"

"The *Daily Telegraph* reports that he is a gentleman."

No one smiled at this last remark, which was made by Phileas Fogg. He rose, bowed to his whist partners, and indulged in a conversation about the robbery. Three days before, a package of bank notes had been picked up by a gentleman from the principal cashier's table. It was not the gentleman's, but he did not return it. So, in a sense, it was his. At least, it would be until he was caught.

As Verne observes, "The Bank of England has a touching confidence in the honesty of the public." No one even knew that the fifty thousand pounds were missing until the bank was closed and the books were balanced. No guards stood by, ready to defend the institution from illegal activities. The cashier had noticed the man taking the money but had thought nothing of it until the loss was discovered.

However, the Bank of England quickly took action when it found its confidence, not to mention the money, misplaced. Detectives were hurried off to Liverpool, Glasgow, Le Havre, Suez, Brindisi, New York, and other parts. The natural zeal of the manhunters was sharpened by a reward of two thousand pounds plus five percent on the recovered sum. They were not proceeding blindly, since they had been provided with an excellent description of the gentleman who had taken the money.

Ralph, as a bank official, thought it unthinkable that the man would not soon be caught. Stuart, the engineer, disputed his conclusion, even after the whist game had started. He had for partner Mr. Flanagan, while Fogg's was Fallentin. Of course, they did not converse until after the first rubber was over. Stuart then said, "I maintain that chance favors the thief, who has to be a shrewd chap."

Ralph said, "But where can he fly to? No

country is safe for him."

Stuart exclaimed with disbelief.

"Where would he go?" Ralph said.

Stuart snorted and said, "I don't know. The world is big enough."

And having provided an opening for Fogg, he waited.

Stuart is derived from "steward," one who manages. And Stuart was an engineer in both a public and a private sense. He was, in fact, Fogg's superior, for all Fogg knew, the head of the entire Eridanean Race. He was the steward, and he was chief engineer of theRace, natal and adopted.

"The world is big enough," Stuart repeated.

Fogg said in a low voice, "It once was."

He handed the reshuffled cards to Flanagan.

"Cut, sir."

After the rubber, Stuart said, "What does your 'once' mean? Has the world grown smaller?"

Ralph said, "Indeed, I agree with Mr. Fogg. The world has grown somewhat smaller. A man can now go around it ten times more quickly than he could a hundred years ago. That is why the search for the thief is more likely to succeed."

Stuart said, "But that is also why it is easier for the thief to get away."

"Be so good as to play, Mr. Stuart," Fogg said.

No one except Stuart was aware of the double meaning in this request.

Stuart was, it must be confessed, as keen a cardsharper as could be found. Even if he had had no native talent, he would have had to be dull indeed not to have profited by one hundred and fifty years of practice. Despite his ability to crook the cards, he was always honest. That is, he was unless the occasion required otherwise. In this case, the occasion required. And so Stuart laid down as his first card that which he had selected, the jack of diamonds. To all except Stuart and Fogg, it meant that diamonds would be trumps. To Fogg it was an order to bet, to take a dare, though not with the cards. What bet, what dare? That depended on Stuart's conversation and Fogg's ability to interpret.

When this rubber was over, Stuart said, "You have a strange way, Ralph, of proving that the world has gotten smaller. Thus, because you can go around it in three months . . ."

"Eighty days," Fogg said.

Sullivan interrupted with a long explanation of why it would only take eighty days. The Great Indian Peninsula Railway had just opened a new section between Rothal and Allahabad, and this would reduce the traveling time enough to make it possible. The *Daily Telegraph* itself had made out a schedule whereby an intrepid, and lucky, traveler might proceed from London and circle the globe with enough speed to be back in London in eleven weeks and three days.

Stuart became so excited at this that he

made a false deal. At least, he seemed to be excited. Fogg knew that the trey of diamonds meant: *On the track. Go ahead.*

Stuart then said that the schedule did not take into account 'bad weather, contrary winds, shipwrecks, railroad accidents, and other likely events.

"All included," Fogg said. He had kept on playing even though the others had stopped.

Stuart was insistent. "Suppose the Hindus or American Indians pull up the rails? Suppose they stop the trains, clean out the baggage cars, scalp the passengers?"

"All included," Fogg replied calmly. He threw down his cards. "Two trumps."

The others looked surprised, not at his cards but at his talkativeness. And they found his attitude irritating. The mirror-smooth calmness and assumption of authority had been noticed by them before, but in general he was a decent chap. His peccadilloes were minor and forgivable because he was an eccentric. Englishmen then loved eccentrics, or at least respected them. But the world was much bigger then and there was room for the unconventionals.

It was Stuart's turn to deal. While shuffling, he said, "Theoretically, you're right, Mr. Fogg. But practically . . . "

"Practically also, Mr. Stuart."

Mr. Stuart had hoped that someone besides himself would initiate the bet. Since this did not now seem likely, he would have to do it. He hoped that the inevitable Capellean—who

was he? the servant nearby? Fallentin?
Flanagan? perhaps, perish the thought, Fogg
himself?—would think that the bet had arisen
naturally. Of course, they were on to Fogg
now or at least suspected him. But he did not
want them to suspect Stuart. Or, at least, to
suspect no more than they did Fallentin,
Flanagan, or Ralph.

In a somewhat indignant manner, he said,
"I'd like to see you do it within eighty days."

"That," Fogg said, "depends on you. Shall
we go?"

Stuart replied that he would bet four thousand dollars that it could not be done.

Fogg calmly insisted that it was quite
possible. One thing led to another, and so the
famous wager was made. Fogg had a deposit
of twenty thousand pounds at Baring's. He
would risk all of it.

Sullivan cried out, and we may judge the
intensity of his passions—real or assumed—
by the fact that an English gentleman would
raise his voice inside the Reform Club. He
cried out that Fogg would lose all by one acci-
dental delay.

Phileas Fogg replied with his curious, and
now classical, remark that the unforeseen
does not exist.

Stuart may have shot a warning look. Any
eavesdropping Capellean would fasten onto
this, worry it as if he were a dog and it the
bone, and find in the marrow a vast suspicion.
He would wonder if some strange hands were
being dealt by strange hands at this card
table.

Or had Stuart sent the message that Fogg was to talk suspiciously?

The latter seems more likely, since Stuart's plan was to use Fogg as a decoy. The time for laying low was over. Now there was a reason for bringing the enemy out, to mark them, and to put an end to them.

Where Stuart got his idea for exposing Fogg is not known. At least, the other log says nothing about its origin. Probably, Stuart was inspired when he read the model schedule for the eighty-day trip in the *Daily Telegraph*. Fogg would not find out until later why Stuart had decided to launch another campaign.

One of the players protested that eighty days was the least possible time to make the journey.

Mr. Fogg made another classical reply. "A well-used minimum suffices for everything."

Another protest that, if he were to keep within the minimum, he would have to jump mathematically from trains to ships and back again.

Fogg made his third classical reply.

"I will jump—mathematically."

"You are joking."

Fogg's rejoinder was, in effect, that a true Englishman does not joke about such matters.

Convinced by this, the whist players decided to accept the wager.

Mr. Fogg then announced that the train left that evening for Dover at a quarter before nine. He would be on it.

He had not known about the bet until this

hour, and he never took the train. How did he know the railway schedules? Had he memorized *Bradshaw's?* In view of his other talents, this seems probable, though he must have done it sometime before 1866, as will be made clear in due course. Thus, he had no way of knowing that trains were still adhering to the schedules of that time. But he would have checked long before boarding, and no doubt he trusted in the resistance against change inherent in the English character.

After consulting his pocket almanac, he said, "Since today is Wednesday, second of October, I shall be due in London, in this very room, on Saturday, the twenty-first of December, at fifteen minutes before nine P.M. Otherwise, the twenty thousand pounds now deposited in my name at Baring's is yours in fact and in right. Here is a check for the amount."

Mr. Fogg's total fortune was forty thousand pounds, but he foresaw having to spend half of that to win the twenty thousand. And this is so strange that it is surprising that no one has commented on it. Why should an eminently practical man, indeed, a far too practical man, one who conducted his life according to the laws of rational mechanics, make a bet like this? He was a man who had never given way to an impulse. Moreover, even if he won his bet, and this did not seem probable, he would not be a guinea richer than before. And if he lost, he was a pauper.

The only explanation is that he was under

orders to make this astonishing and unprecedented move. Even if we did not now have his secret log, we could be certain of that.

As for his forty thousand pounds, the private property of an Eridanean was at the disposal of Stuart when the situation demanded it. Stuart would have sacrificed his own fortune if it were necessary. And so, if Fogg must put his entire wealth in jeopardy, he could assure himself that it was in a good cause.

Far more than money could be lost. He could be killed at any moment. From now on, he would not be an eccentric semi-hermit living obscurely in a tiny area of London. His bet was sure to be publicized quickly. The world would soon be following his journey with hot interest and cool cash.

If Fogg was perturbed by this, he showed not the slightest sign. Of all the party, he was the calmest. The others were quite disturbed. All except Stuart felt that they were taking advantage of their friend with this bet. Stuart's agitation had another case. He knew what dangers Fogg would be encountering.

CHAPTER 4

Verne says nothing about the whist game from this point on. However, the other log does. Fogg had to let Stuart know that he had seen someone who might or might not be their old enemy. Inasmuch as he was as adept with the cards as Stuart, though he had only thirty-one years of practice, not one hundred and fifty, he had no trouble in dealing out the correct combination. Stuart's eyes widened when he saw his hand, and his lips soundlessly formed the dread name. He looked up at Fogg, who slowly lifted his head and lowered it in affirmation.

When it was Stuart's turn to deal, he gave Fogg cards the order of which said: *Proceed as directed.*

But Fogg knew that Stuart would return to his house as soon as the game was over, and the machinery of investigation would be started.

The game of surprises was not yet over. It may be that Stuart had not planned to impart additional information to Fogg. The less any individual in the Race knew, the less he could tell if he were captured and tortured. Fogg's news may have changed his mind. Fogg needed to be on guard even more than Stuart had suspected. And so, when Stuart dealt again, Fogg read a telegraphic but clear message.

The enemy had found a distorter. In China.

If Fogg were shaken by this, he did not show it, of course, and his log says nothing of his emotional state at this time. But he would have been unhuman if he had not been throbbing with curiosity. Who? How? Was this why he was being ordered to circle the Earth? Was this the reason for the inevitable publicity? Was he the decoy? Or, not actually himself but Passepartout? The enemy was to learn that Passepartout had a disorter, and they would try to get it. One distorter was no good; two were needed for transmission.

Then it occurred to him that the Capelleans did have at least one. Rather, they had had one. But this belonged to the rajah of Bundelcund, who was a traitor. According to Eridanean reports, the rajah had been ordered to give it up for use elsewhere. He had refused and so was marked for death by his former superiors. This did not mean, however, that the rajah had gone over to the Eridaneans. Far from it, as an Eridanean agent had found when he had approached the rajah to enlist him. The agent had died horribly.

No, the rajah was not pro-Eridanean. He was only pro-rajah. Intelligence said that he was mad, that he had intentions of finding another distorter, stealing it, rather, and using both in a revolt against the British. First, he would launch a secret war against the British, using his independent raj as a base of operations. The distorters would transmit thuggees, the worshippers of the goddess of death, Kali, into the fortresses and homes of the British officers. The thuggees would strangle the officers in their beds.

The native grapevine would let all India know that the rajah of Bundelcund was behind this and that he had a magical means for sending in his assassins and for getting them out. The rajah's magic could not be fought; his stranglers could go everywhere, not only in India but in the world.

Eventually, there would be another great uprising, but this, unlike the Sepoy Revolt which had been suppressed fourteen years ago, would succeed. It would not fail. At least, this is what the rajah would transmit through the grapevine, though he would know that with only two distorters he could conduct only a very limited warfare. Though the initial transmitter could be used anywhere in the world, the receiver had to be planted at the intended destination. If a Britishman were to be assassinated in his bedroom, the receiver had to be put inside the bedroom. This could be done easily enough by the Indian servants, but if the British caught on to the pattern and imposed strict security measures, planting it would become difficult. The rajah knew this and was reported to have told his closest confidant that he would kidnap Queen Victoria herself and use her as a hostage if he had to do so.

This had not only panicked the Eridaneans. The Capelleans were equally affected. The Earthmen must not discover that there existed, and had existed for two hundred years, two groups of nonterrestrial origin among them. The Earthlings would become hysterical; a relentless hunt by all the governments of the globe would be conducted. This, in the opinion of Stuart, and doubtless of the Capellean chief, could have only one end. The extermination of all Eridaneans and Capelleans. Even if a few escaped, they would have to lie low for a long long time, and the recruiting of new members by adoption or education of their own children would be very dangerous.

Stuart, while playing solitaire with Fogg as a kibitzer for a few minutes, had told Fogg this some time ago. He had also predicted that if the two parties had to be quiescent for a long time, the concept of Eridanean and Capellean would just die out. This was especially probable if all those who were non-human were caught and killed. Their human foster-children could not be depended upon to keep alive the idea of the Race and of the ultimate peril.

There were times when Fogg thought that this might be a good idea.

Then he had to upbraid himself. After all, he and the other humans of the Race were doing all this for the good of the peoples of Earth. Though he would be regarded as a traitor by human beings, if they found out about him, he was actually their guardian angel.

Meanwhile, the rajah of Bundelcund threatened the existence of both Eridanean and Capellean. Once he got hold of another distorter, he would start the first phase of his plan to sweep the British out of India. That completed, he would assume the maharajahship of all India. After that, who knew?

Fogg was well aware that his intended route around the world would bring him close to the borders of Bundelcund. Was he supposed to attempt to get the rajah's distorter?

Stuart sent no message about this.

That meant that he had no orders about that particular affair. And if an opportunity arose to get the distorter, he was free to seize it or ignore it. Perhaps Stuart was sending another agent to try for the distorter while the rajah was being distracted by the threat of Fogg. But why would he send Passepartout with Fogg? The Frenchman had the only distorter the Eridaneans possessed. Why put him near the rajah so the rajah could trap him and get his hands on what he needed most?

Of course, Passepartout's device was the one thing which would draw the rajah away from the fortress-palace of the city of Bundelcund. Though he might come out with an army of thuggees, undoubtedly would be accompanied by an army, he would not be in the rear. He would want to make sure that no one else got a chance to get his hands on the distorter. His general, Kanker, knew about the distorters, though apparently he had not been told anything about their origins. Even so, this breach of security had enraged both Capellean and Eridanean. No one, unless he were of the Blood, should have even the slightest hint of the truth. And if Kanker should get greedy and should come into possession of distorters, there was no telling what terrible things would happen.

The rajah was a very wily person, however, and he would make certain precautions to ensure that Kanker would not realize his ambitions, if he should happen to have any.

But accidents happened, and though the rajah might live to be a thousand years old, he was as subject as anyone to a bullet or to disease.

CHAPTER 5

. It was quite true, as Verne says, that Passepartout yearned for repose. He had been
almost everywhere and done almost
everything. Part of this was due to his nature;
he was not named Passepartout just because
he carried a distorter. Mostly, though, he had
gone here and there, performed this and that,
at the orders of Stuart. Now, called from his
beloved France, he had come to England and
taken up a new trade. Ten English houses had
seen him as their valet in five years. Verne
says he would not take root in any of them. He
always found his masters too impulsive and
footloose. His latest, young Lord Longferry,
M.P., had discharged him because he had
commented on his lordship's drunkenness.
That was true. But Passepartout had deliberately insulted Longferry so that he would be
dismissed. His investigations of the young
nobleman had turned up nothing suspicious.
He seemed to be as innocent of Capelleanism
as the previous nine. Passepartout wondered
why any of them had been put on Stuart's list,
but he did not question Stuart. And when he

was commanded to go to Fogg at once and offer his services, he did not ask why.

Not until he had been given a password by Forster at the agency did he suspect that this case was different. On the way in the cab, he was told more but not much. He had no idea that Fogg was going to get an assignment at the Reform Club. Forster could not have told him because Forster did not know this.

This sparseness of information indicates the strictness of the Eridanean security. It also tells of the loneliness that affected most Eridaneans. He or she had few contacts or intimacy with his or her fellows unless a marriage could be arranged or the singularities of a mission permitted such. The true Eridaneans could not even get married with the idea of having children, since the last true Eridanean female had died several decades ago. However, Stuart was zealous in trying to fix situations so that human Eridaneans could become married and so have children. Otherwise, the Race would die out, and the Capelleans would be victor by default. That is, they would have if they had not also had the same problem as their enemies.

Passepartout seldom got his orders by word of mouth. Almost always it was by code transmitted via playing cards. He would be seated in a restaurant catering to people of his class, and a man at a table by his would be playing patience. Passepartout would be observing the cards with the greatest of interest, of course. And so the cards would tell him in

telegraphic language what he was to do next.
And Passepartout would do it.

He had been in a restaurant in Tours when
the cards informed him he was to go to
London. While eating oysters in a Cheapside
inn, the cards, dealt by a red-faced, fat middle-
aged lady, told him to get hired as valet for a
Lord Windermere. This was the first of his
investigations, all of which had resulted in
nothing Capellean. But Passepartout thought
that some of the things he had uncovered
could be, probably would be, used by the Eridanean chief to the advantage of the Race.

The ninth person he'd worked for had been
General Sir William Clayton of Sallust's.
Passepartout had not ever actually valeted for
the old baronet, since Sir William was absent
from the manor of Sallust's House, Oxford-
shire. He was away somewhere in southern or
south central Africa at this time. Apparently,
he was once again looking for the site of the
ancient city of Ophir, if Sir William's wife was
telling the truth. She was a good-looking
woman of thirty-seven years of age, the
eleventh wife of the seventy-three-year-old
adventurer. Passepartout's predecessor had
been fired when he was caught drinking
brandy from the master's stock. Lady Martha
Clayton had hired the Frenchman to be the
baronet's valet when he got back from the
Dark Continent. Meanwhile, he was to be both
butler and manager of the household, which
included a maid, a cook, a gardener, Lady
Martha, an infant, William, by Sir William's

tenth marriage, and an infant, Martha, by the present wife. Passepartout used "the present" because the baronet's wives did not seem to have much survival value. Except for one who had divorced him, all had died a few years after marrying him. There was no suspicion of foul play in this series of fatalities. The baronet seemed to radiate an aura which attracted beautiful women and then scorched them. Like moths to a light, thought Passepartout.

He did not understand why women kept marrying him, since everybody seemed to know what happened to his wives. But then everybody thinks he or she is special; death isn't going to notice them.

Passepartout was puzzled by his assignment. Sir William's flamboyant lifestyle did not make him a likely candidate for Capelleanship.

Passepartout did not stay long at Sallust's House, however. Apparently, the chief was interested mainly in finding out where Sir William was and how long he would be gone. He had left the country secretly and with no word to his intimates of his destination. But his wife knew, and so Passepartout read, very late at night in the study, a letter she had written but not yet posted to a missionary friend in southeast Africa. She confided to her that Sir William was again on the old quest for Solomon's treasure city. Would her friend report anything she heard about him? Sir William, despite his age, was a remarkably vigorous man, she wrote. (As who should know better than she, who had borne him two children in the past three years, Passepartout thought.) He might be gone a long time. Meantime, their son, Phileas, had died of the colic. But if her friend happened to run into Sir William, she was to say nothing of this. Sir William must not be deterred from his quest.

Passepartout, after five years on the island, was accustomed to the eccentricity of the English. Thus, he was not surprised to find a septuagenarian baronet tramping around in the wilds of Africa after some fabled, doubtless totally nonexistent, city. He was interested when he found out that the dead Phileas was not Sir William's first child of that name. He eavesdropped on Lady Martha's conversations with her crony, the widowed Lady Jane Brandon of nearby Brandon Beeches. And he discovered that Sir William's fourth marriage, in 1832, had resulted in two children, a Phileas and a Roxana. His fourth wife, daughter of an old and noble Devonshire family, had remarried after divorcing Sir William. Lady Martha did not know whom the woman had married, since all her information was based on some scattered remarks by Sir William. She did know that Lady Lorina had hated Sir William so much that she had gotten her new husband to adopt her children. Sir William had not objected to this nor to her wish that he never see her or their children again. This was why, Lady Martha told Lady Jane, Sir William's son by

his tenth marriage would inherit the
baronetcy. His children by Lady Lorina would
inherit nothing. Of course, there had been
some legal difficulties, since the title was
supposed to go to the eldest surviving son.
But that had been taken care of.

Passepartout had thought little of this and
some additional information she had let drop.
When he had ascertained that Sir William
would probably not be back to civilization for
a long time, he was removed from the case.
After his resignation, he was sent into the
service of Lord Longferry, a Member of
Parliament and a drunk. (In those days, the
two were often synonymous.) Passepartout
was startled when he found out that Longferry's Christian name was Phileas. Could
this be a coincidence? Or was it connected, no
doubt in a sinister way, with Sir William and
his Phileases?

During his short stay with Longferry, Passepartout managed to spend some time in the
reading room of the British Museum. It was
necessary to get a recommendation for admit-
tance, but Longferry himself had furnished
this. He had laughed when his valet asked him
for it, as if a member of the lower classes and
a Frenchman at that, could not possibly be
interested in intellectual matters. But he had
consented to send down a note to the proper
authority. Passepartout had then discovered a
very definite connection between the
Phileases, though its significance had been
beyond him at that time. The grandfather of

the present Lord Longferry had been a
Phileas, the original, in fact. He had been a
very close friend of William Clayton in their
youth. Both had gone off to fight with Byron
and the Greeks in their battle for independ-
ence. Captured by the Turks, young Longferry
had died of maltreatment (probably of gang
rape by the homosexual Turks, Passepartout
thought) and of a fever. William Clayton had
grieved for a long time for his dead friend. He
had tried to perpetuate the memory of his
friend by naming two sons after him. The first
had disappeared, as far as the records went.
He looked through the newspapers of 1832
through 1836. He found a notice of Sir
William's and Lady Lorina's divorce (which
had required an act of Parliament), but he
could find nothing about her remarriage.

A record of it had to exist, of course, and
Passepartout intended to track it down. But
he was ordered, via a game of cards, to quit
his present master. He did this by severely
reprimanding the noble for having been
carried home intoxicated early one morning.
Two days later, the cards, dealt out by a
beautiful woman of twenty-five, told him to
seek immediate employment with a Mr.
Phileas Fogg.

Phileas! One more thread, no, cable, rather,
in this mysterious network. Passepartout felt
frightened. What did all these Phileases
mean? Surely an enlightenment would come
someday, and what now seemed so complex
would turn out to be laughably simple.

When he received his first message, he had assumed that Fogg was another of the long line suspected of being Capellean. But during the trip with Forster to Savile Row, Passepartout knew that he was in a different area of the case. The 2° F. signal told him that both Fogg and Strand were his kind. It only remained to be verified by the code words.

After his new master had left, he inspected the domicile carefully. As the valet, he would have done this anyway, but as an Eridanean he was obligated to, if only for the sake of survival. Verne says that the house seemed to Passepartout like a snail's shell. This is a more appropriate comparison than Verne knew. A snail's shell is not only a comfortable home but a fortress. He scoured No. 7 from cellar to garret to determine more than its layout. He wanted to know how vulnerable it was to attackers and what defenses it contained. Curiously, it was its very accessibility to intruders and its total lack of firearms or weapons of any kind which pleased him. This meant that no attacks were expected, and none were expected because its owner did not dream—apparently—that he had any special need for defense.

"Everything betrayed the most tranquil and peaceable habits," Verne says.

No wonder that Passepartout rubbed his hands and smiled. No wonder that he spoke aloud. "This is exactly what I desired! Oh, we shall get along, Mr. Fogg and I! What a domestic and regular gentleman! A real machine! Well, I don't mind serving a machine!"

He spoke aloud for several reasons. One, he was genuinely pleased. Two, his words were designed to reassure any hidden recorders or observers that he and Fogg were only what they pretended to be. Fogg was a rigidly self-controlled English gentleman, and he was a French itinerant who had finally found a snug and unchanging berth.

Passepartout should have known better. The long string of Phileases should have put him on the alert. But he so needed a rest that he allowed his emotions to overcome his logic. Imagine his consternation when his master entered the house, not at the prescribed hour of midnight but at ten minutes to eight or somewhere near that. Because of surprise and apprehension, Passepartout said nothing to Mr. Fogg as he went into his bedroom. He had to be called twice before he went into the master's bedroom. Imagine his dismay on hearing that he was to leave with Fogg for Dover and Calais inside the next ten minutes. Picture his near-collapse when he was informed that they were going to journey completely around the Earth in record time. Visualize the lights bursting in his brain and the shivers running through him when he heard that they would be traveling through India. He knew about the Rajah of Bundelcund. And they would be taking the distorter so close to him!

At eight o'clock, he was ready. Then he

almost collapsed when handed a carpetbag
containing the travel expenses. Twenty
thousand pounds in bank notes!

So it was true, and here was the result of his
investigations into the multi-Phileas! But why
had he had to make sure that Sir William
Clayton was out of reach of news from the
civilized world?

CHAPTER 6

At the end of Savile Row, the two took a cab, which drove rapidly to the Charing Cross Station. Presumably, the street at the end of Savile Row was Vigo, since to walk to Conduit would have taken them further away from their destination. The traffic must have been excessively heavy that night, and perhaps an accident delayed them. Verne says that they arrived at the station at twenty minutes after eight. Since the station is less than a mile from Savile Row, the two could have walked there more quickly. Especially since they were not overburdened. Fogg carried *Bradshaw's Continental Railway Steam Transit and General Guide* under one arm, and his valet carried the carpetbag. Though Verne states that Fogg's house contained no books, he must not have counted the *Bradshaw* as this type of literature. And if Fogg had memorized the *Bradshaw* for the English railways, he had not done so for the continent. Otherwise, he would not have transported the European guide with him. Or perhaps he had committed this to memory, too, but considered that people would think it strange if he did not use such a reference.

At any rate, we may be sure that Verne was guessing or exaggerating when he said that the cab drove "rapidly" to the Charing Cross Station.

However, it could be that Verne's transit time is correct and that something happened on the way which Fogg and his valet would have kept to themselves. Perhaps the Capelleans tried to abduct them. If this were so, then this account is missing an adventure. But Fogg did not record it, and since this is not a novel but a reconstruction of a true story, the gap will regretfully have to be left just that: a gap.

At the entrance to the station, the two were confronted by a wretched beggar woman holding an infant. They were two of the horde that roamed the streets of London. The Western capitals seldom see them now, but then they were an all-too-familiar sight, as common as they are in present-day Bogota, Colombia. The barefooted woman, shivering in the autumnal chill and its fine rain, asked for money.

Mr. Fogg had won twenty guineas at whist, and since he always donated his winnings to charity, and a not inconsiderable sum of his private fortune, he gave her the whole sum.

"Here, my good woman, I'm glad that I met you," he said.

This incident engendered tears in the softhearted Passepartout. His master, after all, was human.

Both men, as a matter of fact, being Eridaneans, were much touched by the poverty, disease, and suffering that afflicted the numerous poor of mid-Victorian England. Such a condition would be wiped out once the Eridaneans had set into motion their long-range program. The ideal society toward which they would strive would be modeled on the state which the nonhuman Eridaneans said existed on their home planet. But before that could be brought about, the evil Capelleans must be exterminated.

What Verne does not mention about this incident, but Fogg does, is what the beggar woman exchanged for money. Fogg received a small piece of paper. It was actually a tiny clipping from a newspaper. It was not only meaningless to any Earthling but of no significance to Fogg. It was a few sentences from an article on the bank theft which had been discussed that very evening at the Reform Club.

Fogg pulled out his watch and seemed to be looking at it. In reality, he was absorbing the article, which lay over the front of his watch. His cupped hand prevented anybody but Passepartout from seeing the clipping, and the good Frenchman was looking through tears at the rapidly departing beggar woman and her infant.

The article had been sent by Stuart, of course. But what did it mean? Something to do with him, no doubt, something he would find out in time, though not, he hoped, too late to do him any good.

He snapped the cover of the watch shut,
enclosing the folded article in it. Later, he
would remove the clipping and swallow it.

There are times, and this was one, when he
wished that communication could be
conducted, if not more openly, at least more
fully. The short cryptic messages often left
him as much in the dark as before, if not more
so, and invariably filled him with uneasiness.
It was true that he did not have to suffer from
anxiety unless he wished to. He could block it
off mentally and so retain his inward
composure. The price (there is always a price)
was that he had to turn the anxiety back on
someday. If he didn't, it stayed undiminished
in the circuit in which he had placed it. Its
current, so to speak, would be added to
anxieties previously shuttled in and switched
into a sidetrack.

Later anxieties would increase the pressure
even more, or, to preserve the analogy,
congest the tracks. Sooner or later, and the
sooner the better, he had to open the switch
and push some of the anxieties out into the
main track. If he didn't, he'd suffer derail-
ments, cerebral wrecks. The pain and the
brain damage would be terrible. He had been
assured of this by that old Eridanean, Sir
Heraclitus Fogg, the being who had raised
him. Sir Heraclitus knew that would happen
from personal experience and from having
observed other Eridaneans.

The baronet, long involved in a particularly

sticky situation, had blocked off his anxieties
and many of his passions. And one day, just
after he had killed two Capelleans in the Paris
sewers, he had been struck down from within.
The pain had lasted for days, and he had been
half-blind and paralyzed on his right side for a
year. Fortunately, Eridaneans, not humans,
had found him. If the latter had come along,
and he had been carried off to a hospital and
given an examination, he might have been
exposed as a nonterrestrial. This had
happened a few times before, but the Eridaneans, or the Capelleans, had heard of it
and managed to hush it up.

Fogg had been only ten at the time. He still
remembered his grief and terror when his
foster-father was brought home late at night
in a van driven by two Eridaneans. The
baronet was the only parent he had, the only
one he deeply loved. His mother had died
when he was four, slain, according to Sir
Heraclitus, by Capelleans. His real father, he
knew, had wanted nothing to do with him and
so Phileas hated him.

Not long after his mother's death, the
baronet had begun to drop hints, to tell little
stories of far-off places and distant times.
Gradually, Phileas had been shown the truth.
And so he had grown up, Earthling by
heredity but Eridanean by education, con-
ditioning, and love. He had not known how
much by love until his foster-father was
brought home from Paris. The thought that he
might die or remain paralyzed shocked

Phileas. Yet, a few minutes later, he was
acting as if nothing ever upset him. He had
blocked off the trauma. And he was still
paying for it. Sir Heraclitus, when well
enough to understand what had happened to
his foster-son, had almost had a relapse.
Quickly, he described to Phileas the results if
he did not start releasing the trauma. It would
build up as other anxieties and shocks were
added to it. One day, the suppressed hurts
would flash forth in a devastating neural
current.

What young Phileas had to do was to construct the mental equivalent of a trickle
capacitor in his circuits. Thus, he could discharge the load slowly. This would hurt, but it
would not be ruinous.

Phileas knew what a capacitor was. He had
learned about it in the laboratory in the cellar
of the manor. It was far advanced over the
Leyden jar or condenser of the time, and he
had been sworn to secrecy concerning it.

Phileas did as directed, though not always
with one hundred percent control. Unfortunately, he had set up in his neural con-
figurations a regenerative feedback. As fast as
he bled off the traumas, these bred new
energy. Sir Heraclitus was puzzled by this
and finally called in Andrew Stuart. This was
when Phileas was twelve, after the bloodsharing ceremony which made him a full-
fledged Eridanean. It had also made him a
sick one for a while, since the elder Fogg's and
Stuart's corpuscles used vanadium, not iron,

for oxygen-carriers.

Stuart had said that Phileas' traumas were feeding off early, and as yet unapproachable, traumas. These had been caused by the desertion of his real father and his mother's death. He had blocked these off through natural, though not desirable, means. And a natural block had, in a sense, to be tunneled to.

Meanwhile, Phileas was suffering the daily uneasiness, shocks, and hurts that all flesh, terrestrial or not, was heir to. Storing and discharging these occupied much of his time, and so he had never caught up with the main task. Though he had kept to a strict exterior or physical schedule these last four years, he was far behind on his interior, or psychic, timetable.

From twelve until twenty-one, he had been busy with his education. This was gotten from tutors, both human and conventional and Eridanean and unconventional. After twenty-one, he was a full-time soldier in the war that had been raging quietly for two centuries.

At thirty-six he had completed a long campaign, though as a spy. He had almost drowned but had been picked up off the coasts of the Lofoten islands by a fisherman. He returned to Fogg Hall to convalesce and await further orders. While there he grew his beard as preparation for his reemergence into the world. His foster-father had become a casualty in the campaign. His bones were on the sea floor, which was just as well if he had to die. Any doctor or anthropologist who got a look at them would be filled with curiosity quenchable only by death.

And his death had been one more great trauma to store and to trickle off later.

Even while Phileas was growing his beard, Stuart was making his long-range plans. This involved Phileas at once, but it also required a schedule which would allow him time for rest and therapy.

Why did Phileas use his own name when he rented out No. 7, Savile Row? No one knows. But in all previous campaigns he had been in disguise and using assumed names. The Capelleans certainly knew nothing of the true nature of Fogg Hall. If they had, they would have raided it. It's probable that Stuart fore-saw that, when Fogg made his bet, he would be highly publicized. Fogg would not reveal his background to any inquiring person. But if some zealous reporter or keen detective backtracked, he might find out where he came from. Stuart did not particularly want anyone to uncover Fogg's origins, but he did not care too much if they were. The humans would only find certain facts which would tell them nothing of Fogg's unhuman connections. By the time the Capelleans found out, it would be too late for them.

This was why Passepartout had been sent to determine the whereabouts of Sir William Clayton. The old baronet was the only one in all the world, outside of a few Eridaneans, who could tell the press where Phileas came

from and how he had gotten there. By the time
that Sir William returned from Africa and
heard the story of the famous dash, the Capelleans would be unable to do anything about it.
They would be dead. Or else the Eridaneans
would be dead. In either case, it did not
matter.

CHAPTER 7

As all the world knows, the story of the bet spread from the Reform Club to the newspapers. Except for the *Daily Telegraph*, the English papers declared Fogg's project to be mad. Nevertheless, there were plenty of people who believed in him enough to put their money down on him, and greater faith has no man. The depth of this sincerity may be judged by the fact that "Phileas Fogg bonds" were issued on the Exchange. Verne goes into great detail about how Fogg's stock rose and fell, so there is no need to repeat it here.

However, for those who have forgotten or who may have somehow missed Verne's book, a week after Fogg had left, his stock dropped to zero.

Mr. Rowan, the commissioner of police, Scotland Yard, received a telegram from a Mr. Fix, a detective for the Peninsular and Oriental Company, a shipping and passenger line.

I'VE FOUND THE BANK ROBBER,

PHILEAS FOGG. SEND WITHOUT DELAY WARRANT OF ARREST TO BOMBAY.

The unbelieving commissioner procured a photograph of Fogg from the Reform Club. He compared it with the description of the man who had stolen fifty-five thousand pounds from the Bank of England. The resemblances were too close to be coincidental unless Fogg had a twin. The unknown origin and background of Fogg, his nongregarious lifestyle, and his rocket-like and totally unexpected departure from England reinforced the suspicions of the police. Fogg was the one.

Fogg's train had taken the two from Charing Cross station to Dover. On the way, Passepartout suddenly recalled that he had left the gas jet in his room burning. Mr. Fogg coldly replied that it must burn—at Passepartout's expense.

From Dover the two took a boat to Calais, and a train from there through France and Italy. At Brindisi, still on schedule, they boarded the P & O ship, the *Mongolia*. This luxurious liner, fed by coal, driven by steam, docked in Suez at 11 A.M., Wednesday, the ninth of October, exactly on time. According to Fogg's notebook, the journey thus far had taken 158½ hours or six and a half days. For this period, the other log of Fogg contained only a few phrases, with some enigmatic references.

Stayed in the cabin. P— brought in the meals. Gave P— a description of N—, and P— is looking for him on the ship. Told P— that the color of N—'s eyes may be different. When I served under him, they were black. But they were covered by contact lenses. N— must have an ocular deficiency or he was wearing them to disguise the real color of his eyes. Latter seems improbable. Why would he need a disguise while aboard the N—? But he can't conceal the extraordinarily wide spacing between his eyes unless he pretends to be injured in one eye and wears a bandage. Or, more likely, a large patch over one eye. Told P— to look for these.

Should have killed N— while aboard the N— and taken the consequences. But a thousand years are not easily thrown away. Not conscience but longevity doth make cowards of us all.

At Suez, the man who had sent the telegram to Scotland Yard was waiting on the dock. Mr. Fix was short and thin and had sharp intelligent-looking features, bright foxy eyes, and eyebrows incessantly rising and falling as if subject to shock waves. He was a detective who had been sent to Suez to apprehend the Bank of England robber if he should be trying to escape via the Eastern route. Mr. Fix had been provided with a good description of the

wanted man, but he did not need it. He had
known beforehand that the thief and Mr. Fogg
looked like twin brothers. He was cursing
softly now because his superiors (Capellean,
not police) had not permitted him to "find"
and arrest Fogg the day after the theft. But no,
they wanted to make it appear that Fix had
"happened" to come across Fogg during his
walk from his house to the Reform.

All must appear natural and unforced. The
arrest could take place three or four days
after the theft; there was no hurry. First, Mr.
Fix must find an excuse for being in Fogg's
neighborhood. Then he would "accidentally"
see Fogg, note the resemblance to the thief,
and take him into custody. There was little
chance of keeping him in jail long or of bringing him to trial. This seems to have been overlooked by Verne, though he was only one of
many millions who did not consider carefully
the weakness of the case against Fogg. Aside
from the startling physical similarity of Fogg
and the criminal, there were no grounds for
charges. Mr. Fogg would have had his valet's
testimony that he had been in the house until
11:30 A.M. the morning of the theft. At least
two dozen people could testify that he had
entered the Reform Club at the regular time
and stayed there long after the theft had
occurred.

The mystery about the case is why the
police of the public paid any attention to Fix's
identification of the robber as Fogg. Any
policeman on the beat could have established

in a short time that Fogg could not possibly
have been the culprit. The only explanation
for this mistake is that the robbery occurred
in the morning and that Forster, the valet,
could not be found to testify that his master
had indeed been home that morning. Forster
must have been sent out of the country on a
mission from which Stuart could not recall
him even to save Fogg's reputation.

However, why did Fix go to Suez before he
knew that Fogg would be leaving England and
travelling on the *Mongolia?* The answer is
that, though the Capelleans often
manipulated people and events, they could
not always manage things to suit themselves.
Fix, though a Capellean, was also an em-
ployee of the police department. When
ordered by the police chief to go to Suez, he
had to go. He could have played sick and so
stayed in the country. But his Capellean
superiors must have decided that Fogg might
be apprehended by a non-Capellean
policeman.

And so Fix took train and steamer to the
Red Sea port. Meanwhile, his superiors
prepared to tip off the police through an
anonymous note. Fogg would be brought in
for questioning. If the Capelleans could
abduct Forster, Fogg would have no witness
to verify that he had been home and not at the
Bank of England. As it turned out, the Capelleans had taken too much time to carry out
the plot. Forster had disappeared, which was
fine for their plans, except that they had

hoped to get their hands on him and extract all the information he contained. But Fogg himself had left England.

We may imagine what the Capelleans did, since we are as logical as the Capelleans. This unexpected defeat of their plans might be fortunate. If Fogg were arrested by Fix, Fix would not have to turn him over to the authorities. On the journey back to England, an "escape" by Fogg would be arranged. Fogg would disappear, apparently into hiding. But he would be hidden in some Capellean secret chamber. There the same methods planned for Forster would be applied to Fogg. The original idea had been that Fogg would be held in jail for a day or two before an investigation determined that he must be innocent. But he would be "rescued." He would suppose that those who effected his escape would be Eridaneans. He would discover his error when it was too late for him.

And so Fix received a message that he should intercept Fogg at Suez. Fix was happy about this. He went at once to the British consul and informed him that a passenger who remarkably resembled the thief would soon step off the *Mongolia*. After hurrying back to the dock, he scanned every face of the disembarkers. The man he was looking for did not get off. Fogg, as we know, was discreetly staying in his cabin.

As chance would have it—or was it chance? —a passenger asked him how to get to the consulate. He was a short stocky fellow with

thick wild hair, bright blue eyes, and a slight
French accent. He showed Fix the passport he
was carrying. On reading the description
thereon, Fix was startled. It was of the man
for whom he was looking. The Frenchman,
Passepartout, was taking his master's
passport to be stamped by the consul. This
was not necessary, since this was British
territory. Fogg, however, wished to validate
the times and places of his journey so that the
bettors of the Reform Club would have no
doubt that he was not cheating. This was also
unnecessary, since his word was good enough
for his friends at the Reform.

He also, we may be sure, wanted the Capelleans to know where he was. Only thus could
he make sure that the hunters would not lose
his track.

Why, of all the people standing on the
wharf, did Passepartout pick Fix to ask the
way to the consulate? Was this not more than
a coincidence? On the other hand, how would
Passepartout have known that Fix was a
Capellean? They did not carry placards pro-
claiming their identity.

Passepartout, however, had had much
experience with the police. Just as Fix had
bragged to the consul that he could smell a
crook, so Passepartout could smell a cop. The
Capelleans, like their enemies the Eridaneans, had many of their people in the
police departments. They could be very effective there. Being lawmen, they could often act
outside the law with impunity if they were

discreet. So Passepartout may have calculated that a policeman might also be a Capellean.

It is more likely that Passepartout recognized Fix as a detective and thought that a policeman could give the proper directions. In any event, Fix directed him to the building, which was only two hundred steps away on the corner of the square. Since the British flag would have been flying over it, and there would have been signs indicating its function, it is strange that Passepartout did not see it. So, after all, he may have just been testing out the nervous little Capellean.

Fix informed the valet that, if the passport was to be stamped, its owner must appear in person with it. Passepartout returned to the ship. Fix at once hastened to the consul. He told him that he believed that the thief was on the *Magnolia.* The consul must detain Fogg when he came to have his passport visaed. Fix needed time to get a warrant for his arrest from London via telegram.

This the consul refused to do. Unless a warrant was on hand, the consul must permit Fogg to go on his way.

The master and servant shortly thereafter appeared, and Fix helplessly observed the stamping of the passport. He decided to follow the two. Fogg had returned to the cabin to eat his breakfast there, but Passepartout was around the wharf. He readily answered Fix's questions. He told him that since they had left in such a hurry, he must buy some

shoes and shirts while in Suez. Fix offered to
take him to a shop. Passepartout accepted
with thanks. On the way, the Frenchman consulted his watch to make sure he had enough
time to shop and then get back to the steamer.

"You have plenty of time," Fix said. "It is
only twelve o'clock."

Passepartout was astounded. His watch
indicated only eight minutes to ten.

"Your watch is slow," Fix said.

Passepartout exclaimed with disbelief. His
watch, he said, did not vary five minutes in a
year. It was an heirloom; it had originally
belonged to his great-grandfather. And it was
true that he was proud of the chronometer as
a perfect timepiece. But he also dangled it
before Fix to get a reaction which had nothing
to do with watches per se. It was necessary to
know if the Capellean, if he were one, suspected that a distorter was concealed therein.
Fix, however, seemed interested only in Passepartout's lack of knowledge about time zones.
He informed him that his watch was still
keeping London time. This was two hours
behind Suez time. He should regulate his
watch at high noon whenever he passed into a
different zone.

Passepartout acted as if this suggestion
bordered on sacrilege.

"I regulate my watch? Never!"

Fix patiently, if in a nervous manner, said,
"Then it won't agree with the sun."

Passepartout's reply was typically Gallic.

"So much the worse for the sun. The sun

will be wrong!"

Fix was silenced for a few moments by this vehemence and disregard for natural laws. When he recovered, he said, "You left London suddenly?"

"I believe so! Last Friday at eight o'clock in the evening, Mr. Fogg came home from his club. Three-quarters of an hour later, we were off!"

"But where is your master going?"

"Always straight ahead. He's going around the world!"

Fix was startled by this. Or, at least, he seemed to be. Perhaps his superiors had not notified him as yet of the wager.

"Around the world?"

Passepartout then told Fix that the trip must take no more than eighty days. As for him, he did not believe the reason given for this unexpected departure from the "snail's shell." There must be another reason for this madness.

This may have convinced Fix that the Frenchman was only an innocent fellow-traveler. If so, he could learn much by being friendly with this fellow.

Whatever Passepartout's role, he was certainly telling the truth about Fogg's intention of going eastward.

"Bombay, is it far from here?" Passepartout said.

"Rather far. It's ten days by sea."

"And in what country is Bombay?"

"India."

"In Asia?"

This ignorance may be excused in a peasant or an illiterate worker in the factory. But would a man whose name means "Goes Everywhere," and who has been everywhere, be so lacking in such elementary geographical knowledge? Hardly. Passepartout was merely continuing to act the role allotted to him. To reinforce this image, he told Fix of the gaslight he had forgotten to turn off. His master was charging him for this, justly, it must be admitted, which meant that he was losing sixpence a day more than he earned.

Fix did not care about the man's troubles. After saying good-bye to the valet, he sent off a telegram for a warrant of arrest. He then packed a small bag and boarded the *Mongolia* a few minutes before it left the dock. He also, we may be sure, sent a coded telegram to his superiors in London. He would receive their reply in the telegraph office in Bombay.

CHAPTER 8

The *Mongolia* was scheduled to traverse one thousand three hundred and ten miles in one hundred and thirty-eight hours. Fogg ate his four meals a day, breakfast, lunch, dinner, and supper. During this leg of the trip, he did not stroll on the decks, but he did not entirely confine himself to his cabin. If he had one passion, aside from a desire for regularity, it was for whist. This game, the precursor of bridge, was then the rage of England. He found three equally intense lovers of the cards and spent most of his time with them at the table. These were a tax collector on his way to Goa, a priest, and a brigadier-general in Her Majesty's service at Benares. All were not only excellent players but untalkative, which pleased Fogg. He may have joined them originally to determine if one of them had any message for him from Stuart. But no, all were what they appeared to be, and whist was the only thing in which they were interested.

Passepartout had informed Fogg that Fix was aboard. Fix, he said, claimed to be an agent for the P & O and was going to Bombay on business. This could be true. But what was his business? Assassinating the two, arranging for their abduction, or what? Neither were aware yet that Fogg was wanted by the law. Fogg was still puzzling over the clipping given him by the beggar woman. He would have to find some means to clarify this, but at the moment he did not know how. He could have sent a message to Stuart at Suez or Aden, where the ship also stopped en route to Bombay. It was certain, however, that Fix would find out to whom Fogg had cabled, and this would not be allowed to happen.

Fogg had a quiet talk with his valet. He quoted the newspaper article from memory. Passepartout suddenly perceived the likeness between Mr. Fogg and the description of the thief. Why Fogg, for whom the unforeseen did not exist, had not seen this before is inexplicable. The only answer is that it was unthinkable to him that anybody could associate him with anything dishonest. Though he was an Eridanean, he was also an English gentleman. Yet it was he who had pointed out to his Reform Club whist partners that the robber was no robber but a gentleman.

"What a coincidence!" Passepartout said. "Who would have thought of such a thing occurring? And expecially at this time?"

Fogg was suddenly cured of his blindness. Now that he could perceive the facts unshrouded by his egotism, he saw exactly what had happened. But Passepartout still thought that it was only an unlucky chance.

"No," Fogg said, "far from it. This has been brought about by you-know-whom. One of them was made up to look like me and sent out to steal the money. If we had not left so abruptly, I would now be in jail. Stuart saw what was going on, though I cannot understand why he did not warn me sooner."

"Perhaps he only began to think about it after the subject was brought up at the Reform," Passepartout said. "He had no time to get a message to us at our house. In any event, it would have aroused the curiosity of you-know-whom if a message had been delivered to you. So he chose the beggar woman, who may or may not be one of us. But then why did he himself not deliver the clipping when he said good-bye to us at the station?"

"Because Flanagan, Fallentin, and Ralph were also there. They seem to be innocents, that is, not you-know-whom, but he did not want to take a chance."

"But what could a mere clipping tell you?"

"He knew that I would soon see the connection. I should have known it immediately. But my pride prevented it. And though the description does fit me, in general that is, it is vague in particulars."

"What will we do?"

"Proceed as planned," Mr. Fogg calmly replied.

"But if you are arrested at Bombay?"

"All taken care of."

Passepartout did not ask him what his

plans were. He would only have received a
cold stare and rightly so. If he were to fall into
the hands of the enemy, the less he knew the
better. Nevertheless, Fogg did tell
Passepartout to encourage the drinking in the
bar with Fix. Passepartout, who had a strong
head for strong liquor, considering he was a
Frenchman, was to pretend to have his tongue
loosened by the pale ale and whiskey with
which Fix was daily plying him. He was to tell
Fix nothing except what he would have known
if master and valet were exactly what they
pretended to be.

Passepartout reported that Fix was continuing the hints he'd made during their first supposedly chance meeting on the *Mongolia.*
These were that Fogg's trip was a blind for
some other mission, possibly diplomatic. Fix
also kept urging the Frenchman to adjust his
watch to the sun. Fogg told Passepartout to
shadow Fix to determine if he was communi-
cating with anybody.

At thirty minutes after four in the afternoon, the two world travelers stepped onto
the soil of Bombay. Verne says that Fogg gave
his servant some errands to do after telling
him he must be at the railroad station at eight
that evening. And then, with his clockwork
gait, he proceeded to the passport office. He
exhibited no curiosity whatever about the
architectural wonders of this jewel of India.
This was to be expected from his character.
But it probably was also due to the fact that
he had seen them before and more than once.

Verne reports a strange incident in the restaurant of the railroad station. Fogg ordered a giblet of "native rabbit" which the proprietor highly recommended. Tasting it, he rang for the owner. Staring coldly, he said, "Is this rabbit, sir?"

"Yes, my lord. Jungle rabbit."

"And this rabbit didn't mew when he was killed?"

The owner protested at length.

Fogg said, "Remember this. Cats were once considered to be sacred in India. That was a good time."

"For the cats, my lord?"

"Perhaps for the travelers as well."

By which we know that Fogg was not altogether without a certain dry wit. But by this curious conversation Fogg had determined that the proprietor was an Eridanean and that he had seen nothing suspicious to report. There had been no doubt in Fogg's mind, or in his tongue, that the animal was what it was claimed to be. If the owner had said, "For the rabbits, my lord?" instead of, "For the cats, my lord?" Fogg would have known that the owner had something important to impart.

Fogg's own final statement signified that he had nothing else to say and that all was well as far as he knew.

This was not the first time this had occurred. When Fogg was a new member of the Reform Club, a waiter had brought a rabbit instead of the beef he always had for dinner. During the course of the conversation

—kept subdued because he did not wish the
waiter to get fired—Mr. Fogg had received
instructions. Stuart had not been able to
deliver a message via the cards because of
urgent business elsewhere. The same mix-up
with rabbits had taken place twice more but
at widely separated intervals of time. After
all, if rabbit was mistakenly brought to him
too often, some Capellean might get
suspicious.

It was not too long after the restaurant
incident that another and unfortunate
incident occurred. Passepartout, though an
Eridanean, was also human. He allowed his
curiosity to lead him into the splendidly
pagan pagoda of Malabar Hill. He was
unaware that Christians were forbidden to
enter this holy place. Not only the Brahmin
but the British law prohibited this desecration. Passepartout was forced to knock
down several priests while they were beating
him and tearing off his shoes. The latter act
was motivated by the injunction against anyone, even the faithful, wearing footgear in the
temple. Lacking these, and also lacking the
package of shoes and shirts he'd purchased,
Passepartout fled. Fix overheard the valet
explain to his master what had happened.

Fix had been about to follow them on the
train, but this changed his mind. Though the
warrant from London had not yet arrived, he
could see to it that the two were arrested for
an offense committed in India. He stayed
behind to inform the authorities of the

offenders' identity.

The two got into a carriage with Sir Francis Cromarty, the brigadier-general who had played whist with Fogg on the *Mongolia*. This looked suspicious, but if Sir Francis was either Capellean or Eridanean, Fogg did not record it. Further events validate that he was what Verne says he was. Sir Francis had observed the eccentricity of his companion and wondered if a human heart did really beat beneath that cold exterior. Also, having learned from Fogg about the bet, he considered their journey to be useless and nonsensical. Of course, he had no way of knowing that Fogg was traveling to save the world, not just to girdle it.

At eight o'clock the next evening, the train stopped some fifteen miles beyond Rothal. The conductor shouted that all passengers should get off, an announcement which amazed the three. Passepartout, sent out to inquire about it, returned alarmed. They had stopped here because the railway ended here. A further inquiry revealed a disturbing situation. No one had bothered to inform them that, contrary to what the London papers said, one could not ride the rails from Kholby to Allahabad.

Sir Francis was angry. Fogg was unperturbed. Very well. All was foreseen. Fogg knew that, sooner or later, some obstacle or other would present itself. Due to the speediness of the trip so far, Fogg had gained two days. At noon on the twenty-fifth, a

ship would leave Calcutta for Hong Kong.
That was was the twenty-second. They had
almost three days to get to Calcutta. That they
might have to go on foot for seventy miles or
more through jungle and over mountain was
not something to worry about—for Fogg.

The restless, ever curious, Frenchman,
having investigated possible means of conveyance on his own, returned with good news.
They could continue on an elephant!

They proceeded to a nearby hut where they
were introduced to a Hindu. Verne says that
Fogg talked directly to the native. This means
that the Hindu could speak some English or
Fogg used the local dialect of these Khandesh
people. Since Sir Francis might have
wondered how he, supposedly a stranger to
India, could have mastered this, Fogg must
have refrained. Possibly the general did the
interpreting and Verne did not bother to note
this. In any event, there was no language
difficulty.

Yes, the Hindu had an elephant. His name
was Kiouni. But Kiouni was not for sale or
hire. He was very valuable; he was being
trained to be a war elephant.

Mr. Fogg offered ten pounds an hour for the
use of the animal. No? Twenty? No? Forty?

Would Kiouni be for sale for a thousand
pounds?

At this point, Sir Francis took Fogg to one
side. He begged him not to ruin himself. Fogg
coldly replied that he never acted rashly. He
would pay twenty times what the beast was

worth if need be.

Twelve hundred?

No?

Fifteen hundred?

No?

Eighteen hundred pounds?

No?

When Fogg offered two thousand pounds, Passepartout almost fainted. He could hear the money in the bag boiling away.

Two thousand?

Yes!

The Indian was afraid to ask for more because he might lose it all. The sum would enable him not only to live comfortably the rest of his life but would make him the biggest man in his community.

None of the three Europeans knew how to ride an elephant nor how to keep from getting lost if they could. A young and intelligent man of the Parsi faith then offered his services. Fogg quickly accepted this, promising a large sum in payment. An hour after they arrived, the three Europeans, with the Parsi, rode off. Sir Francis and Fogg sat on each side of the howdah; Passepartout straddled the saddle-cloth between them; the mahout rode on the beast's neck.

Their guide assured them that if they went directly through the jungle, they could lop twenty miles off the journey. Passepartout went pale, because this meant entering the territory of the rajah of Bundelcund. British law did not extend into it, and if the rajah

were to discover that they were within, they
would be in for it. He stroked the watch.

Fogg did not hesitate in ordering the
shortcut taken.

At noon they had left the dense jungle for a
country covered with copses of date trees and
dwarf-palms. The pachyderm's long legs soon
left this behind, and they were on great arid
plains on which were sickly-looking shrubs
and huge blocks of syenite. This stone, Fogg
informed Sir Francis, was an igneous rock
largely composed of feldspar. It derived its
scientific name from the ancient Egyptian
city of Syene, where it was found in large
quantities.

Sir Francis merely grunted in reply. He was
hanging onto the side of the howdah, which
moved up and down with a motion like a
small boat's in a choppy sea. Passepartout
also found the motion upsetting and sickening. He had no inclination to meditate on what
would happen if they encountered Bundelcundians. If he had, he might have wished that the
meeting would be fatal, since he would rather
die than continue this ride, and would soon do
so anyway if it did not cease. Then they did
see some natives, and these gestured
threateningly. The Parsi, however, urged the
beast to a faster speed, and the Hindus did not
try to pursue them.

By eight that evening, they had crossed the
principal chain of the Vindhya Mountains.
They stopped at a ruined bungalow to rest in
it for the night. The elephant had carried them

for twenty-five miles, twice as fast as they
could have gone on foot in this rough country.
Allahabad now lay only another twenty-five
miles away.

Verne says that the Parsi built a fire against
the cold night and that they then ate the
provisions they had brought from Kholby.
This is confirmed by Fogg's secret log. They
resumed, as Verne says, at six o'clock next
morning. But Verne's account of the time
intervening is not at all accurate. The guide,
according to Verne, watched the sleeping elephant. Sir Francis slept heavily. Passepartout
dreamed uneasily of the jolting journey. Fogg
slept as peacefully as if he were in bed in No.
7, Savile Row.

This is not a likely picture. Anybody who
has for the first time in a long time ridden all
day on a horse would know how sore they
would be and how hard sleep would come.
Magnify the soreness and fatigue by a third
and add to that the inevitable distress
occasioned by eating the food of tropical
jungle aborigines, and you have an excellent
idea of their state. The truth, as revealed in
the other log, is as follows.

CHAPTER 9

Though their trip had been speedy, it had not been nonstop. All three Europeans had frequently required the Parsi to halt the elephant while they dashed into the bushes. Toward the end of the day even the imperturbable Fogg looked ·pale. Before they went to bed, master and servant stepped out into the thick jungle to perform certain bodily functions they felt almost too weak to perform. Fogg listened serenely, if sympathetically, to Passepartout's groans, moans, and complaints until they were finished with their duties—or hoped they were.

He said, "Have you been checking your watch, as I impressed on you that you should?"

"But certainly . . . . "

"And?"

"And nothing! No signals of any kind! Which is indeed fortunate! If there had been, then we would be certain that that pig of a rajah . . . "

"Speak more quietly," Fogg said. "It would be easy for someone to approach unnoticed in this dense forest."

"Pardon, sir, but it is possible that I did not hear the tiny gong which announces that another . . . "

"Do not use that word."

" . . . another, er, watch, is activated and broadcasting. The noise made by the beast's motion and the creaking of the howdah, not to mention our groans, made it difficult to hear."

"It's quiet enough now."

"Except for the screaming and chattering of those monkeys and the yelling of those birds. And the Parsi says that we will hear leopards and tigers tonight."

"It will be quiet enough in the bungalow," Fogg said. "You will keep the watch beside your ear tonight."

"But certainly! I had planned to do just that. And if the signal comes?"

"We will answer it."

"Name of a pig!"

"In our own fashion," Fogg said. "However, there is one way we can assure that it is sent."

"Assure it?" Passepartout said. He had been pale before: now he looked as white as one of the demons in the legends of the Hindus.

"There is no need to repeat myself. When the others have gone to sleep, you will set it on *transmit*."

Passepartout's eyes swelled like a pouter pigeon's chest.

"But why? We will be instantly whisked . . . "

"I am not finished. You will do this very briefly. Flick it off and on and then wait. If, in ten minutes, there is no indication that another device is on, you will repeat the *transmit*. For a half-second only. You will repeat this pattern for two hours, after which I will take over."

"What do you plan? What could we do if we did get a signal?"

"That is arranged," Fogg said. "If you get a signal before your two hours are up, wake me at once."

Passepartout did not like the idea of having to stay awake when he was so tired. He discovered, however, that he would not have been able to sleep in any event. His muscles felt as if they were ropes which had been used to lift heavy stones all day; his bones, it seemed to him, had been twisted as if someone had been trying to make corkscrews out of them. His nerves were like harp strings which vibrated to every sound as if they were sounded by ghostly hands. The sudden maniacal laughter of birds, the screaming of some large animal far-off—a leopard?—and a distant roar—a tiger?—made him jump as if Fogg had kicked him. Soft slitherings and rustlings in the thatch of the ceiling did not contribute to his relaxation. And the apprehension with which Fogg's unknown plans filled him built up like dough in an oven.

He heard the Englishman's regular

breathing and wondered how he could go to
sleep so soundly and so quickly. Sir Francis
was quietly groaning and turning every few
minutes; evidently, he was finding it difficult
to drop off. What if the brigadier-general
were still awake when, or if, a signal came?

After a while, unable to lie still, the Frenchman arose and stepped outside the bungalow.
The moon had risen and was shedding an
effulgent light on the hillside. The vast bulk of
Kiouni and the small body of the mahout-
guide were black under the shade of a giant
tree about twenty yards away.

A loud cracking made him leap a few inches
off the ground. His heart accelerated. Were
the thuggees approaching through the bush
with their garrots in hand, intending to
strangle the foreigners and so sacrifice them
to the goddess Kali without the spilling of
blood? Was a wild elephant coming toward
them with a vast malice in its vast heart? Was
a herd of the dangerous wild buffalo or
savage wild pig about to attack them?

Passepartout sighed, and his tired heart
beat more slowly. No, it was only Kiouni tearing off a branch of the tree to feed his huge
stomach. He munched while his belly
rumbled as if it were a distant but mighty
cataract.

Verne says that Kiouni slept all night, for-
getting that the poor beast had been traveling
all day and had had nothing to eat. Kiouni
needed sleep, but needed food more, since an
elephant requires several hundreds of pounds

of forage a day to maintain his strength. Kiouni had gone to sleep, standing up, for several hours after arriving. Now hunger pangs had awakened him, and he was eating, indifferent to the noise he was making or its possible interference with the sleep of the humans.

Though the mountain air at night was cold, Passepartout perspired heavily. *Mon dieu!* he thought. What could they do if they were transported into the heart of the rajah's palace? Their only weapons—pitifully tiny— were the jackknives he and Fogg carried. And would not the rajah be prepared for them? Would he not have many of his soldiers lined up around the distorter, all armed with rifles and swords? Would not he, Passepartout, and his mad master be helpless to resist capture or slaying? Far better to be killed at once. To fall into the hands of a Capellean meant days of the most terrible torture. Ah, if he did not quit perspiring he would catch a cold which would quickly transform itself into a fatal pneumonia.

Look! The Parsi, who had said he would stand watch over his beast, had lain down on the ground and was even now snoring so loudly that he could be heard through the elephant's stomach stormings. Wretched creature! Had he no sense of duty? How could the Parsi sleep while he, Passepartout, suffered? Was all the world asleep except for the sinister predators of the jungle, the voracious Kiouni, and himself?

He held the watch up to his ear and listened. It emanated nothing but its steady ticking, measuring Time, the shadow of Eternity, while Passepartout and the universe grew older. But the universe, though doomed to die eventually, would be here a long long time after Passepartout had become dust and less than dust. Dust which a tree would draw up within its woody body and which some elephant would strip off and digest in its stomach and then eject and which the ground, not to mention some bugs and birds, would eat and then eject. So Passepartout, in a million dissociations, would go through eternity being taken in and driven out, though, thank God, unconscious of all the indignities and nastinesses. Unless the Hindus were correct and he, as Passepartout, a whole, would be reincarnated again and again.

Yet he could live in his body for a thousand years if he escaped accident, homicide, or—here he crossed himself, since though an Eridanean he was also a devout Catholic—he killed himself. Why throw away a millennium by allowing himself to be sucked into the trap assuredly set by the rajah of Bundelcund? Was this not suicide, and was not suicide unforgivable? Would Fogg agree to this reasoning, this inescapable logic, if it were set before him?

Alas, he would not!

But perhaps the rajah had no intention of sending out a distorter wave. Perhaps he was sensible and was snoozing away at this very moment, no doubt in the soft arms and on the soft breasts of some beautiful houri or whatever the Hindus called their wives. That would be much more rational than sitting up late at night and sending out signals. But men, alas, were not always—or, in fact, were seldom—rational.

As if to affirm this conclusion, the watch emitted a ringing sound.

Passepartout jumped again, and his heart thumped as if it were a trampoline on which fear was performing. The dreaded had indeed happened!

For a second, Passepartout thought of keeping the news to himself. But, despite his terrors, he was a courageous man, and it was his duty to inform the Englishman. First, though, he must send the return signal.

As soon as the ringing stopped, he pushed down on the stem of the watch and quickly twisted it one hundred and eighty degrees to the right and then set the hands on the prescribed numbers. Immediately after, he returned the hands to the correct time—his correct time, anyway—and returned the stem to its original position. Then he hurried into the bungalow to wake Fogg up.

Fogg awoke easily and was on his feet at once. After listening to Passepartout's excited whisperings, he said, "Very well. Now, here is what we shall do."

Passepartout had been as pale as moonlight on still waters. Now his skin looked like that moonlight after it had been passed through a bleach. But when Fogg was through talking, Passepartout obeyed at once. His first task was made easier because the Parsi was still sleeping soundly and soundily. His snores were terrible enough to frighten off a tiger. Passepartout led Kiouni away. When they were half a mile down the southern slope of the mountain, the two men climbed up the rope ladder and rode him the rest of the way. Kiouni did not like being taken away from his feeding, but he did not trumpet. He went slowly because his eyes could not pick out obstacles easily in the moonlight. Also, he had to be careful about stepping into holes. The weight of the beasts is such that even a four-inch misstep may break their legs.

About an hour later, the two were at a distance which Fogg judged sufficient. Passepartout dismounted; Fogg remained on the elephant.

"But will not Sir Francis and the guide be able to hear the sounds even from here?" Passepartout said.

"Possibly," Fogg said. "However, the mountain itself and much forest is between us. They should deaden the sounds. They may believe they are hearing a distant temple bell. In any event, there is nothing they can do about it. When we return, we shall tell them that the elephant ran away and we went after it."

Passepartout shivered. *"When* we return . . . !"

It would be more realistic to say "if," not "when." Nevertheless, he admired the optimism of the Englishman and deeply hoped that it was not ill-founded.

During the journey, Passepartout had three times swiftly adjusted the watch to send out signals. The received signals were now coming every twenty seconds.

"Set it so it will go on *transmit* in five minutes from now," Fogg said. "But make sure that its field is wide enough, since it must include Kiouni. And make sure that it will automatically go on *receive* five minutes after its transmit mode is terminated."

Passepartout, his teeth chattering, opened the back cover of the watch and set it as directed, turning three tiny knobs. He placed the watch in a small hole he had dug in the ground with his knife. It was necessary that the device be below the ground level of those to be teleported. Also, the hole would keep the elephant from accidentally stepping on it if he should move, though Passepartout hoped that the beast would stand still. If he did take too many steps in any direction, he and his riders might find themselves cut in half.

He scrambled back up the rope ladder and pulled up the rope after him. He coiled it on the floor below one of the howdah seats. Mr. Fogg was already sitting on the neck of the beast. He had closely observed the command words and hand and touch signals used by the mahout. He used them now as if he had been in the profession for years. So far, the animal had obeyed him. Would it continue to do so when it suddenly found itself elsewhere and surrounded by hostile humans?

Passepartout, unable to consult his watch, mentally counted off the seconds. He was sitting on the saddle between the howdah seats, his unfolded jackknife in his hand. He felt pathetically helpless, and he wondered what the nine hundred and sixty years of life that he was throwing away would have been like. Ah, to see what 2842 A.D. held for him! Or even 1972! When the Eridaneans had exterminated the verminous Capelleans, then they could change the world. Would it take more than a hundred years? Would not Earth be a paradise, a veritable Utopia, with all war, crime, poverty, disease, and hatred wiped out forever? Why should he be denied the fruits of his labor because of this madman whose placid back was now before him?

But if a cause is to win, it must do so over the bodies of martyrs, as someone, probably an Englishman, had once said. It was his misfortune to be one of those martyrs. Still, a martyr should not sacrifice himself unless the cause could profit by it. There would be no profit to anybody tonight except the rajah of Bundelcund.

Yet, had not Fogg said that, for him, the unforeseen did not exist?

But what if he had foreseen that the rajah would die but they would die too?

No, Fogg was a gentleman, and he did have a kind heart. He would not ask his servant,

and his colleague, to be killed also. Not unless
it was necessary. Passepartout thought, his
heart drooping now like a flag on a breezeless
day. But what could they do with only small
knives against rifles and spears?

"Ah, *mon* . . .

And they were there . . . *Dieu!*

Fogg had not been as blind as Passepartout
had thought. A spy had long ago managed to
report where and in that manner the distorter
was located and guarded. Fogg had not told
Passepartout about this simply because he
was not sure that the situation had not
changed since the report. It would not do to
have Passepartout all set for one environment
and suddenly be faced with the unexpected. It
might throw him too much off balance. The
poor fellow was in a state of terror as it was.
Indeed, Fogg would have left him behind if he
had not been sure that Passepartout would be
thoroughly capable once the action began. No
genuine coward would have survived to the
age of forty in this secret war. Nor would
Stuart have entrusted his mission to anybody
who had not proved himself many times over.
To fear is not to lack courage.

His main concern was the behavior of
Kiouni. His training as a war elephant was
only half-completed. Even a seasoned old
veteran might go into hysterics.

The transit was made instantaneously.
There was no sense whatsoever of passage
through time or distance. Their ears were
battered with a great clanging as if they were

standing a few inches below a bell as large as
the bungalow. Its sound was shattering, and
Fogg and his aide, though holding the jackknives with their fingers, had to thrust the
ends of their thumbs into their ears.

Kiouni bolted; his trunk was raised and he
was, seemingly, shrilling panic through it. He
could not be heard above the hideous
clanging, which, as always, tolled nine times.
This auditory phenomenon accompanied the
operation of a distorter at both the receiving
and transmitting ends. The site of the watch
they had left behind would be loud with nine
clangs, loud enough to carry faintly to Sir
Francis and the Parsi even with some miles of
mountain and forest deadening it.

The theory accounting for the noises was
that the distortion of the space in the area
around the devices caused a condensation and
bending of the electromagnetic field of the
Earth itself. The return to a normal state
resulted in atmospheric disturbance and
consequent clangings. This theory was
disputed, but it did not matter what made the
noises. They were unavoidable and, unfortunately, acted as an alarm.

Fogg saw at a glance that the rajah had not
moved the distorter since the report. Its
location was something that only an Oriental
would dream up.

They were in a vast room lit by thousands of
gas jets. It soared perhaps six stories, ending
in a great white dome. The room itself was
circular with a diameter of perhaps two

hundred yards. Its circumference was set
with over three hundred tall and narrow archways—a quick estimate—with a mosaic walk
about ten feet wide inside it. This ran completely around the chamber. The walk was set
about an inch above the level of the great pool
that constituted most of the surface level of
the place. The floor was mostly a body of
water, and in its center was a circular islet of
smooth red marble. This had a diameter of
forty feet. Kiouni and his riders had appeared
in its exact center, though they did not stay
there long.

Kiouni had begun running madly almost at
once around and around the edge of the islet.
Elephants are splendid swimmers, but even in
his panic he had not cared to plunge into the
water. The reason, Fogg perceived as he rode
around and around, was the large number of
large crocodiles in the pool.

Fogg set himself to calming the beast. While
engaged in this seemingly hopeless business,
he felt a tap on his shoulder. He looked back
and then upward. Passepartout was pointing
at the ceiling. Fogg saw a square of blackness
appearing in the center of the white dome.
From it, suspended on a cable, a car was
descending. Six dark faces topped by white
turbans stared over the sides of the car.

Fogg looked at the archways around the
walk. They were still empty.

Passepartout then pointed at the center of
the islet. He indicated what they had missed
before because the bulk of the elephant had

been between the rajah's distorter and the two men, and both had been too occupied since to look for it.

The device must have been set in the circular depression in the center of the islet. Certainly, it had not just been placed in the hole so the newcomer merely had to stoop over to pick it up. It would be placed within a defense of some kind. What alarmed Passepartout was that the distorter, contained in a watch, was disappearing. It had been placed on top of a cylinder set about an inch below the level of the islet's surface. Now the cylinder was sinking swiftly into the shaft.

The islet must be hollow with a room beneath the surface. Men below were operating the machinery which raised and lowered the cylinder of stone. They would remove the device from the top of the cylinder and take it to a safe place. Then the rajah's men would take care of the intruders.

Kiouni had not slowed down in his circular dash. There was no more time for endeavoring to control him. Fogg gestured at Passepartout to take his place, and he rolled off the neck of the beast. His agility would have drawn applause from the professional acrobat, Passepartout, under different circumstances. But the Frenchman was too busy hanging on.

As Fogg slid down the gray wrinkled side, he pushed himself away, landed facing the elephant's side, fell back, but kept on walking backwards and so saved himself a hard fall on

the marble. Whirling then, he yanked from a
vest pocket a watch, twisted its stem, looked
down into the hole, and dropped the watch.
From first to last, despite his swiftness, he
managed to perform with an air of unhurried-
ness, of perfect aplomb.

The men above him and the men below may
have, undoubtedly did, cry out. he could not
have heard them since his ears were still
ringing. But he did look up and saw, not unexpectedly, that five in the car were brandishing sabers and one was holding a rifle. This
looked like a modern rifle, perhaps the
Mauser adopted by the Prussian army only
the year before. Those in the car could see
that the invaders had no firearms. Since no
smoke had resulted from his dropping of an
object into the shaft, they must have believed
that, if it were a bomb, it had failed to go off.
Possibly, they had not seen him drop the
watch, since his body had been between them
and the shaft. Nor would they believe they
had to shoot the intruders; they were trapped.
They could take their time, dispose of the
elephant if it failed to calm down, and
overpower the men. Meanwhile, the rajah
would have retrieved the distorter in the
room.

Fogg believed that the rajah was down
there, since it was unlikely that he would
allow anyone but himself to handle the
invaluable device. In fact, Fogg was certain
that there was only one man below, the rajah.
The fewer who saw the distorter, the better. It

would be, in the eyes of the Hindus, a magical device, one that many would do anything to possess.

Mr. Fogg turned, having extracted and set another watch. With a smooth motion, he tossed it upward into the car, which was now about two and a half stories above the islet. The actions of those he could see became very agitated. Two dived out of the car into the pool. The car disappeared in a spurt of flame surrounded by smoke. The blast was dimly heard by the two men and Kiouni, but they felt it as if it were a giant hand slapping them. Bits of thin steel and flesh and bone rained over them.

Fogg was knocked off his feet. Passepartout came tumbling off Kiouni's neck. The elephant whirled and began running in the opposite direction along the edge of the islet. Passepartout fell without injury, rolling on the floor and coming up on his feet as if at the end of an act. His hair was wilder than ever, and his blue eyes were huge. Fogg returned to the hole in the center while smoke from the explosion, blown downward at first, rose around him. He knelt down and looked into the shaft. The watch case, for it had contained no watch, could be set to explode its contents or to convert them into a gas. This would be expelled at a high rate of speed to fill any small chamber. Its effect dissipated almost immediately so that he did not have to fear breathing the air coming up from the shaft.

Mr. Fogg's face kept its serenity, but his log

records his astonishment and alarm at what
he saw. The cylinder had continued to sink
into the shaft in the floor of the room below.
Even as he watched, it stopped with its top
about three feet above the floor. Beside it lay
a short, stocky dark-skinned man dressed in
gorgeous garments. His wrists and fingers
were covered with bracelets and rings
bearing pearls and jewels that only a very rich
rajah could afford. His hair and beard were
gray, and his hook-nosed face was wrinkled.
Fogg knew that the gray and the wrinkles
were only makeup. Rajah Dakkar of Bundelcund had not wanted his agelessness to be
rumored about. Such a story would have
brought him to the attention of the Eridaneans far sooner than it had, and the British
might have become aggressive if they thought
he had a secret for prolonging life.

The rajah had opened the lid of the cylinder
before it had stopped sinking. If it had not
been for the anesthetic gas, he would have
been out of the room by now with the distorter. But the device, encased in a big golden-
plated watch with several inset diamonds, lay
nine feet directly below Fogg. He only had to
remove from around his waist the magnet and
the long thin silken cord to which it was
attached and to drop it straight down. The
gold covering would not be affected, but the
steel plates and the steel works within would
be sufficiently magnetized. And then he could
pull the treasured object up by the cord.

But a man was standing by the marble

cylinder and reaching out for the device.
Something stopped him, perhaps a sense
which told him that he was being observed.
He looked upward. Fogg did not cry out,
though how even he kept his self-control is
difficult to understand. He knew the man. His
beard was gone, and the eyes were no longer
black but a dark gray. Fogg might not have
recognized him now if it had not been for the
extraordinary width between the eyes.

The man was now wearing the uniform of
an officer of Her Majesty's Indian Sappers,
which accounted in part for Fogg's failure to
recognize at once that he had seen him only
recently. Once the effect of the uniform
passed, Fogg saw the resemblance between
him and the man he had seen standing in the
doorway near the Reform Club. Yes, it was he.
The man he had served under, the man in the
doorway, the man now about to take the distorter were the same. But how had he arrived
ahead of Fogg? Had he come via a distorter?

The man mouthed one word, faintly.

"Fogg!"

So, he did not recognize Fogg as a former
member of his crew. If he had known, would
he not have wanted to let Fogg be aware that
he had penetrated his disguise?

Fogg uttered the man's name softly.

"Captain Nemo!"

CHAPTER 10

Fogg records in his secret notebook many things that were puzzling about this man's presence, though he had no time to think of them then. Why was he, a Capellean of good standing as far as Fogg knew, with the traitor rajah? Or had he talked Dakkar into believing that he himself had become a traitor? How had he gotten here? Why had he not been overcome by the gas?

The last could be accounted for by a quickness in running out of the room when the watch fell. Or perhaps he had been outside and had just entered.

Fogg let the magnet fall down the shaft onto the watch. Nemo had no weapons; his holster was empty. Doubtless, the rajah permitted no one except the most trusted guards to be armed in his presence. Nemo, acting on his reflexes, shot his hand toward the non-existent gun, realized the situation, cried out —Fogg heard it faintly—and dodged away. Fogg could no longer see him. But if he believed that the watch was another bomb, gas or explosive, he would leave the room and

perhaps slam the door behind him. Yes, there
was a muffled slamming noise. But he might
come back at once. He might be behind armed
men whom he'd sent into the room to
determine if the watch case held anything
deadly. Or, quick thinker that he was, he
might perceive the significance of the cord
attached to the case, guess it held only a
magnet, and would come charging back in
with a gun.

He would also be sending armed men into
the huge room. Fogg was surprised that none
had appeared by now; at any moment he
expected to hear the explosions of rifles. He
glanced up and looked around. No figures
were emerging from the archways. So, the
rajah had wanted as few people as possible to
be near the distorter. He had had faith that a
few men in the car above and he and Nemo
below could take care of the Eridaneans.

But the soldiers would soon be here.

Now another distraction occurred.
Passepartout was pulling one of the men out
of the water who had dived out of the car. He
was doing it with all possible speed to get out
of the way of Kiouni, still racing along the
perimeter. The explosions had frightened the
huge saurians in the water long enough for
one man to get away. The other had not been
so lucky. Some crocodile, quicker to recover
than the others, had seized him. Only the
roiling of the water as the crocodile turned
over and over, trying to tear a leg or arm off,
showed where the man was.

Fogg had not time to shout at Passepartout to abandon the man if the elephant came around too fast. He turned his attention back to the shaft, lifted the magnet again, swung it a little to one side, and dropped it. This time it fell squarely on the rajah's watch, and Fogg drew it up swiftly.

Before he had gotten it out of the hole, he saw the face of the rajah, now recovered, directly below him. It was contorted with rage, and he held in his hand a Colt revolver. He pointed it upward. Fogg could either drop the device and fall back out of the way or be shot. In fact, even if he dropped it, he might not get away in time.

The rajah's face passed from rage to triumph. Fogg decided that he would have to try to dodge. If he continued to draw up the device, he would be shot anyway. His only chance, not a very good one, was to throw himself to one side at the same time yanking up on the cord. If he did not get the distorter away from the rajah, then he was stuck here. And he would be stuck later in various unpleasant ways.

The rajah cried out in English for him not to move or he would get a bullet between his eyes.

Fogg wondered how the rajah knew he was an Englishman. He also wondered if the rajah's reputation as a marksman was deserved. Next to a certain Captain Moran of the Indian Army, the rajah was supposed to be the best hunter in India.

He had just made up his mind to throw himself to one side, since death was better than being captured alive in any event. A shadow fell on him. Something half-dark and half-glittering sped down the shaft. As if it had sprung out of some hidden magician's compartment on his body, the handle of a knife was sticking out of the rajah's throat. He had had to lean backwards to point the gun up and so had left his throat exposed.

Dakkar's eyes glazed, and he crumpled. As his revolver hit the floor, it discharged. There was a shout, and a soldier fell into view face down. He must have been struck by the ricocheting bullet.

Fogg serenely pulled the magnet and device up, turned the magnet off by pressing the stem on the watch case which held it, pocketed the case, reset the magnet, and lowered it down the shaft again. He then proceeded to draw up the revolver.

"Where did you get that throwing knife?" he said.

"From a man whom I rescued from the crocodiles," Passepartout said. "Alas, not reptiles but a pachyderm was what he should have feared."

He pointed at a gruesome object, what was left after Kiouni had found him lying in his path. The beast had stopped running now, but it was still trumpeting, and its eyes looked dangerous. Its feet and trunk and tusks were splashed with blood.

"Splendid," Fogg said, and Passepartout

smiled with pleasure.

"I learned more in the circus than just to tumble and to walk a high wire, sir."

"Obviously."

"So what now, sir, if I may presume?"

"There is a very dangerous man in the palace," Fogg said. "If he were in London, he would be the most dangerous man there. Or anywhere. He should be killed, but that is impossible now. Indeed, if we do not make an expeditious retreat, we shall be the ones to suffer death. Still . . . "

"Yes, sir?"

"Never mind. We must not test probabilities too far. Ah, I see the soldiers are coming through the archways. Get up on the elephant quickly."

"Without a rope ladder, sir? Besides, he does not look as if he would give permission, ladder or not."

"If he will not give permission, we leave without him."

Fogg removed another watch from his pocket. He set it and placed the magnet between it and the distorter. The three were now bound together by the magnetic field. He lowered the trio into the shaft a few inches. He had nothing to put on the cord to keep the three objects from slipping further except the body of the trampled man. He did not have time to drag the corpse to the shaft and place it on the cord. The first fire from the guns of the soldiers was ringing in the dome. Fortunately, the Bundelcundians were excited and were, probably, poor marksmen to begin with, as were many of the ill-trained natives of that day. Moreover, only five had rifles; the rest were equipped with matchlock muzzle loaders, unrifled weapons with not much accuracy. But as soon as enough came in, the volume of fire would ensure their hitting their target. The elephant, big as he was, would be hit even if no one was firing at him. Wounded, he might turn on the two men, who would have no place to go except into the pool.

Fogg shot three bullets from the rajah's revolver as cooly as if he were on the firing range. Three soldiers dropped. The others ran behind the scanty shelter of the archways. Fogg removed the last of his watches and hurled it. This struck just beyond the edge of the walk, skittered across it toward an archway, and stopped. It began whirling and emitting a thick smoke. This quickly spread over the walk on that side of the room and out across the lake. The winds were blowing it from the archways, helped by the draft created by the opened trapdoor in the top of the dome. Cries of fear and a number of loud coughs came through the smoke.

Still holding onto the end of the cord, Fogg approached the swaying beast. He started to speak softly the loving words he had learned from the mahout, then realized that the beast could not hear these. He spoke more loudly while he held one hand out to the beast. It watched him with rolling eyes, but Fogg's composure and the lack of fear-scent steadied

Kiouni. Fogg had thrust all disturbing emotions into another circuit of his mind—he would pay heavily for it later—and was as cool and unafraid as he looked. The elephant allowed him to get close and lowered his trunk to feel along his clothes. Passepartout got to the extreme other side of the islet, crouched, and then ran straight toward the animal's tail and pulled himself on up and over onto the animal's back. Fortunately, he managed to get hold of the howdah before the startled beast began running around again. Fogg had hurled himself to one side just in time and then he stood near the shaft and began trying to quiet Kiouni down again.

The Frenchman threw out the rope ladder, which trailed along a few inches on the floor. He got onto the beast's neck and did his best to imitate the Parsi. This, with Fogg's renewed words, brought Kiouni to a standstill. By then, some of the soldiers had run out from the cloud to the far side of the pool and begun firing. Even so, the smoke hindered them.

Fogg climbed up the ladder quickly and drew the rope after him. Kiouni was urged toward the shaft, finally coming to another stop a few feet from it. This was as close as Fogg dared get him, since soldiers might now be in the chamber below. He was not certain that this was close enough, but he must take the chance.

"Transmit, for the love of God! And of Passepartout!" the Frenchman cried.

"Transmit! Transmit!"

A shout came from above. Passepartout looked upward, and his eyes rolled.

"Mother of Mercy! They will shoot straight down! They cannot . . . "

His words were beaten into thin sheets by the terrible nine clangings. And they were deaf again, though happy. At least, Passepartout smiled. The expression of Fogg, holding to the cord minus its load, did not change. A second later, both were busy hanging onto Kiouni. It took half an hour to get the nerve-shattered animal back to the buried distorter.

Arriving at the desired spot, Passepartout descended from the elephant, dug up his watch, cleaned its surface, and reattached it to his old watch chain.

On the slow journey back up the slope, Passepartout said, "Sir, is it permitted to ask a question?"

"Certainly," Fogg said, "though the answer may not be permitted."

"One certainly carried an unusual number of unusual watches."

"That is an observation, not a question."

"But where are these deadly watches obtained? I have seen nothing to indicate their existence. No one could have slipped them to you en route, surely?"

"They were originally in my bureau in my house. A man who runs his life by the watch would not seem out of character if he had some spare chronometers."

"But how did you, sir, get them past my

eyes? I am not altogether dull-eyed."

"They were in my vest from the beginning."

"Ah! And if a prying Capellean had found them and opened them for examination?"

"The first one to be tampered with would have blown up in his face."

"But, sir, I might have found one and, being curious . . . "

"Then you would have discovered that there are certain things into which you should not pry."

Passepartout was silent for a while. He wiped the sweat off his face and said, "And the rajah's distorter? Was that a bomb you attached to it?"

"Set to go off when we were transmitted."

Passepartout exclaimed with delight.

"And now we will return to London? We have killed a major Capellean and destroyed their distorter."

"That is the third question, and you stated that you had only one in mind."

There was another silence. A leopard screamed in the distance. Mr. Fogg said, "We will not return. The bet has not been canceled."

"And this dangerous man of whom you spoke?"

"He is the one I told you to watch for while we were on the *Mongolia*. And there are no more watches."

Passepartout wished to ask more questions but was deterred by Fogg's tone of finality.

CHAPTER 11

When they returned to the bungalow, they found the Parsi still snoring beneath the tree and Sir Francis in the same position in which they had left him. They restored Kiouni to his spot beneath the tree where the beast, half-asleep, began ripping off branches and stuffing them into his mouth. Fogg and Passepartout crept into the bungalow, lay down, and this time both slipped away.

Two hours later, they were awakened by the Parsi. Mr. Fogg asked him if he was tired because of standing watch all night. The Parsi replied that he did not feel in the least fatigued. He could go for several days without a wink of sleep. Mr. Fogg, of course, made no comment.

At six o'clock, two refreshed and two tired men crawled onto the elephant. Kiouni, despite lack of food and sleep, seemed to have vast reservoirs of strength. He went almost as speedily as the day before. Nevertheless, the guide remarked about the beast's tendency to shy at any sudden movements of the brush or the animals in it. And they had to pause for

half an hour to allow Kiouni to eat and so
quell some of the rumblings in his stomach.

They passed down the lower branches of
the Vindhya Mountains and near noon went
by a village on the Kani River, a branch of the
great Ganges. The mahout steered Kiouni
away from habitations for safety's sake. Mr.
Fogg agreed privately with this decision. The
dead rajah's men would be out looking for
them. There was no reason to trouble the
Parsi and the general with the story of last
night, which, in any event, they would not
have believed.

When Allahabad was twelve miles away,
they stopped by some banana trees to refresh
themselves and Kiouni. Around two, they
plunged into another dense jungle. Passepartout was happy that they were so hidden in
this but was apprehensive about their
nearness to the capital city of Bundelcund.
Two hours later, they were still in the dense
forest, though the Parsi said that they would
soon be out. Passepartout was about to ask
him how soon was soon when the beast
suddenly stopped.

"What the devil now?" Sir Francis said,
sticking his head out of the howdah.

"I do not know, sir," the Parsi said.

They heard voices, as of many people, coming through the jungle. After a few minutes,
they could distinguish both voices and
musical instruments of brass and wood. The
Parsi descended, tied Kiouni to a tree, and
wriggled away through the bush. In a

moment, he returned.

"A procession of Brahmins approaches. We must hide."

He untied the rope from the tree and led the animal with its riders into the green thickness. From their vantage, the three on Kiouni could see the procession. First came priests, then many men, women, and children. The crowd was singing a sad chant intermingled with the beat of tambourines and the clash of cymbals and the wailing of pipes and the strumming of various stringed instruments. After the crowd came a large car with huge wheels drawn by four zebus.

Sir Francis, seeing the hideous statue in the car, whispered to the others, "It's Kali, the goddess of love and death."

"Perhaps she is of death," Passepartout said. "But of love? That old hag? Never!"

The Parsi gestured for silence.

A mob of long-bearded and naked old fakirs were dancing wildly around the idol and cutting themselves with knives.

After them came more Brahmins. They led a young woman who did not seem to be a voluntary member of the parade. Despite her dull expression and dragging steps, she was beautiful. Her hair was black, and her eyes were brown, but her skin was as free of pigment as any Yorkshireman's. She wore a gold-edged tunic and a light muslin robe which clung to a splendid figure. Bracelets, rings, and earrings set with jewels of many kinds loaded her down.

Accompanying her were men evidently charged with seeing that she did not run away. These carried sabers and long decorated pistols. Four of them also carried a palanquin on which lay a richly dressed corpse.

Fogg said nothing. Passepartout hissed with astonishment. The body was that of the rajah of Bundelcund.

Behind it were musicians and more dancing bloodied fakirs.

Sir Francis, looking sorrowful, said, "It's a suttee."

When the parade had passed, Fogg said, "What is a suttee?"

This seems a strange thing for the highly knowledgeable Fogg to ask. Perhaps Verne inserted this question to give Sir Francis a chance to enlighten the reader.

"A suttee is a voluntary human sacrifice. The woman you've just seen will be burned at dawn tomorrow."

"Oh, the scoundrels!" Passepartout cried.

"And the corpse?" Mr. Fogg asked.

"It is that of her husband, an independent rajah of Bundelcund."

Fogg said, emotionlessly, "Is it possible that these barbarous customs still exist in India? Why haven't we put a stop to them?"

"They have been terminated in most of India. But we have no power in the savage areas and especially in Bundelcund. The whole district north of the Vindhyas is the theater of unceasing murders and pillage."

"The miserable woman!" Passepartout said. "Burned alive!"

Sir Francis explained that if a widow somehow got out of the sacrifice, she would be treated with utmost contempt by her relatives, indeed, by all who knew of her refusal to become ashes with her husband. She would have to shave her head and exist on the scantiest of food. She would be less than a pariah, because even a pariah had his own kind to associate with. Eventually, she would die of shame and heartbreak.

Sir Francis did not know that this was not exactly the case with this poor woman. If she could have escaped from Bundelcund, she would have gone to live with her relatives in far-off Bombay. These were Parsis who did not hold with suttee. This sect, descended from Persian fire worshippers whose prophet was Zoroaster, had customs as different from the Hindus as those of the Orthodox Jews from their Gentile neighbors.

The Parsi did not agree with Sir Francis.

"The sacrifice is not willing," he said.

"How do you know that?"

"Everybody knows about this affair in Bundelcund."

This statement is another of the many puzzlers in *Around The World In Eighty Days*. The Parsi lived only thirty miles from the borders of Bundelcund. Yet, what with the mountains, the jungle, and the isolation of his small village, he might as well have lived three hundred miles away. The

Bundelcundians were hostile to his people and were not likely to exchange news with him through the so-called grapevine, even if it existed. And how would he know that the rajah had died? He had spoken to no one except the three Europeans since the journey started, and the rajah had died only the night before. Yet Verne says he knew all about it.

The truth seems to be that none of the travelers could possibly have known about the situation of Verne's story were as he reported it. Fogg and Passepartout knew, of course, that the rajah was dead. But they could not say so, and Verne was unaware of what had really happened that night.

However, the Parsi did say that the rajah's widow was drugged with fumes of hemp and opium. This would have indicated to him that she had been put into a state wherein she would not disgrace herself or the community by resisting.

This is what happened. Verne, like every good novelist, had inserted some remarks of a purely fictional character to inform the reader swiftly about what was going on.

Still, would the impulse to save the woman from this horrible rite have been strong enough for Fogg to act on it? Why should he have endangered his all-important mission and the wager to attempt a seemingly hopeless rescue? Was it just humanity that caused him to interfere? Perhaps it was. Perhaps there was also the fact, unrecorded by anyone, that Fogg fell in love at first sight with the beautiful woman. But the log reveals that there was another, and no doubt stronger, motive. An Eridanean had been planted in the heart of the rajah's palace. This was the one who had slipped out a description of the domed room in which the rajah kept his distorter. She, for this Eridanean was female, had gotten as close to the rajah as it was possible for anyone to get. Her beauty and charm enabled her to attract the rajah's attention easily, and from this to marriage was another easy step.

Fogg had been told all this a long time ago by Stuart via a whist game. This is why, just as the journey was about to be resumed, Fogg said, "Suppose we save this woman?"

Sir Francis exclaimed, "What, save this woman, Mr. Fogg?"

"I have twelve hours to spare. I can devote them to this."

"Why," Sir Francis said, "you *are* a man of heart!"

"Sometimes, when I have the time," Fogg replied.

Sir Francis must have wondered about this man whose emotions could apparently be turned on or off as if they ran through a spigot. What he did not know, of course, was that Fogg could not decide whether or not he would have a certain emotion or not. The emotion came, willy-nilly, but he could shunt it aside, store it in neural circuit where the emotional charge ran around and around the track, like a current in today's super-

conductive circuit. But he could not kill the
emotion, because it would not die. Sooner or
later, he had to pay for the storage, and he
would pay double or treble the bill by the time
he released it.

The two other Europeans were all for this
idea. But what about the Parsi guide? He
could not be expected to risk his life, but he
might agree to stay behind and wait for them.
Even this would be dangerous for him.

He answered that he was a Parsi and that
the woman was a Parsi. He was in this with
them all the way.

Verne says that the Parsi knew all about
her. Probably, Verne got this from Fogg's
public log and inserted the informational
conversation about her in the Parsi's mouth
for the benefit of the reader. In any event, we
know that she was a famous beauty, the
daughter of a wealthy merchant of Bombay. If
she were that famous, then the Parsi may
have heard about her after all. Travelers
coming through his remote village may have
gossiped about her.

The woman's name was Aouda Jejeebhoy,
and she had been educated in an English
school in Bombay. This, plus her light skin,
enabled her to pass as a European. She was
related to the wealthy Parsi who had been
created a baronet by the queen. He was Sir
Jametsee Jejeebhoy, whom the curious reader
may find listed, with some biographical
details, in Burke's *Peerage*.

The Parsi said that after her parents had

died, she had been forced to marry the rajah.

(This, of course, was what the rajah and the public believed. She had succeeded in making it look as if she were a victim. If she had been eager to marry him, she would have aroused his suspicions.)

The Parsi, however, was right in saying that she had fled as soon as the rajah died but had been captured and returned to the capital city. The rajah's relatives were insistent that she perform the suttee, since they did not wish her to inherit the rajah's wealth.

This was probably true, Fogg thought. If Nemo had found out, or even suspected, that she was an Eridanean, he would have saved her from the suttee. She would be too valuable as a source of information for him to allow her to be wasted on the funeral pyre. But it was possible that Nemo no longer had any influence in Bundelcund and was helpless to prevent her—to him—too-early death.

The Parsi guided the travelers to the temple of Pillaji, where the distressing ceremony was to take place. Thirty minutes later, they were hidden in a dense copse about one hundred and sixty-seven yards from the Brahmin temple. Kiouni made much noise by tearing off branches and eating them, but this could not be helped. The beast was very hungry, and any efforts to stop him might result in his making even more noise. Fortunately, the distance from the crowd, the uproar it was making, and the thick vegetation that surrounded the travelers would keep the

Bundelcundians from noticing the sounds the
elephant was making.

Fogg questioned the guide about the layout
of the area around the temple, its interior
design, and the behavior of the Hindus at such
occasions. Verne says that the Parsi was
familiar with the temple. But why would a
Parsi ever have gone into a Hindu temple,
especially one in hostile territory? Perhaps,
being intelligent, and hence curious, the Parsi
had picked up his knowledge by questioning
various Hindus of his village, or travelers,
who had worshipped there. The Pillaji temple
seems to have been a famous one.

The party waited in the copse until night
fell. Meanwhile, they were still apprehensive
about being discovered. Kiouni had not
stopped feeding, and now and then children
wandered off from the crowd and came close
to the hiding place. Once, three ten-year-olds,
playing some sort of hide and seek, started
toward the copse. They were quite close when
the mother of one came after them. Kiouni
was stuffing some broken branches into his
mouth at that time, so there was no snapping
and cracking of wood to attract her. Also, the
wind was blowing toward the travelers and
helped to carry the noise away from the
crowd.

Even so, they had some anxious moments.

As the sun set, the noise of the mob began to
die. Kiouni had by then stripped half of the
trees, but, his belly full, was now dozing. The
celebrators were not only worn out; they were

sleepy from the effects of liquid opium mixed
with hemp. This use of such drugs and some
other features of Verne's description of them
indicate that the Bundelcundians did not
belong to a conventional sect of Hinduism.
The Bundelcundians were, after all, devotees
of Kali and undoubtedly considered
unorthodox even by other branches of this
particular worship. There were elements of a
pre-Hindu religion in the Bundelcundian
religion, probably adopted from the original
inhabitants, the small dark peoples who now
survived only in the mountain jungles.

Fogg's record validates Verne's description,
so we can accept it as true that these Kalians
did indeed use opium and other drugs.

After dark, the Parsi stole out to observe the
situation at close range. He found that all the
mob were lying in a stupor, children included.
The unfortunate exceptions were the priests
and the guards, alert within the temple. Fogg,
hearing this, was unperturbed. They would
wait on the chance that the people in the
temple might go to sleep later.

At midnight, it became apparent that the
guards intended to stay up all night. Fogg
gave an order, and the travelers went out into
a night which lacked a moon, since it was
covered by heavy clouds. They stopped at the
rear wall of the temple and began chipping
away with their pocketknives. Fortunately,
after one brick had been removed, the others
came out without much labor. Once, they had
to retreat into the woods because the guards

were disturbed by a cry. This caused Sir Francis and the Parsi to argue that they should give up their rescue attempt. Whatever had caused the cry, the guards would now be even more vigilant. And daylight would soon come.

Fogg replied that he wished to stay until all hope was gone. Something might happen to their advantage.

Passepartout, watching from the branches of a tree, had a sudden inspiration. Without a word to the others, he got down off the tree and slipped off. His act was motivated only by humanity. He had no idea at that time that the woman was a fellow Eridanean.

At dawn, Aouda Jejeebhoy was brought out of the temple. The crowd recovered from its stupor, and the voices and the music became as loud as before. Aouda struggled until she was held over burning hemp and opium and forced to breathe. Sir Francis, greatly moved by this pitiful scene, grabbed Fogg's hand and found in it an open knife. But Fogg did not rush into the crowd brandishing the knife in a vain effort to save her. Verne says that, at this point, Fogg and the other two men mingled in the rear ranks of the crowd and followed it to the pyre. This is obviously not true, since they would have been noticed at once and set upon. In actuality, they remained at some distance and took care to hide behind bushes.

Verne fails to say what Fogg thought of Passepartout's unauthorized disappearance. Fogg records that he had assumed that the

Frenchman was still up in the tree posted as their lookout.

The three men saw the now senseless woman placed beside the corpse. They saw the oil-soaked wood of the pyre being ignited with a torch. Fogg seems to have lost his self-control. He was about to dash through the crowd when Sir Francis and the Parsi grabbed him. Despite their efforts, he broke free and was about to launch himself again when something unexpected and terrifying happened. The whole crowd, screaming with terror, threw itself on its face and cowered.

The dead rajah had sat up, gotten to his feet, lifted Aouda in his arms, and was now coming down from the pyre. Smoke flowered about him as if he were a devil carrying a poor lost soul through the fires of Hell. He walked through the prostrate mob straight to the party in the rear, all of whom had come out from their concealment.

The reanimated rajah, as everybody knows, was Passepartout. In the darkness, while the crowd slept, he had stripped the corpse, buried it under sticks of wood, put on its clothes, and then lain down in the posture and place of the dead man. In fact, the dead rajah was directly below.

A few moments later, Kiouni, aroused from his sleep, bearing five on his back now, was tearing along as if he fully understood the necessity for a speedy departure. Cries and gunshots sounded behind him, and a bullet pierced Mr. Fogg's hat. The fire had by then exposed the naked body of the rajah. The worshippers of Kali at once understood not only that they had been duped but in what manner. Inasmuch as they had no elephants or horses at hand, they were soon hopelessly outdistanced.

CHAPTER 12

Passepartout was delighted with his exploit. Sir Francis shook his hand. Fogg said, "Well done," though he must have thought that the valet, who was, after all, under his command, should have consulted him before acting. He was, however, eminently pragmatic. And it was the Eridanean custom to act independently if the situation required.

Sir Francis told Fogg that the woman would never be safe in India again. The fanatics of Kali would track her down and strangle her.

At Allahabad, the young woman waited in a room in the railroad station while Passepartout purchased suitable clothes for her. Though Verne does not say so, he must have bought clothes for himself, too. When he entered Allahabad, he was still wearing the garments he had taken from the rajah. His own had been burned in the pyre.

On the train to Benares, Aouda fully recovered. She was astonished, of course, since she had expected to awaken in the Parsi Heaven. Fogg made no mention at this time of their Eridanean connections. He pretended to her to be what the world thought him, an overly eccentric English gentleman. He did offer to take her with him as far as Hong Kong. There, it seemed, she had a Parsi cousin who was a rich merchant.

At Benares, Sir Francis, who had to rejoin his brigade, bade them a fond farewell. He said that he would never forget their adventure, and neither Fogg nor Passepartout enlightened him on the one that he had missed.

On the twenty-fifth of October, exactly on schedule, the party arrived at Calcutta. The two days gained on the trip from London to Bombay had been lost during the journey across India. Verne says that it is to be supposed that Fogg did not regret the loss. He spoke more truly than he knew.

As they left the railway station, a policeman politely asked the two men to follow him. Aouda accompanied them to the police station. There they were held for trial, which would begin at 8:30 that morning. They were not told why they were detained, which seems strange since British law required that they be so informed. Aouda said that it was because of their interference with the suttee. Fogg replied that that was highly improbable. Who would dare complain to the authorities? Whatever happened, he would not desert Aouda. He would go with her to Hong Kong.

Passepartout, wiping the perspiration from his forehead, cried, "But the steamer leaves at noon!"

"We shall be on board at noon," Fogg said.

At the stipulated time, the three were brought into the courtroom. Here they discovered the nature of the charges brought against them. It was not the affair at the temple of Pillaji which had caused their arrest. It was that at the temple of Malabar Hill in Bombay.

Fix, whom we last saw in Bombay, had traveled with the three priests to Calcutta. Because Fogg and party were delayed in the rescue of Aouda, Fix and party had beaten them to Calcutta. There they had complained to the British authorities of Passepartout's desecration of the temple. Fix, who had paid their passage, had also promised them that they would collect a large sum in damages. On seeing Fogg and party arrive, he had gotten a policeman to detain them.

Sitting inconspicuously in the crowd in a corner, Fix observed the trial. He was delighted at the sentence. Passepartout was fined three hundred pounds and given fifteen days in jail. Since Fogg, as master, was responsible for his servant, he was sentenced to seven days in jail and fined one hundred and fifty pounds.

Fix knew that there was now time for the warrant to arrive. And while Fogg was on his way back to England as Fix's prisoner, many things could—and would—happen to Fogg.

Mr. Fogg, however, claimed his right to bail. Fix became cold at this point but warmed up when he heard that bail would cost each prisoner a thousand pounds. Then he became cold again when Fogg paid the amount from his carpetbag.

Passepartout insisted that the shoes left behind in the temple be returned to him. They were, whereon he complained that they not only had cost a thousand pounds apiece, they pinched his feet.

Fix, hoping that Fogg would never leave two thousand pounds behind him, shadowed him. To his consternation, he saw the party board a small boat and head for the steamer *Rangoon*. There was nothing he could do except follow them to Hong Kong. So far, he thought, he had certainly failed to "fix" them. He did succeed in getting onto the *Rangoon* without being seen by the Frenchman. But first he left orders that the warrant, when it arrived, should be forwarded to Hong Kong.

Fix stayed in his cabin as much as possible. While there, he considered the addition to the party. Where had she come from? Who was she? Was she an Eridanean? The latter seemed more probable, since Fix could not conceive of the coldly inhuman, or inhumanly cold, Fogg taking a mistress.

Suffering from cabin-fever, and convinced that Passepartout might give him more information, Fix left his quarters. This was on the thirtieth of October; the next day, the *Rangoon* would stop briefly at Singapore.

Fix located the Frenchman, who was promenading on the first-class forward deck. Pretending to be surprised at finding him aboard, Fix greeted him. He explained to Passepartout that unexpected business at Hong Kong was responsible for his being on the ship. He had not been on deck before because seasickness had kept him in bed. He expressed astonishment on hearing from the Frenchman that a young lady was now with Mr. Fogg—though in a separate cabin, of course. Passepartout told the story of the rescue, their flight, their trial, and the bail. The woman, Fix discovered, was to be left at Hong Kong with a relative.

Fix, hearing this, thought that perhaps she was not an enemy after all. Disappointed, he gave up his plan to get Fogg arrested at Hong Kong on a morals charge. Fogg's behavior toward Aouda was, according to Passepartout, irreproachable.

Fix invited Passepartout to have a drink of gin on him. Perhaps this time the Frenchman would drink enough to unlock the door of his discretion.

Later, Passepartout, having sent Fix reeling home to his cabin, reported to Fogg. This fellow, Fix, was undoubtedly trailing them. Whether he was just a detective or a Capellean remained to be seen.

Not much happened at Singapore, according to Verne. While the *Rangoon* coaled up, Fogg and Aouda took a long drive through the city and the surrounding country. Fix shadowed them so skillfully that they did not observe him. Passepartout, however, had shadowed Fix for a while, saw whom he was

following, and went off to carry out some
errands. At eleven o'clock, a half an hour
ahead of time, the ship left the English-
founded colony.

When Fix returned to his cabin, he
discovered waiting in it a man whom he had
met once before. We know this because it is
recorded in Fogg's secret log, though he was
not aware of the meeting until much later.

The man was sitting in a chair, his long
well-muscled legs extended straight out, the
posterior edges of the heels of his expensive
boots on the deck. Though he was about forty
years of age, he had the physique of an athlete
of twenty-five. His waist was narrow; his
chest was broad and deep; his shoulders were
wide. His nose was long and straight. His
mouth was thin. His chin jutted out. His forehead was high and bulging. His eyes were a
pale gray and set so far apart that they could
cover one hundred and eighty degrees. He
was smoking a long thin cigar the make and
aroma of which Fix could not identify. It had a
certain salty tang to it.

"Sit down, Fix," the intruder said in Capellean. "Do you have anything of interest to
report?"

Fix sat down as if he could not obey the man
fast enough. His nervousness became even
more manifest as he told what had happened
from the day he met the *Mongolia* at Suez.
While he talked, he could not keep from
wondering if his guest was one of the Old
Ones or an adopted human. Those wide-

spread eyes and the superhuman and chilly intelligence in them! But he dared not ask. In any event, it made no difference. He was under the orders of this person, man or alien. And he was a deadly person. An utter lack of compassion emanated from him in an almost visible aura, if a negative quality could be said to radiate.

At the end of Fix's lengthy account, the man straightened up in the chair. "You will continue to follow him, all the way back to London, if need be. And continue to make friends with this Passepartout. He is undoubtedly an Eridanean. That watch which he refuses to adjust to the sun sounds suspicious. It may contain a distorter. One of them is carrying a distorter."

This man was the one whom Fogg had called Nemo when he had seen him in the rajah's palace. Nemo knew that Passepartout was Fogg's accomplice. He had not seen him during the raid, but the soldiers in the dome had described the Frenchman. That he did not bother to tell Fix this was a mistake due to his arrogance. Fix was only an underling and a not very competent one at that in his opinion. Why should he tell Fix that he knew for certain that Passepartout was Eridanean? He had stated that the Frenchman was Eridanean and that should be enough for Fix.

That, however, was not enough for Fix. He assumed that the man's statement was based on suspicions only. As far as he was concerned, Passepartout could be just a human.

Fix had some questions and some suggestions, but he did not voice them. This man was evidently one who gave orders and did not care to have them questioned. Fix would be glad when he left.

"Both Fogg and Passepartout," the man said, "are aware that you are probably not just a detective. I don't know why they haven't killed you or tried to extract data from you. They must know that you may try to eliminate them at any moment and that you can easily do so. Still, they may be waiting to act until their plans develop further. They are iron-nerved, intrepid, and intelligent—for Eridaneans. As I have good reason to know."

He puffed on his cigar for a while. Fix wished he would tell him just why he had such good reason to know. He also thought that he had identified at least one of the elements in the odor of the tobacco. Seaweed? But, if so, it was a fine seaweed, for the smoke was certainly pleasant enough, even to a non-smoker.

The man, as if reading his mind, said, "This is the next to last cigar. Then I go back to the more easily procured."

He puffed again and said, "I think I'll save it for a special occasion. Such as the demise of Fogg, who, by the way, has something familiar about him. Where have I seen him before?"

Fix sweated even more heavily. If a superior talked too much to an inferior, it could mean that he no longer cared if the underling knew

too much. The underling would soon be dead.
But what had he done? Where had he failed?
He had carried out all orders, and it was not
his fault that London had not sent the
warrant.

The man, whose expression had been
unrelieved by any sign of emotion, unless
coldness is one, now smiled.

"I can't tell you what is going on. But I can
tell you that never have affairs looked so good
for us. There is a very important operation,
perhaps the most important in our history,
going on right now that will undoubtedly
bring an end to our war with the Eridaneans."

Fix sat up. "Incredible!"

"Not if I say so," the man said.

"Pardon me, sir. But an end!"

"Yes, an end."

"But they would never make peace with
us!"

The man quit smiling.

"You think strangely, perhaps too
strangely. Did you really imagine that we
would make a treaty with those demons? Or"
—he stabbed the cigar as if it were a knife—
"do you *hope* that we will? Peace will be
declared only when every Eridanean is
peaceful. That is, with the peace of death."

"Pardon me," Fix stammered, the sweat
running down into his eyes. "I was so taken
aback by your news!"

"Yes? Well, this near-total isolation, this
secrecy, this noncommunication, is correct
for soldiers in the field. But it has had a

deleterious effect, too. How can you keep a community of interests, a secret nation, together if the members lose their sense of community, of communion, of commonness, as it were?

"The truth is that if it weren't for one thing both Eridanean and Capellean would have become extinct long ago. Most of the Old Ones are dead. Even they, with one or two possible exceptions, are second or third generation. All the females of the Old Ones have been killed during the war or are sterile. Some trace element necessary for conception seems to be lacking in the soil of Earth. This is no secret, so don't look so surprised. The original ships only contained five females apiece, and both we and our enemies chose the females as the prime target in our war. But you know this. Or has this secrecy been carried so far that no one has told you?"

Fix thought that the man, however hard he looked on the surface, and doubtless was, was still human. He was "visiting," trying to re-establish some sense of being Capellean. On the other hand, he might just be testing him or softening him up for something unpleasant.

Fix felt lonely only because he had been away from home so long and was in a country he did not like at all. In London, he had a wife (a Capellean, of course) and three children. The children had been conditioned from the time they started to talk. They were now listening to stories from him and his wife of far-off planets and space flight and galactic war. They thought these were fairy tales now, but in a few years they would, if they passed certain tests, be admitted into the blood brotherhood. An Old One would contribute some of his blood to be mingled in their veins.

Fix loved his wife and children. He liked to come home to them after a hard day or night of tracking down criminals, arresting them, and occasionally beating them up in the inter-rogation cells. Only, of course, if he was absolutely certain they were guilty and they had committed some terrible crime such as murder, child abuse, or sodomy. If the mundane life of a policeman got dull, and it often did, it was relieved enough by the sudden secret codes, the esoteric messages, the missions against the evil Eridaneans. But he liked his missions to be on home soil. After all, he was English.

"Two things only have kept us from disinte-grating," the man was saying. "One, fear of death if we should defect. Two, the strongest by far, is the possibility of living for a thousand years. Most men and women would sell their souls—if they had any—for this gift. But, of course, being brought up as a Capel-lean or Eridanean is the glue that holds us together. And we do have ideals. We do intend, once the enemy is out of the way, to steer the world into peace, prosperity, freedom from disease and pain, and brother-hood."

He puffed again, sending out thick green stormclouds, smiled like lightning, and said,

"This world will be ruled by the only ones who have the ancient knowledge to do it. Us. And our grandchildren may be among the aristocracy, Fix."

"Yes, sir."

"In any event, you are now forty years old and won't become any older, physiologically speaking, for about eight hundred to nine hundred years. But you can be killed, Fix. And our enemies want to kill you. So we must kill them first. Isn't that right?"

"Yes, sir."

"But it is better to take them alive first so we can find out who the others are and so catch them, too."

"Yes, sir."

"So you will play your role. And Fogg and Passepartout will play theirs until we lower the curtain on them. Meantime, what are your thoughts on this woman?"

"Possibly an Eridanean," Fix said.

Since Nemo's conversation indicated an uncertainty about Aouda's true identity, it may safely be presumed that he had never seen her before. The rajah of Bundelcund had evidently kept her hidden in his seraglio, and Nemo had left Bundelcund immediately after the rajah's death.

"It seems unlikely," he said, "that the two Eridaneans would have risked their lives for anyone besides another of their kind."

"I don't know about that, sir, if I may be so bold," Fix said. "That Fogg is a strange one. No fear there, if I may say so, sir. And he is an

Englishman, sir."

"Would you have rescued her?"

"Yes, sir. As an Englishman, sir. As a Capellean, no, sir, not unless I had orders to do so."

"And which do you think is the most human
action, Fix?" the man said with a hint of a
sneer.

"Most human, sir?"

Fix was silent for a moment, then smiled.

"Being human, sir, if I do say so myself, and
capable of both of the actions you mentioned,
I'd say neither is more human than the other.
As for a question of heart, sir, what is the
word for that ... cumpass ... ?"

"Compassion, Fix. I can quote you its dictionary definition, as I can every word in the
dictionary and in the Encyclopedia Brittanica
of 1871."

But I doubt if you really *know* the word,
Fix thought. The word is the shadow, but
what about the substance? His mind knows,
but it's not connected to his heart. And that's
where the only knowing worth knowing is.

What the man had said about the millennium medicine, as Fix called it, made sense,
though. He wanted to live for a thousand
years. He wanted desperately for his children
to share in that long life. But there was a
chance that at least one of his children might
not be permitted to do so. If the chiefs decided
that the child was too emotionally unstable,
that he or she might blab to the world, then
that child would share neither in the Blood or
the elixir. And his little Annie, his beloved

little Annie, showed signs of hysteria.

The man suddenly stood up. He was very tall, at least six feet five inches tall. And, now that Fix considered it, under that cultured English voice was the faintest of brogues. Was this man of Irish descent?

"I shall be out of sight," the man said. "But I shall be close. When the time is ripe, you'll hear from me. Meanwhile, play your part. And delay Fogg as much as possible without being obvious about it. Let's hope that the warrant will be waiting for you in Hong Kong. If it is, we'll attempt to keep him from arriving in America on time or at all."

No greetings. No good-byes. He walked out boldly, though he shut the door softly enough.

Mr. Fix said, "Whew!" He pulled out a handkerchief to wipe his face. He felt as if a tiger had decided not to eat him after all. The room reeked of the essence of predator. It was nothing he could smell, or anybody could smell, unless he had that extra set of nerves in his nose. Just as he had boasted to the British consul that he could smell a criminal, just so he could smell the human tiger in a human. In this case, the man stank of both criminal and tiger. Fix would have felt sorry for Fogg and Passepartout if they had not been Eridaneans. And, even so, but no, he must never feel like that. He must never think of the enemy as anything but vermin and deadly vermin at that.

Still, he was glad that man with the widely spaced gray eyes had not ordered him to assassinate the two.

The story that Verne tells of the tribulations of Fogg from this point until he was at the 180th meridian is well-known. The events of that period are briefly outlined here for those who have read the story so long ago that their memory of it is vague.

Aouda, it was evident, fell in love with Fogg. That gentleman, if he were aware of her emotion, betrayed no knowledge of it. Passepartout could not understand why Fogg did not respond to this adoration. Certainly, he would have.

A storm put the *Rangoon* twenty hours behind schedule. Fix, though rendered seasick by the tempest, had a consolation. Perhaps the delay would allow time for the warrant to arrive at Hong Kong, and he could then arrest Fogg.

There were times, though, that Fix wished that the warrant would not get there in time. Once he put the handcuffs on Fogg, he would have to participate in the abduction and torture of Fogg. No, he wouldn't. *That man* would not take him along with Fogg, since it would seem strange if he, Fix, were to disappear also. He would have to play the outraged detective who had been incompetent enough to lose a prisoner.

Fix felt better thinking about this. He did not contemplate the fact that he would be just as responsible for whatever happened to Fogg as if he himself were torturing and then murdering, no, killing him; whatever was done to him was not enough.

At last the storm subsided and with it Fix's perturbed and guilty thoughts. The *Rangoon* was a day late; Phileas Fogg seemed doomed to miss the steamer for Yokohama.

Passepartout was afraid to inquire about the Yokohama ship. Better no news than bad news. Fogg did not hesitate, however, and he received good news. The steamer had been held up for one day for repairs to a boiler. They would make it on time after all. This was indeed fortunate, not to mention an absolute necessity. If he had missed this ship, he would have had to wait a week for the next steamer. He was still twenty-four hours behind schedule, but this was not disastrous.

As he had sixteen hours to spend at Hong Kong, Fogg took advantage of it to see that Aouda was put under the protection of her cousin, Jeejeeh. Fogg had by now ascertained that she was the Eridanean spy. But, since neither of them had orders about her, she would remain in Hong Kong until she received them. At the Exchange, Mr. Fogg inquired about her cousin. He was informed that two years had passed since Jeejeeh had left China. He had retired and now he was supposed to be living in Holland. Fogg returned to the Club Hotel, where he had installed Aouda in a room.

Verne says that she did not comment on this turn of events which left her alone and unprotected. Instead, she merely asked Fogg what she should do.

Serenely, he replied, "Go on to Europe."

She is supposed to have said that she could not intrude or in the least hinder him on his voyage. Fogg replied that she would be doing neither, and he sent Passepartout to obtain three cabins on the *Carnatic*.

This scene is quite in keeping with Fogg's character. But it is not quite what happened.

Fogg did not like to leave her alone in Hong Kong. He could have given her money to support herself for a while or to buy passage to England. But he did not wish to leave her exposed to poverty, to white slavers, or to the thuggees of Kali, who might come after her even in China. Moreover, the Capelleans might have identified her by now as an Eridanean, and if she were alone here, she would stand little chance of surviving. And it is likely, though he did not show it then, that he reciprocated her love. This emotion may have influenced his philosophy of rational mechanics. A rational mind has to consider all known factors, and personal emotion is certainly a part of the universe.

In any event, he told her that he doubted that she could do anything in Hong Kong for the Race. Since she had proved herself to be an exceptionally competent agent, she should accompany them. Three were stronger than two. She could keep an eye on Fix and for other Capelleans who were probably on this ship. Of, if not aboard, waiting for them in Yokohama or America.

Fix, meanwhile, was despondent. The warrant had not arrived. That it would come in a few days was no solace. Hong Kong was the last piece of British territory. The Fogg party would leave that by tomorrow. If only he could find some means of detaining them long enough.

While pacing back and forth on the quay, he met Passepartout. The Frenchman smiled at him as if he knew what was going on in his mind. No doubt he did. Passepartout asked him if he had decided to go to America with them. He did not ask Fix why he would do so. Fix, gritting his teeth, said he would be on the *Carnatic*. Together, they went to the ticket office. The clerk informed them that the repairs had been made sooner than expected. The ship would leave that evening, not tomorrow.

This gave Fix an idea. He invited Passepartout to a tavern on the quay. He knew that it held an opium den and that there he might get Passepartout to smoke a pipe of opium if he got him drunk enough. Fogg might then be delayed by a search for his missing valet. While they drank, with Passepartout downing two to Fix's one, Fix revealed that he was a detective and that Fogg was the wanted bank robber. He was still not convinced that the Frenchman was an Eridanean. If he were only a valet, his sense of duty to the law might make him desert his master. That would at least save his life. Fix was convinced that, even if Passepartout were innocent, the gray-

eyed man would probably order him killed.
Passepartout could identify Fix as the man
who'd trailed them, and the gray-eyed man
would want no investigations of Fix by Eridaneans.

Besides, Fix had become rather fond of the
chap. He would never have admitted this to
Gray Eyes, but there it was.

The result of this sojourn in the opium den
was that Passepartout passed out, and Fogg
and Aouda were forced to leave without him.

There is no need to recount the adventures
of the Frenchman after he awoke. After some
tense, but comical, episodes in Yokohama, he
was reunited with Fogg. They caught the ship
to America just before the gangplank was
raised.

Passepartout did fail to notify Fogg of the
early departure of the liner. The ever-
resourceful Englishman chartered a pilot
boat. This sailed to Singapore, where he
caught the *Carnatic* and proceeded to Yokohama. Fix was deeply chagrined by this
course of events. At least, he told himself that
he was. The few impulses of gladness he put
down to flaws in his character, flaws that
could become fatal for him if he did not
master them.

Adding to his chagrin, was his indebtedness
to Fogg. That gentleman not only permitted
Fix to go with him on the pilot boat but
insisted on paying his passage.

Fogg was motivated by a desire to keep Fix
handy. He might have to seize a Capellean and

extract data from him. Moreover, he suspected that others of his kind—if Fix were a
Capellean—were on the ship. If these made
contact with Fix, Fogg might spot them.

Fix knew this. He also knew that if they
were all just what they pretended to be, Fogg
would have treated him as generously. He did
not like knowing this. It make Fogg too
likable.

Verne says that Passepartout, on meeting
his master in Japan, did not inform him that
Fix was a detective who intended to arrest
Fogg. This was not true. Even if Verne's
surface tale was valid, it would be difficult to
account for Passepartout's silence. Verne had
him say nothing because it was necessary for
his plot. Fogg must be kept in ignorance of
Fix's mission. Otherwise, Fogg would have rid
himself of Fix and so not have been arrested
when he landed in England.

CHAPTER 13

The ship which Fogg took for San Francisco was the *General Grant*. This belonged to the Pacific Mail Steamship Company and was a paddle wheel steamer also fitted with three masts bearing large sails. At an expected speed of twelve miles an hour, it would cross the Pacific in twenty-one days. Fogg calculated that he would disembark at San Francisco on the second of December. From there he would travel by train to New York City, arriving on the eleventh of December. From New York he would take a ship to England. The twentieth of December would see him in London, ahead of the required arrival date of the twenty-first.

Verne says that, nine days after leaving Yokohama, on the twenty-third of November, the ship crossed the 180th meridian. Fogg had gone exactly halfway around the Earth since this imaginary line was at the antipodes of London. Though Fogg had only twenty-eight days to traverse the second half of his journey, he had actually completed two-thirds of his circuit. To get to the 180th meridian, he had been forced to make long detours. But the course from then on would be comparatively straight.

On this twenty-third of November, according to Verne, Passepartout made a happy discovery. His watch, which he had not adjusted to the various time zones, now agreed with the sun.

Passepartout, Verne says, did not know that if the face of his watch had been divided into twenty-four hours (like Italian watches), the hands of his watch would have indicated the true chronometry. They would have shown him that it was not nine in the morning but nine in the evening. That is, they would indicate the twenty-first hour after midnight, exactly the difference between London time and that of the 180th meridian.

As we know, Fogg had no watches, having expended them in Bundelcund. Verne did not know of the incident at the rajah's palace, but he also says nothing at this time of Fogg having a watch. Why this gentleman, who conducted himself strictly by the chronometer, lacked a timepiece, Verne does not say.

Fix had stayed in his cabin until the twenty-third, when he felt that he must leave it or go mad. While walking on the forward deck, he ran into Passepartout. He also ran into blows of the fist from the seemingly enraged valet. Passepartout was genuinely angry at the trick that Fix had played on him. But even if he had not been, he would have pretended to be. The role he was playing demanded it. Besides, if Fix were a Capellean, it was fun to pummel him.

Fix tried to defend himself but soon found that the Frenchman was the superior boxer. Lying on the deck, he said, "Are you finished?"

"Yes—for this time," Passepartout said.

"Then let me have a word with you."

"But I . . ."

"In your master's interest."

They sat down in an area distant from the other passengers, who had regarded the encounter with enthusiasm, some even making bets.

"You've thrashed me," Fix said. "Good. I expected it. Now listen. Until now I've seen Mr. Fogg's adversary. But I'm now in this with him."

"Aha! You're convinced he's an honest man!"

What the devil is this one up to now? he was thinking.

"No," Fix said coldly. "I think he's a rascal."

He proceeded to tell Passepartout his plan, which was to help Fogg win his bet. He would, however, only be doing this so he could get him back on English soil. There it would be determined whether or not Fogg was innocent.

"Are we friends now?" Fix said.

"No," Passepartout said. "Allies—perhaps.

At the least sign of treachery, I'll twist your neck."

Passepartout had a double meaning in his threat, of course.

Verne then says that, eleven days later, on the third of December, the ship entered the bay of the Golden Gate. Mr. Fogg had not gained or lost a day.

This is true, but Verne did not know what happened the next few days after Fix was knocked to the deck.

While we do not know exactly what Fix and the gray-eyed man were up to during the time they were out of Passepartout's and Fogg's sight, we can reconstruct their activities from Fogg's other log.

At one in the morning, Passepartout was wakened from a fretful somnolence by the ringing sounds from the watch at his ear. He listened for a moment, ascertaining that the series of sounds formed no code he recognized. He hastily put on some clothes and left the cabin. He did not observe the figure standing in the shadow of one of the large life-boats on davits some fifty feet away.

He was standing watch because Fix was in bed with diarrhea and a high fever. Nemo was not pleased with this course of events, both because it was inconvenient and because it showed him that Nature was even stronger than he. And since he did not care to be seen by any of Fogg's party, he could not leave the cabin when the sun was up. He did have a disguise available. The beard was actually a false one, which he could discard in favor of a false moustache. A wig would give him the appearance of a man approaching old age, and putty would make his nose bulbous. To remove the noticeable wide spacing between the eyes, he had a set of glass eyes to which he attached false eyelids and flesh-colored false skin. The glass eyes were thin shells with blue irises, one-way glass which both the Capelleans and Eridaneans had inherited from the Old Ones along with a few other devices far in advance of Earthling science. These could be set within the hollows of his eyes so that his eyes seemed to be closer together.

Unfortunately, half of the vision of each eye was obstructed. Nemo did not like to use them unless the situation absolutely demanded that he do so. He had elected to stay in his quarters, coming out only at night. Now he was just about to light a cheroot when he saw the Frenchman's cabin door. If it had opened a few seconds later, Passepartout would have seen the light of his match. Cursing (his way of delivering thanks for having been saved from observation), he replaced the cheroot in its case. From his belt he drew a Colt revolver.

He had hoped he would not have to use it, since the noise might alarm the occupants of cabins near Fogg's. He waited hidden in the shadow of the lifeboat until Passepartout had knocked on Fogg's door and been admitted. He started toward Fogg's cabin but had to dodge back under the lifeboat. The door had

swung open again. Passepartout emerged and
went to Aouda's cabin, next to Fogg's, and
knocked. There was an exchange of words,
which Nemo could not hear, through the
crack by the slightly opened door. Nemo supposed that Aouda was requiring Passepartout
to give a password, even though she must
recognize his voice. In less than two minutes,
Aouda came out dressed in a robe, her black
hair hanging to her waistline. Both
disappeared into Fogg's cabin.

Nemo walked softly to the door and applied
to it a stethoscopic device, another
inheritance from the Old Ones. The moonlight
falling on his features, showed his alarm,
followed by a look of determination. Though
he hated to make the noise, there was only one
way to enter the cabin. He lifted his right boot
and gave the lock a mighty kick. Few locks
could have stood up under a kick from Nemo,
who was extremely powerful. The lock tore
out, and the door banged into the wall with
Nemo swiftly leaping through the doorway.

A glance showed him that the three were
unarmed. They were sitting at a table. Passepartout's watch, illumined by the swinging
petroleum lamp attached to the ceiling, lay on
the table. That it was there confirmed Nemo's
suspicions that it contained a distorter. In the
silence that followed his crashing entrance,
he could hear, faintly, the ringings from the
watch. And he recognized the Capellean code.

Nemo, pointing the revolver at them, shut
the door behind him. Passepartout started to

rise. Nemo shook his head. The Frenchman
sat down. His eyes and Aouda's were wide,
and their skins were pale. Fogg sat as still as
if he were in a tintype. His was the only calm
face at the table.

"You will slowly rise and move over against
the bulkhead," Nemo said. "You will then
slowly turn around until you face it. You will
then place your palms flatly against the bulkhead."

Though he voiced no curses, he must have
been thinking them. The pulses indicated an
immediate and emergency action for any
Capellean possessing a distorter. Nemo
would not have ignored any such call, even
from the lowliest. This message was sent by
the highest chief of them all. It was directed at
the Capellean who was bringing the recently
found distorter from China. But it also
pleaded that anyone else who might possess a
distorter should use it if the Chinese agent
failed to reply.

Whoever answered was to set his device on
transmit, though he must, of course, make
sure that no one would come across it while it
was left unguarded. That the chief would
allow a distorter to be left behind showed how
desperate the occasion was. Moreover, that
the chief thought that the rajah of
Bundelcund was still alive but was willing to
take a chance on being transmitted by him
indicated the desperation of his situation.

Also, the chief said, if at all possible, bring
two men. Three would be preferable, but he

could manage with two. He did not say why he wanted the two men.

He would prefer that all be Capellean, but if that was not possible, the man in China—or whoever else might be listening in—must pick up two Earthlings at gun's point and bring them along.

Nemo, having been out of touch with other Capelleans so long, did not know what was behind the message. But it changed his plans for the three Eridaneans. Why did Fix have to be sick at this time? Someone had to be at this end to insure that Nemo and the chief would be transmitted back if need be. If they were not, then Fix would have to take care of the distorter. They were too valuable to lose.

And why did not the Chinese agent answer? Was he sleeping? Was he drunk? Was he in the hands of bandits? Or, horrible thought, had he been taken by Eridaneans? If so, they would have the distorter, and even if they did not know the Capellean code, they could set the distorter on *receive* on the chance of scooping up whoever was at the other end. Or, even more unthinkable, they might transmit a group of heavily armed men.

Still, the intelligence report was that the Eridaneans only had one distorter left. And that was on the table before him. But intelligence reports were not always reliable.

Nemo wanted to go to the chief's aid at once, but he had to make certain preparations which would take at least ten minutes. Perhaps fifteen.

At his orders, Passepartout tore the bed sheets into strips. While he was doing this, Nemo, using one hand, pressed the watch stem to send a message to the chief. Then he held the gun on Passepartout while the Frenchman bound his master's hands behind him and his ankles together. Aouda then tied up Passepartout in similar fashion. Nemo struck her over the head and bound her. With the three strips left over, he gagged the three. For a moment he contemplated using his knife to finish them but decided against it. The chief wanted three bodies, but he needed them alive and able. Very well, he would get them.

First, he must make sure that they could not roll over and so get out of the door, which could not now be locked. He tore off other strips and bound the legs of the three together. Then he soaked the clothes of the three with petroleum from one swinging lamp. He set three other lamps near them so that if they moved in any direction, the vapors from the oil would be ignited by the flames of the three burning lamps.

He pocketed the watch and, closing the door behind him, went after Fix.

Fix was in a half-delirium. When he finally understood what Nemo wanted of him, he protested. He could not possibly walk to Fogg's cabin and then carry the watch back to his own cabin.

"Then you will crawl," Nemo said. "But you had better run, since the noise is going to wake up the entire ship. If you fail to get away with the watch, you will die. I'll make sure of that."

"I just can't do it," Fix muttered.

"Then you will die now," Nemo said.

Fix tried to get out of his bed but fell on the floor.

Nemo swore at him. Nature was proving once more that she was stronger than he.

Or had she?

He picked up Fix and hoisted him over his shoulders and carried him out onto the deck. He hoped that he would encounter no insomniacs strolling the deck, or any of the crew. If he did, he could explain that his friend was drunk and that he was making sure he got to his bed. But he did not want any strange events to be observed by anyone who might remember after the uproar had died down.

If Nature was against him that night, so was that other lady, Chance.

An officer did see him with his burden when he was halfway to Fogg's cabin.

Nemo explained that Fix had been sleeping on the deck and was either drunk or sick. He was returning him to his cabin.

"You are going the wrong way," the officer said. "Mr. Fix has his quarters back there."

"Ah, yes," Nemo said. "I must have gotten turned around."

"I doubt that Mr. Fix is inebriated," the officer said. "He has been very sick, as you must know if you are a friend of his. No doubt, he wandered out onto the deck in a delirium. I will call the doctor and make sure that he is restrained. And I'll see he has a nurse."

"You are very kind," Nemo said, wondering if he could kill the officer and drop him over the railing.

That was taken care of a moment later when they encountered a sailor. The officer insisted that the sailor help Nemo carry Fix back to the cabin. The sailor stood by while the officer went off to rouse the doctor and a nurse. Nemo wished to leave at once but knew that the crewmen would think it strange if he did not show concern for his "friend."

He was not, however, restrained from signaling to his chief the changed situation. He went into the water closet, took out the watch, and sent the coded message. The chief replied that he was not in that much of a hurry now that he knew help was on its way. Nemo wished to ask where the chief was and why he needed so many people, but he heard the doctor enter and thought it better not to stay in the closet too long. He had to get back to Fogg's cabin.

Even so, six more minutes passed before he was able to leave. The captain himself appeared and demanded an account. Nemo gave it. The captain seemed to be satisfied. Nemo said that he would look in on Fix in the morning, and he said good night. He hurried back hoping that Fix would be well enough in the morning to go to Fogg's cabin and pick up the watch. After all, it would be taped to the underside of the table. Even if the crew investigated the cabin, which they might well do once they observed the broken lock, they might not see the watch. Fix could gain entrance later and remove it.

He also hoped that the three Eridaneans would not decide to sacrifice themselves. If they set themselves afire, they would defeat his intention of taking them along. And the fire would bring the attention of the ship to that cabin.

If that happened, then he would go to his own cabin and transport himself to the chief. If need be, they could come back to the *General Grant*. It would mean a change in plans, which the chief evidently did not wish. But that could not be helped.

Nemo also wondered where the chief had gotten his distorter. As far as he knew, the one found in China was the only one the Capelleans possessed. But he did not know everything. That cursed secrecy was an evil not always necessary.

With such thoughts, he entered Fogg's cabin.

The next few empty moments, he had no thoughts at all.

The empty lamp swung against his head as he entered.

When he awoke, he was lying tied up in a fetal position on the table. He knew then that they had taken the distorter from him and secured it to the underside of the table on which he lay.

Passepartout, at Fogg's bidding, looked outside. On returning he said, "No Fix in sight,
sir. Could Fix be what he claims to be? Surely,
if he were a Capellean, Nemo would have
called him to his assistance? He would need
him to guard the distorter."

"That could well be," Fogg said. "You will
inquire after him sometime this morning.
After we return."

Passepartout said, "You are determined to
carry out this, if I may say so, mad project?"

"I am."

"Will I be accompanying you and this man,
sir?"

"Assuredly."

"We were lucky last time, sir. But now . . . "

"We must find out what is behind this."

Passepartout sighed but said no more.

On a chair lay the weapons which had been
taken from various hiding places in Nemo's
clothing. There was a knife which had been
strapped to his left leg, another in a scabbard
on his right leg, one in a sheath suspended
from his belt in the rear, and a small
cylindrical object the function of which Nemo
declined to explain. Passepartout, however,
found out how to operate the thing. A small
slide on its side, if pressed, would obviously
discharge the cylinder's contents from a hole
at the other end. Pointing the end close to
Nemo's face, he said, "Now, sir, please illuminate me. Or I will activate this and so possibly
extinguish you."

Passepartout had no intention of doing so,

since Nemo might wish to die to escape questioning. Nemo suspected this, but he could not be sure. And he did not intend to commit suicide unless he were in a far more hopeless situation.

"It will expel a stream of cyanide," he said.

"Very clever," Passepartout said. He gave it to Aouda to use in case Fix should appear.

Fogg said, "Miss Jejeebhoy, you will reset the distorter for *receive* a minute after we are gone. But I do not believe that you should stay in this cabin. The door cannot be locked, and we can't be sure that Fix won't be coming along. As soon as we've made the transit, you will take the distorter to your cabin and tape it to the underside of your table."

"Why not leave this man . . ."

"Nemo," Fogg said.

"This Nemo here?"

"I do not trust him, however capable Miss Jejeebhoy is," Fogg said. "He has enormous strength and great intelligence and resourcefulness. If we could get loose from our bonds while unobserved, he might be able to do so, observed or no."

Nemo had been hoping that they would reveal just how they had gotten loose, but they were keeping this a secret. He would find out someday; he swore to that.

"Besides," Fogg said, "seeing him bound and gagged may disconcert whoever is at the other end. You may gag him now, Passepartout."

"The clanging will undoubtedly awaken

everyone on the ship," Fogg said. "And Fix, if he is a Capellean, will know what is transpiring. If anyone knocks, tell them you are frightened and won't come out. Open the door for no one."

"I understand," Aouda said. Her voice was so soft, so lovely that Passepartout's heart bounced as if on a trampoline. How could Fogg resist such a woman, who so openly adored him?

Aouda said, "The bell-like sounds will have to remain another of those mysteries of the sea."

How prophetic her words were, though even she could not have foreseen that from that night there would be, not one, but two marine mysteries.

Passepartout crawled under the table and set the watch to activate within four minutes. He and Fogg climbed onto the table and stuck their fingers in their ears.

CHAPTER 14

The three men found themselves aboard another ship.

This, however, was a small sailing ship, and the sun stood at an altitude indicating some time around nine in the morning. Fogg knew that this would place them somewhere in the Atlantic, probably between the 15th and the 30th meridians. After this hasty calculation, he had no time for scientific matters.

They had dropped a few inches from the air onto a small deckhouse near the forepart of the ship. They were so close to a mast projecting from the roof of the deckhouse that they could reach out and touch it. Near them, piled on the roof, was an untidy mass of canvas.

The only other human being in sight was on the deck about twenty feet away where he would be sure to be out of range of the distorter field. Pieces of white cotton stuck out of his ears, and he held a revolver.

The sailor did not shoot at once because he must have thought that the two armed men were Capelleans and the bound man was the "slave" he had requested. It was true that he had expected only one Capellean and two bound men and a bound woman, but this may have further contributed to his astonishment. He could not grasp the idea that the situation had been changed.

Nemo, though painfully deafened by the nine clangors, nevertheless acted quickly. He straightened out and pivoted on his side, his long powerful legs coming around to strike both his captors across their ankles.

Passepartout, with the acrobat's quickness of reaction, leaped into the air. Fogg, who should have foreseen this move, since he claimed that the unforeseen did not exist, was knocked off his feet. His shot went wide of the sailor and, of course, informed him that all was not as it was supposed to be. The sailor fired at Fogg, missed, perhaps because of the roll and pitch of the ship, and then ran along the deck toward the stern. Passepartout bounded down in pursuit, even though armed with only one of Nemo's knives. He slipped, fell, rolled, and was back up on his feet at once.

Fogg had sprawled forward, and so was unable to keep Nemo from rolling off the roof of the deckhouse. He fell heavily on his side, and Fogg was after him a few seconds later. However, Fogg did not think there was much Nemo could do from then on. To make sure, he struck Nemo over the head with the butt of his revolver. Blood welled out from the wound, and a second later he suffered from another wound. The sailor, having turned once to fire at Passepartout, had missed. The bullet went downward and hit Nemo in his right arm.

Fogg left the limp and bleeding body and hastened after Passepartout. The sailor had taken refuge behind the rear of the aft cabin, just forward of the wheel. Passepartout waited for Fogg at the companionway to the fore cabin. This could be entered by a sliding door which was already shoved to one side.

Since they had not been in a confined space, and the distorter had been, the clangings had not affected their eardrums as much as the previous time. Their hearing was restored enough so that they could hear each other if they put their heads closely together and shouted. Fogg told his comrade to wait there while he inspected the interior of the aft cabins. Perhaps there was another entrance at the other end of his deckhouse. He had to make sure that the sailor did not try a surprise attack by using this. Before reemerging from the doorway, he would give the password. Thus, if the sailor had entered the other end, and overcame or killed Fogg, he would not be able to take Passepartout unawares.

"I saw the upper part of the wheel over the top of this house," the Frenchman said. "There was no one at it."

"The ship seems to be deserted except for this Capellean," Fogg said. "Very strange. But doubtless it can be explained. This seems to be a brigantine. And it's going on the star-board tack."

"Pardon, sir?"

"With the wind from the right. The jib and foremast staysails are set on the starboard tack. The ship is headed westward."

"Jib? Foremast staysail, sir?"

"The headsails. At the front of the ship. The two middle sails, those triangular-shaped ones, attached to the long boom projecting from the nose of the ship. The lower fore-topsail, the fourth from the bottom of the main mast, seems to have been set, but its head has been torn, probably by the wind.

"The foresail and upper fore-topsail are missing. I would judge that they have been blown from the yards. The main staysail, the lowest of the three triangular sails attached between the two masts, is down. It's that heap on the forward house. The aftersails have been removed. All other sails are furled, even the fore-and-aft sails. The main peak halyards, ropes for lowering and raising the sails, have been broken. Most of them are gone. Before the mainsail can be set, the halyards will have to be repaired. The seas are somewhat heavy, but the ship is not yawing much, that is, changing direction. But we can inspect the ship at a later time. I'm telling you this now so you'll have some idea of what to do if I don't return."

That was not nearly enough for him to know what to do, Passepartout thought.

Fogg, holding the revolver ready, entered

the cabin. The open door gave some light. There was a window on the bow end, but it had been covered with a piece of canvas secured by strips of plank nailed into the side of the cabin. The floor was wet, though there was no standing water. This could be accounted for by a heavy sea or rain having come in from somewhere. There was a clock without hands secured upside-down by the two nails to a partition. A table held a slate log and a rack—called by the sailors a fiddle— which kept dishes from sliding off. The rack held dishes but no food or drink was visible nor were there any knives and forks. A piece of canvas evidently used as a towel was on the rack.

Fogg also saw a stove and a swinging lamp.

He looked at the slate log, which would have been used by the chief to make notations while on deck.

"H" stood for the hour; "K," for knots. Though the log said it was for Monday the twenty-fifth, the date was nautical, not civil. The day would have started on noon of the twenty-fifth, not midnight. The twenty-fifth, for the ship, would end at noon of the twenty-sixth, after which it would be November twenty-sixth.

Today was November twenty-seventh. Something had happened at eight in the morning on the twenty-fifth, or a few hours later, to prevent the mate from continuing the log. When the record ended, the island of St. Mary's was about six miles to the southwest.

H	K	COURSE WIND	MONDAY 25th
1.	8		Comes in fresh
2.	8		
3.	8		
4.	8		
5.	8		
6.	8		
7.	9		
8.	9		At 8 P.M. fresh
9.	8		Got in royals & topg.
10.	8		sail
11.	8		
12.	8	E. by S.West	M.P., rainy
1.	8		
2.	8		
3.	8		At 5 made the island
4.	8		of S. Mary's, bear-
5.	8		ing E.S.E.
6.	8		
7.	8		
8.	8		
9.			At 8 eastern point
10.			bore S.S.W. 6 miles
11.			distant
12.			

On the port, or left, side of the cabin was the pantry. Fogg, entering it cautiously, found an open box holding moist sugar, a bag with several pounds of tea, an open barrel of flour, an open box of dried herrings, some rice and kidney beans in containers, some pots of preserved fruit, cans of food, and a nutmeg. These were all dry.

Fogg went back into the mate's cabin and looked around again. On the starboard side was a small bracket holding a tiny vial of oil for, he guessed, a sewing machine. This was still upright. If very heavy seas had been recently met, it would have been thrown to the deck. The bed was dry and showed no damage from water.

He looked under the bed and drew out the ship's ensign and its private signal: WT. The letter "W" had been sewn on. Also under the bed was a pair of stout sailor's boots, designed for bad weather but apparently unused. There were also two drawers. One held some pieces of iron and two unbroken panes of glass. The lower drawer held a pair of log sunglasses and a new log reel but no log line.

The next cabin, the last, was the captain's. He doubted that the sailor was in it. If he had entered it, he surely would have made his presence known by now. However, Fogg entered it slowly, and he kept to the sides of the cabin after he got in. There was a skylight through which the sailor might shoot if he crawled onto the top of the deckhouse.

A harmonium, a reed organ, was by the partition in the center of the cabin. Near it was a number of books, mostly religious, by their titles.

A child's high chair was on the floor along with a chest containing bottles of medicinals. A compass minus its card was on a table. A portable sewing machine was in a case attached to the bulkhead.

Under a bed, Fogg found a scabbarded sword. He removed it, thinking that he could use it. It seemed to be of Italian make and had probably been an officer's.

By the port side of the cabin was a water closet. Still cautious, because the sailor might be hiding there in ambush, Fogg looked within. Near the door was a damp bag. It looked as if it might have been wet by rain or spray entering through the half-covered porthole on the opposite side.

Curious, Fogg entered the closet. He opened the bag and found ladies' garments, all wet, inside. So the captain had been accompanied by his wife and small child.

The starboard side held two windows, also covered by canvas cut from a sail.

There were no signs of violence anywhere, and the cabin had no aft exit.

Fogg returned to the deck, though not without giving the password first. Passepartout said that the sailor had shown his head around the corner several times but had ducked back each time. Fogg told Passepartout what he had observed. He gave him the pistol, saying, "You hold that man with this. I'll go back to check on Nemo and inspect the fore deckhouse."

With the sword in hand, he walked slowly down the starboard side. Though his gait made him a better target for the sailor, he did not believe that it made him a good enough one. What with the wind and the motion of the ship, accuracy was not to be expected from a revolver at this range. Evidently the sailor, if he saw Fogg, had the same thoughts. No shots were fired.

Just before arriving at the fore deckhouse, Fogg went over to the port side. He looked around its corner. Nemo was gone.

Torn strips of sheet were evidence of Nemo's great strength. He had burst them apart with sheer muscularity. His boots lay by the strips.

Before he had returned on the starboard side, Fogg had looked down the port side. Nemo's still figure had been on the deck. So, the wily fellow had waited until Fogg was out of sight, because he knew that Passepartout, watching for the sailor, would have his back to him.

Fogg spun around, hoping that Nemo had not passed him going aftward while he was going forward. But he had. He was running barefoot, as swiftly and as silently as a tiger. He was only about ten feet from the Frenchman's back.

Fogg gave his first yell in years and ran toward the two. Passepartout, half-deafened, did not hear him. Nemo struck him on the back of his neck with his left fist. The Frenchman was hurled face forward into the deckhouse wall. He crumpled, and Nemo picked up the revolver. Grinning, he turned toward Fogg. Triumphant he might look, but he was pale, and blood ran down his right arm and dripped from his hand. His right arm seemed to be useless, since it hung down at his side and, though right-handed, he held the revolver in his left.

Fogg half-spun to port and raced toward the deckhouse. If Nemo was firing at him he could not hear the reports, but the knowledge that he probably was made him increase his speed. He went around the side of the deckhouse and then to its forepart. Hidden momentarily from the two enemies, he stood there, breathing hard. So now events were suddenly in Nemo's favor. Passepartout was out of the action, perhaps forever, and Nemo and the sailor each had a revolver.

After making sure that Passepartout could not imitate Nemo's feat, the two would proceed toward the bow. One would come along the port rail; one, by the starboard rail. Their paths would converge at the place where Fogg now stood. He could attack one with his sword, but the other would quickly join the man he attacked. At point-blank range, they would not miss.

The fore deckhouse was about thirteen feet square and six feet above the deck. It would contain the fo'c'sle or crew's quarters, the galley, and, perhaps, a cabin for the second mate. It would not afford a good hiding place or even a mediocre one.

Fogg looked upward. He could still run to one of the rope ladders formed of transverse ropes called ratlines and attached to the shrouds, pairs of ropes from the mastheads which gave lateral support to the masts. If he went up a ladder, he could at least get away from them for a while. If he then went out onto the yards, he would force them to use both hands while getting close enough to him so they would not waste their bullets. Perhaps he could attack them then with his sword. If he were an acrobat such as Passepartout, he might go up the main mast to one of the middle triangular sails and ascend by its ropes to the aft mast. If he could get down quickly enough, while the two were still aloft, he could seize the wheel and change the direction of the ship. If it swung around violently enough, it might dislodge the two.

Fogg did not, however, follow his desperate plan.

Instead, he slid open the wooden door on the forward cabin and darted inside. This was on the port side of the deckhouse and seemed to be the second mate's. It held a sea chest the examination of which Fogg deferred. He went through another sliding door into the crew's quarters, placed closest to the bow. His log does not mention his feelings at this point, but we may suppose that even the face of the imperturbable Fogg lit up with delight.

There, as he had hoped, was the watch, taped to the ceiling of the fo'c'sle. He tore it loose and, holding it to his ear, ran out of the entrance onto the deck of the bow.

The watch was emitting, in Eridanean code, a stream of ringing sounds. Aouda had set her distorter on *receive*.

If he set the Capellean distorter for *transmit* he could escape. That meant leaving the enemy distorter, Passepartout, and the explanation of the mystery of the ship behind him. As for the first, he must submit to it if he were transmitted. As for the third, it was better to survive at the price of ignorance. As for the second, it was probable that Passepartout was dead. He was doomed even if Fogg stayed here and tried to fight with only the sword.

He stood for about five seconds, five seconds during which his enemies would be approaching.

Six seconds after this, the two Capelleans were dismayed—and deafened again—when nine clanging sounds seemed to tear the air around them and buffet their eardrums. Both, we may presume, swore at the same time they turned pale. Both, we know, started to run into the cabin under the assumption that they would find only the device. The foxy Eridanean had undoubtedly taken the only way out. He must have removed the distorter from the ceiling and taped it to the underside of a table and been transmitted back to the *General Grant*.

Nemo must have been blaming himself for not having first retrieved the device. But he could console himself with the thought that if he had done so, he, instead of Fogg, might have been trapped in the deckhouse.

The Capelleans met at the forward entrance of the deckhouse. The sailor arrived first and so was ahead of Nemo in entering the fo'c'sle. He halted because, to his astonishment, the watch was still taped to the ceiling. That was all he saw. The edge of Fogg's sword struck the top of his head. He dropped; the revolver fell from his hand. And Fogg picked up the revolver.

And Nemo? After the first moment of chagrin, not unmixed with panic, he backed out of the companionway.

The affair had not suddenly become reversed. It had just evened out. Neither side held a particular advantage at this moment. Both were armed. Fogg was shut up in the deckhouse, but Nemo was losing blood and strength.

The gray-eyed man got onto the top of the deckhouse and proceeded to remove his coat and his shirt. He tore his shirt into strips and bound them around the arm. The wound, fortunately, was only a flesh wound, and blood seemed to stop flowing after a few moments. Nevertheless, he might as well have had only one arm, and the gorilla-like power of his muscles had drained out of him.

He decided that he could afford to desert his post for a few minutes. Fogg would not dare to make a dash for the outside. At least, not for a while. Nemo would finish off the other fellow and then return to the deckhouse. Fogg would still be crouching near a bulkhead or under some furniture. He would know that Nemo could break the deckhouse windows and fire from there. If he had not been so overwhelmed by the thought of Fogg escaping, he would have done that at once. Of course, if he did use the windows, he stood a good chance of receiving Fogg's bullets in his face. It would be discreet to remain away from them.

Eventually, Fogg would be driven out of the deckhouse by thirst and hunger. He would not have access to the galley. Nemo had ascertained from his chief that the galley was partitioned off from the fo'c'sle and second mate's cabin. Even if Fogg knocked a hole through the partition, he would not find much food. Most of the supplies were kept in the pantry, which was in the deckhouse aft.

Nemo moved softly away from the roof of the deckhouse only because it was his nature to do so. He did not have to fear that Fogg would hear him. Fogg would still be defeated by the clangings.

Nemo had proceeded about thirty feet toward the stern when the nine clangings struck again. He whirled. What the devil was Fogg doing now?

Had he indeed departed this time? Or was he setting the same trap? And, if he had gone, would he not be quickly back with help?

There was nothing to prevent Fogg from setting the distorter to revert automatically to *receive* within a certain time.

But Fogg might be hoping that he would think just this and so rush in to turn the distorter off before Fogg & Company would return.

Nemo was in a highly indecisive state, a foreign one to this man of great intelligence and speedy action. If he entered either entrance to the fore deckhouse, he would be exposed to fire from a man whose coolness and accuracy with arms had been proven in Bundelcund.

Moreover, Fogg would be in semidarkness. The windows were covered by shutters, and while he could destroy these to let some light in, he would be exposed. Fogg would expect him to try that and so would be ready for him. The deckhouse was built of thin planking through which Fogg's bullets could find him even if Nemo stood to one side while tearing off the canvas coverings.

He stood on the deck for a minute, and then he turned away. If only Fogg did not find the papers on the chief. The distorter itself would have to be abandoned. That could not be helped.

And if only Passepartout were not dead.

Nemo did not expect Fogg to surrender to save Passepartout. That happened only in novels. Fogg would know that he would be killed if he did surrender. Nemo would no longer consider keeping him as a prisoner.

The two of them might possibly be able to sail
the ship to some port, but Nemo could not
stay awake long enough for this. And he could
not take any more chances on a live Fogg. The
Englishman was too wily.

Passepartout was sitting with his back
against the bulkhead of the main cabin. His
forehead and nose were bloody, and his eyes
were dull.

Nevertheless, he spat at Nemo.

"Good! You are still alive!" Nemo said.

Passepartout did not reply.

Nemo searched him but found no weapons.
He picked up Passepartout with his left hand,
his revolver stuck in his belt, and propelled
him forward. The Frenchman sprawled out
onto the deck, but, after being raised again, he
managed to stay on his feet.

"If your master is willing to make a bargain
by which we will all gain, though some loss by
all is inevitable, then you will stay alive,"
Nemo said.

He pushed Passepartout ahead of him with
the end of his revolver until they had reached
the fore deckhouse. Standing by the entrance
to the second mate's cabin, Nemo shouted out
the terms. His own voice sounded distant, and
he was not sure that Fogg was yet able to hear
him. Or, for that matter, that he was even in
the cabin. Fogg could have slipped out while
he was busy with the Frenchman, but he did
not think so.

After a short silence, Fogg's voice came
faintly.

"Very well! Provided that you tell me what happened to the people on this ship. I don't expect you to tell me anything about your own people which might reveal your secrets."

"I can't tell you much because our man didn't have much time to impart anything but a bare outline."

To hear him, Fogg had to be close to the door. Perhaps if he were to make two quick shots, one on either side of the door? The bullets would go through the thin planking. But no, it was too risky.

"It all seems mysterious," Nemo said. "But similar things have happened before and doubtless will happen again. As you may have observed, there are signs of a hasty departure but none of violence. The vessel has a cargo of seventeen hundred barrels of alcohol contained in spruce and red oak barrels. This is highly volatile, and any rupture of barrels could be a source of explosion or fire. But such was not the case. This ship was not abandoned because of that.

"The sailors left their clothing, sea boots, oilskins, and their tobacco pipes. So the situation was of such a nature that it let no time for taking articles which a sailor would normally not leave behind. Especially the pipes. It is obvious that the misfortune did not occur during meal time, since there are no places set for meals.

"According to . . . to our man . . . "

"His name was Edward W. Head, and he was the cook and steward," Fogg said. "He

had his papers on him. That his name was
Head is significant, I believe. He must be your
chief."

"Only a coincidence," Nemo said. "We have
abandoned that ancient, but useless, custom
of using names which indicate a person's
function."

"Perhaps," Fogg said.

Nemo wondered what else he had found on
Head.

"Is he dead?" Nemo said.

"Yes."

"You may have noticed that the navigation
book, sextant, and chronometer are missing,"
Nemo said. "Evidently the captain—his name
was Briggs, by the way—had time to grab
these. Other articles, such as clothes, were
left behind. Nor were provisions from the
pantry stored on the yawl."

"The yawl? What about the main lifeboat,
the longboat?"

"That was left behind at New York. It was
damaged during the loading of the barrels.
Several fell out of the sling on it, and Captain
Briggs did not want to delay the ship while it
was being repaired. The yawl could hold ten
people, but it was smaller and not as
seaworthy as the longboat."

"The last hour marked on the deck log was
eight A.M., November twenty-fifth," Fogg said.
"And after that?"

"Between nine and ten o'clock, the *Mary
Celeste* was within several miles of the Dollabarat shoals," Nemo said. "Those are

dangerous shoals about three and a quarter miles southeast of the Formigas rocks. The Formigas are, it is thought, the peaks of submerged mountains. The *Mary Celeste* was not close enough to be in any peril and would have passed on safely, but . . . ''

Nemo wondered why Fogg was having him give this lengthy explanation. Was he hoping to drag out the time before their departure because he had planned some trick which required time to prepare?

Well, there was nothing he could do about it. But if things suddenly went wrong for him, he would kill Passepartout at once. And perhaps this prolonged talk might turn to his advantage, if he could think of something.

"One of those inexplicable but frequently occurring calms befell the ship. At any other place, the *Mary Celeste* could have ridden it out. But now, her sails sagging, the ship was borne by the currents toward the Dollabarat shoals. These have taken many a victim. And it looked as if they would soon fasten their teeth into the hull of another. Captain Briggs had the light sails furled and the mainsail lowered and the ship hove to on the starboard tack. This was to ensure that, if the wind should rise in time, it would blow against the sails and stop its headway. Then the yawl might catch up with the ship, and the crew could board it.

"After this, the captain ordered that the ship be abandoned.''

"The yawl lay across the main hatch. This

was unsecured while a section of the port rail, which you no doubt saw is missing, was removed. There was no time for a leisurely departure; everything was done in a few minutes. The yawl was lowered without tackle, and the main peak-halyard was unroven. It was used as a towline for the yawl with an end still attached to the gaff.''

(The gaff was the spar upon which the head of a fore-and-aft sail was extended. The halyard was about four hundred feet long, and where it was fastened to the gaff it would be about eight feet above the deck.)

"The captain took the ship's papers, chronometer, and sextant. A sailor tried to get a compass; that is why the binnacle is displaced and the compass was broken in the haste to extract it. There was no time to get the other compass. The ship had drifted too close to the rocks.

"At this point, Head refused to get into the yawl with the others. He believed that his only chance of survival lay in using the distorter. If he were in the yawl, he would have to leave behind both the distorter and witnesses. He could, of course, shoot the nine people in the boat, but his revolver held only six cartridges at a time, and he might be overpowered before he could reload or perhaps even before he had finished firing. He decided to take his chances on the ship itself. If he could get the attention of . . . of one of us who had a distorter, he could be transmitted. Still better, if he could get enough men transmitted to the

Mary Celeste and the calm did not last, then he could sail it to Europe."

Why, Fogg wondered, had Head taken passage on a brigantine as a cook and steward and not proceeded to Europe by a steam liner? Was it because he thought that the Eridaneans would be looking for him on the passenger ships? Had he hoped to slip across on this sailing ship, quit or desert at Gibraltar, and from thence go in disguise to England? What was he carrying that was so valuable? The distorter? That was certainly valuable enough, but why had he not waited in America until the Chinese agent got to England so he could transmit himself to there? Another Capellean could have brought the distorter at a later time. If it were the distorter itself that was responsible for all this secrecy and haste, he could understand Head's actions. But he felt that there was some other reason.

Stuart, if he were aware of Head's existence and his mission, would have set his people to look for Head. Because of the overstrict security system, he had not informed Fogg of this. Or, perhaps, all this had started after Fogg left England and Stuart had not been able to get news of this through to him.

Fogg determined to make another search of Head's body before he left the cabin.

Nemo said, "Captain Briggs raved when Head refused to get into the yawl. He called him a coward and a mutineer and threatened him with all the consequences of mutiny. But there was little he could do and no time to do it in if he could do it. The yawl departed and presently was at the end of the towline. Briggs was waiting to see what would happen. If a breeze arose in time, the ship would sail away from the shoals. The yawl would be rowed up to it while the line was taken in, and the *Mary Celeste* could be boarded. He must also have thought that Head, to regain favor and get any charges dropped, would steer the ship and give any other assistance he could.

"But a wind did arise, filling the square sails, and the ship moved away from the shoals. It was however, going westward in a direction opposite to its original course. The towline became taut and was pulled at an angle away from the ship. It broke. The yawl, though rowed desperately toward the ship, could not catch up."

"And why didn't Head bring the ship about?" Fogg said.

"Because he was afraid that he could not depend on Brigg's gratitude. Briggs was a stern New England skipper who would probably arrest him and charge him with mutiny even if Head had saved the whole company."

Was Nemo telling the whole truth? Had the sudden strain really snapped the towline? Or had Head severed it to make sure that Briggs would not get back aboard? By the time the yawl made land or its passengers were picked up by another ship—if they did not perish before this at sea—Head would be long gone.

As for the story of the panicky and premature abandonment, that could be true enough. About two hundred and thirty-two derelicts were found every year. Sometimes, the crews were picked up by other ships. Sometimes, they were never seen again. Sometimes, the reasons for the hasty desertions were unknown. A fire, an explosion, too much water in the hold. Sometimes, no reasons could be found by the investigators.

The case of the *Mary Celeste* was only one of many—if it were ever found. Many ships were just swallowed up by the ocean.

"The ship went through several squalls, hence the damage to the sails and the wetness of the floors and garments in some of the cabins," Nemo said. "There was little that Head could do about them, and they were not serious. He was mainly concerned with making contact with our people who had distorters. He did not even bother shutting the doors or the fore and lazaret hatches though he did wash the dishes.

"He was beginning to despair, because if a violent storm did hit the ship, it would surely go down with him aboard."

"He will despair no more," Fogg said.

CHAPTER 15

Fogg told Nemo to wait a few minutes before the truce arrangements were put into effect. This delay would upset Nemo, who would wonder what Fogg was up to. Fogg did not worry about this. He only wanted time for another inspection of the corpse.

Being a very tidy man, he cleaned up the blood on the floor with a piece of canvas. Later, he would use seawater to remove all traces of blood from the floor and water and lemon juice to cleanse the sword. The latter he would put back in its scabbard under the captain's bed. Fogg wished to leave the ship much as he had found it.

He stripped the body, felt the clothes, and then ripped them open with his jackknife. He found nothing in them. The boots were taken apart, but these revealed nothing. Head seemed to have all his original teeth; there were no caps concealing hollows in which objects could be kept. With some repugnance, he probed the anal cavity but found it to be only as nature intended it.

Possibly, the skin bore schematics or

writing in some type of invisible ink. He had no means to bring these out. Should he drop the body into the sea or take it back to the *General Grant* for more tests? There was bound to be a hullabaloo because of the three series of clangings, and when these sounded for the fourth time, announcing his arrival, more uproar would ensue. Every cabin might be searched, and it would be more than embarrassing to try to explain Head's corpse.

Before finishing his examination, he pulled on the corpse's hair again to make sure that a shaved head with a code on it was not below a wig. Head's hair seemed to be his own.

Fogg arose and went to the doorway. He declared that he was ready to start disarmament proceedings. Passepartout thoroughly frisked Nemo while Nemo held his revolver at Passepartout's head. The Frenchman announced that Nemo seemed not to have concealed any weapons since the inspection on the *General Grant.*

Nemo frisked Passepartout with the same results.

Passepartout then moved away, stopping when he came to the railing.

Nemo grasped the barrel of his Colt in his right hand, which retained enough strength for this task. He prepared to eject the cartridges from the magazine. Fogg threw the sword and jackknife and Head's knife outside. He stood in the doorway, holding his revolver by the barrel. Together, as Passepartout slowly counted, the two got rid of their cartridges.

Fogg stepped outside onto the deck, his cartridges in one hand. Nemo backed away until he was by the starboard railing. Fogg backed away to the port railing. At a signal from Passepartout, both men, one by one, in unison, tossed their cartridges into the sea. Fogg had removed his coat and shirt before coming out of the deckhouse to ensure that he would not be able to palm any cartridges. This was unnecessary, since the cartridges could be seen sailing away over and into the sea.

Passepartout threw the knives into the ocean. Nemo had permitted the Frenchman to do this because he did not think he was in a condition to hurt him even if Passepartout did come at him with a knife.

Nemo had wanted the sword to go overboard, too, but Fogg had insisted that all articles aboard were to be restored to their original positions, except for Head, of course.

This was a ticklish moment. Nemo could make a dash for the sword. If Passepartout picked it up first, Nemo thought he could dodge the first feeble slash and close in with Passepartout. Even if Passepartout threw it overboard, Nemo would have the others at a disadvantage. Wounded though he was, and still suffering a strong headache from the two blows on his head, he felt that he was physically superior to the combination of the others.

It was then that Fogg reminded him that Aouda was waiting at the other end with the cyanide expeller. She had orders to use it if Nemo appeared alone.

Despite all this, Nemo suddenly decided that he would attempt to overpower them. If he could get Fogg over the railing and into the sea, he could deal easily enough with the Frenchman. He would not kill him, because he might need him to transmit the proper code to Aouda. But there were many ways to make him yield that information. And if Passepartout should somehow refuse, or die, then he would send a message to the man from China. The fellow surely must be listening by now. Or, if that failed, he would turn the ship around toward the east again and hope that another ship would sight the *Mary Celeste*.

It was at this moment that Nemo was stricken with a fit of shaking. Whether it was the first time or not, we do not know. Fogg was startled, because he had not observed anything like this while serving under Nemo. From later accounts by another Briton, the fits became more numerous and one phase of them became permanent. What the nature of the disease was, no one knows. Perhaps his neural charges, restrained too long, damped a part of his brain.

In any event, on this occasion Nemo began shaking violently all over. This lasted for about a minute, after which he seemed to regain a partial control. Now only his head,

with the face thrust forward, oscillated in a
curiously snake-like fashion. This, with his
high domed forehead and the large widely
spaced eyes, made him look like a king cobra.

After perhaps sixty seconds, the nervous
motion ceased. He had become even paler,
and he looked very weary. He passed his
hands over his eyes and groaned loudly
enough for Passepartout to hear him.

"Great God! Enough! Enough!"

Then he said, "I can't do it!"

Neither of the Eridaneans knew what he
meant by this, but we may deduce that he had
planned a final attack on them but now
realized that he could not carry it out.

Passepartout took the sword to the
captain's cabin, cleaned it as required by
Fogg, and put it back in its scabbard under
the bed. When he returned, he found that
neither Fogg nor Nemo had moved.

The next step was to dispose of Head's
corpse and clothing. Nemo had recovered
enough to assist with this. While Fogg held
the feet of the body, Nemo supported the
other end with one arm. He failed to let loose
of the corpse at the same time as Fogg, and,
for a second or so, his hand passed over
Head's face. Fogg thought nothing of this
incident except that it indicated Nemo's
sickness and consequent lack of coordination.

The fo'c'sle was cleaned up so that no traces
of blood remained. Fogg brought an open box
from the lazaret. He placed it upside-down on
the deck. This was near the opening in the

port rail left by its removal for access of the yawl. Its underside held the distorter, set for *transmit* in three minutes.

The three crowded upon the box and linked arms. Fogg was counting on either the roll of the ship sending it into the water after the weight on it was relieved or heavy seas carrying it off. He hoped that the transmission would take place before the three men were precipitated off the box by the ship's rolling. He had given Aouda more instructions, and she, using the watch which Fogg had purchased for her in Hong Kong, timed the action exactly right. She turned her distorter on about six seconds before Fogg's began operation. The three, accompanied by the ear-paining clangings, appeared on top of the table in Aouda's cabin.

Aouda had thrust the end of the expeller up toward Nemo's face. He made no motion until told by Fogg that he could leave. He looked slightly surprised, as if he had expected that, now he was outnumbered, he would be taken prisoner again. Certainly, if the situation had been reversed, he would have taken advantage of it. He bowed and walked out of the cabin into a crowd of near-hysterical passengers.

Since they could not hear yet, Fogg and Aouda communicated with pencil and paper.

Yes, Aouda wrote, there had been much running about and screaming. After a while, most of the passengers, chattering loudly but over their panic, had returned to their cabins. Some had stayed on deck; some had repaired to the bar, which was opened at their insistence.

The two series of clangings which had followed Fogg's activation of the distorter to fool the Capelleans had brought everybody boiling onto the decks again. Some passengers had insisted that the center of the noise was in the cabins near Aouda's. Yes, a passenger check had been made, and an officer had talked with her through the door. Yes, she had overheard the discovery of the shattered lock on Fogg's door, and crewmen had been searching for him. But in this turmoil, who could find whom? The broken lock could be attributed to the efforts of a thief to get into Fogg's cabin while the panic was on.

Fogg thought that it was unfortunate that this could not be kept out of the newspapers. Both Capelleans and Eridaneans, reading of the mysterious bell-like noises on the *General Grant* would know that the distorters had been used. They would be watching the ship when it discharged its passengers.

The reader is doubtless wondering why Verne did not describe the mysterious noises. The answer is that he would have if Fogg had been in any way connected with them by the authorities. Of, if there had been a logical explanation for the noises, Verne might have included them. But since the bell-like sounds were only one more of the many mysteries of the sea, Verne, as a disciplined novelist, did not see why he should include the incident. If he had included every interesting, but irrelevant, event, *Around The World In Eighty Days* would have been twice as long.

It is also possible that Verne never even heard about the clangings.

Late the next day, Passepartout met Mr. Fix on the promenade of the forward deck. Though somewhat pale and shaky, Fix had regained most of his strength. Nemo had told him all that had happened. Fix, Nemo said, was to continue to play innocent. He must say nothing of his sickness to Passepartout, who would guess that was why Fix had not accompanied Nemo.

Fix told Passepartout that he had been sleeping peacefully until the first of those terrible belling noises awakened him. What did Mr. Passepartout know about these?

The Frenchman said he knew no more than anybody else. After some small talk and some large drinks, he returned to Fogg. Perhaps, he said, Fix was only a detective.

Fogg replied that could well be. And now, would he sit down with Miss Jejeebhoy and hear what Fogg knew about Nemo? There was no sense in keeping it secret any longer, if, indeed, there had ever been any sense in it. They should understand what sort of man they were up against.

In 1865, Fogg had been summoned by the chief to a secret meeting. He, Fogg, had been on a long mission in the eastern Mediterranean. But he had been replaced by another and told to hurry to London. That he was to

have a tete a tete with the chief and not get his
orders via cards or other means indicated the
seriousness of the situation. On a train to
Paris, Fogg was surprised to see the chief
enter his compartment. The chief said he had
reason to believe that the proposed meeting
place was under Capellean surveillance. So he
had intercepted Fogg in France.

The chief had learned that the man called
Nemo (no one knew his true name) was about
to launch a very disturbing project. The word
"launch" was used in a double sense, since
this project involved a submersible vessel.
After the vessel had been built, it would
venture onto the seas on a pirating expedition.

"Ah, the *Nautilus!*" Passepartout said. He,
like most of the world, had read in 1869 Professor Pierre Arronax's narrative, edited and
agented by the everbusy Jules Verne.

Fogg continued. "This Nemo has an
inventive genius which is, alas, not dedicated
to the world's good. It has been devoted to the
good of the Capelleans, of course, who ration-
alized that the goal justifies the means.

"Nemo had almost completed the submersible vessel, which was far beyond anything
else in its scientific advances. Part of the
ingenious devices which enabled it to operate
derived from knowledge handed down by the
Old Ones. The rest was due to Nemo's almost
superhuman intelligence. The submersible
would bring in an enormous amount of
wealth, both from looting ships and recovering sunken treasure. With this at their dis-

posal, the Capelleans could make much more effective war on us. For one thing, they could hire great numbers of criminals to use against us. These, of course, would not know the ultimate identity of their employers, but they would not need to do so."

"I never suspected that the *Nautilus* was of Capellean origin!" Passepartout cried. "But Arronax's account makes him out to be a hero!"

"Yes, for those who have not read the account carefully," Fogg said. "A close reading soon evaporates the clouds of the Byronic hero which Nemo managed to gather about himself. He was, to put it simply, a pirate. A bloodthirsty money-hungry pirate who sent hundreds of the innocent to a watery grave. It is evident that he kept Professor Arronax, his valet, Conseil, and the harpooner, Ned Land, alive only because of his need for intellectual companionship and to feed his ego. Conseil and Land were not his mental equals, but if Nemo had killed them, Arronax would have refused to talk to him.

"Nemo, as I said, is a mathematical and engineering genius. But even he, if he were only an Earthling, could not have designed and built the motors to drive the *Nautilus* at fifty miles per hour or have created the metal alloys to withstand the pressure of the ocean at forty-eight-thousand feet. He told Arronax that it was electricity which propelled the submersible. Was it this or the power of the atom itself that he used? In either case, he

must have had access to some information
handed down by the Capellean Old Ones.
From this he deduced the rest, though it took
a great genius to do that.

"One of our spies learned of the orders
Nemo had placed with various industries all
over the civilized world, including the States.
After all, the Americans, whatever their other
deficiencies, are splendid engineers. Nemo
was bringing these specially made parts to a
remote island and putting them together
there. Our chief told me to get admitted into
Nemo's confidence and to sabotage the vessel.
I obeyed the first and expected to be able to do
the second. Through certain channels, I
learned that Nemo was recruiting a crew
from different countries. Most of these, poor
deluded fellows, were patriots. They came
from countries which lay under the heels of
oppressors. Nemo told them that he would be
waging a deadly war against the oppressors.
He hinted that he himself came from a land
which was suffering under British rule. To
make it appear that he was an Asiatic Indian,
he wore glass lenses which gave his eyes a
black color, and he often talked as if he had
been exiled from his native country after an
unsuccessful revolt against the British.

"He even had a common ship's language
which he taught the crew to master enough to
obey commands in this tongue. This, I believe,
was the dialect of Bundelcund. Nemo had
spent much time in Bundelcund, a good part
of it as the aide to the rajah before the rajah

became a traitor to the Capelleans. In fact, I would not be surprised to learn that Nemo had talked the rajah into becoming a renegade. Nemo's motto should be, not *Mobilis in mobili*, the swift among the swift, but *Aut Nemo aut nemo*. Either Nemo or nobody.

"Be that as it may, I was enlisted as Patrick M'Guire, an Irishman who hated the English. I was part of the crew that terrorized the seas from 1866 through 1868. I was equally guilty of sinking all those ships, since I had to play out my role. I told myself that these would have been sunk anyway. I had to cooperate in this so that I could sooner or later stop Nemo's nefariousness. In fact, without me aboard, the *Nautilus* might operate for decades. Nevertheless, I felt guilty.

"And imagine my state when I learned, after the affair was over, that I had participated in sinking a vessel on which my own father was a passenger. I was guilty of fratricide."

At this point, Aouda, tears coursing down her cheeks, put her hand on Fogg's. He did not seem to notice it. At least, he did not withdraw his hand.

"That it was not intentional did not ease my conscience one bit.

"From the time that the *Nautilus* plunged into the sea on her maiden cruise, I looked for an opportunity to sink her and with her its commander. But in those crowded quarters, where a dozen eyes are always on you, I had no chance. After we rammed the *U.S.*

Abraham Lincoln, we picked up Arronax and his companions. Events went much as the professor described them, though much happened of which he was ignorant.

"And then we were pulled into the maelstrom off the Lofoten Islands. Even that mighty whirlpool might not have defeated us if I had not had my first chance to act. While the others were occupied at their posts, and frozen with the terror of the maelstrom, I destroyed the circuits which controlled the steering."

"Ah, then it was you who was responsible for sinking that accursed submersible!" Passepartout said.

He had completely abandoned his original concept of Nemo as a battler against evil, a tortured and lonely genius whose only mission in life was revenge against the oppressor.

"Yes. But I should have blown it up long before that, even though it meant that I, too, should die. Arronax, Conseil, and Land, as you know, escaped. So did I. So did Nemo. Perhaps others did. I do not know. I thought at the time that I was the only survivor. Several months later, I was back in London. The chief and I assumed that Nemo had died. Then I saw him on the second of October in the shade of that doorway near the Reform Club."

"But," Passepartout said, "is this man all bad? What about the portrait of the woman and two children which Arronax said hung on

the wall of Nemo's cabin? Did not the good
professor see Nemo stretch out his arms to
the portrait, kneel before it, and sob deeply?
Does a man with no heart behave so?''

"He undoubtedly does not lack all senti-
ment," Fogg said. "It has been established
that even the most hardened criminal may
love his mother, his wife, his children, or his
dog. I do not know the history of his familial
connections. To tell the truth, I was surprised
to learn that he had a wife and children. But I
do not think that his marriage could have
lasted long. His intellect is so lofty that he
regards all others, man or woman, as mental
pygmies. And he is an excessively imperious
and moody man. Perhaps his wife left him,
taking the children with her. That may be why
he wept. His self-image was bruised; if anyone
were to leave, it should be he.

"At any event, he did not always have the
portrait on the wall. You may have noticed, in
Arronax's account, that he himself observed
the portrait only after being on the *Nautilus*
almost a year and a half. Surely, if he had
seen it before, he would have commented on
it? Now I, who was aboard from the
beginning, only saw it put up twice. Both
times were on July second; it was a second of
July when Arronax witnessed the sad scene.
This date must have some significance to
Nemo, but of what only he knows."

"Then, sir, if I understand you aright,"
Passepartout said, "Nemo was not an Indian
patriot who gathered a crew from all over the

world to fight oppressors. He was a pirate."

"Most of his crew were patriots, yes. But Nemo was using them. They believed that he was turning his treasures over to underground organizations to finance their revolutions. No such thing. Most of the wealth went either to the Capellean exchequer or into his own bank accounts.

"As for the portrait, the woman and children looked very European; they looked far more English than Hindu."

"But Aouda looks European."

"She could pass for a Provencal or an Italian, true."

"Pardon me, if I persist, sir," Passepartout said. "What about the professor's final scene with Captain Nemo? Did he not hear Nemo sobbing, were not his last words, 'God Omnipotent! Enough! Enough!' Did not Arronax wonder if this was an outburst of sorrow or a confession of remorse?"

"You observed the fit suffered by Nemo while we were disarming on the *Mary Celeste?* Nemo looks, and is, a giant in stature and strength. And he has, like all Capelleans, the elixir which should enable him to live to a thousand years. This, as you know, increases resistance to disease. But it does not make us invulnerable to disease. I am certain from my observations that Nemo is doomed to last no longer than most men. He is inflicted with some sort of nervous malady. Its effects have been few so far. But they will increase. And part of this affliction is an infrequent but blinding and sickening headache. Perhaps this is caused by a tumor, though I suspect that damage caused by undischarged traumas is responsible. But when he was crying out, 'Enough! Enough!' he was, I believe, calling for a cessation of his pain. That he, a zealous atheist, called on God indicates the extent of his torture. And that he spoke English in this painful moment, when a man is likely to revert to his native language, is significant."

"He did not speak in French? But Arronax . . . "

"Failed to mention that it was in English. No, Nemo is a native of some English-speaking land, most probably of Ireland. He could speak Gaelic fluently when talking to one of his Irish crewmen, though it was evident that it was not the speech he learned from his parents. I, though, posing as an Irishman, claimed to be from Dublin and ignorant of all but a few phrases of the Celtic."

"Poor man!" Aouda said. "To be suffering so and thus doomed to die early when he could live to a thousand years! Indeed, the elixir will only prolong his agonies. Without it, he would die in a few years, his sufferings mercifully ended."

"Do not waste sympathy on him," Fogg said. "Nor allow his sickness to cause you to underestimate him. We must be on guard the rest of our voyage on this ship. I do not trust him not to break his oath to us to keep the peace until we land at San Francisco."

CHAPTER 16

Mr. Fogg, as soon as he landed in San Francisco, learned that the next train for New York City left at six in the evening that day. He took rooms for the three in a hotel and then started out for the British consulate with Aouda. He had gone only a few steps from the hotel when he ran into Passepartout. The Frenchman was waiting for him so he could get permission to buy some Enfield rifles and Colt revolvers. Verne says the Frenchman wanted them in case they were attacked by Indians en route to the American Midwest. Both he and Fogg, of course, were thinking more of the defense against the Capelleans than against the Sioux or Pawnee.

A few paces further on, Fogg met, "by the greatest chance in the world," Mr. Fix. The detective pretended great surprise. Could it be true that he and Mr. Fogg had crossed the Pacific Ocean together and not once encountered each other? Since Fix owed Mr. Fogg so much, he would like to accompany him. Could he go with him on his tour of this pleasant American city, so agreeably Old-

Worldish in many aspects?

Mr. Fogg said that he would be honored, and Fix went with the two. On Montgomery Street, the three ran into a great crowd. Every place was jammed with people yelling and screaming slogans and carrying big posters and flags.

"Hooray for Camerfield!"

"Horray for Mandiboy!"

Fix said that it was a political meeting and hence to be avoided. Americans got violent when they encountered opposition to their political beliefs, and the two parties were out in force today. Mr. Fogg may have thought that the same could be said for Englishmen— and it was true in those days—but he did not say so. Instead, he made another of his classical remarks.

"Yes, and blows, even if they are political, are still blows."

Shortly thereafter, a fight did break out. The three British subjects found themselves caught between the Camerfieldians and the Mandiboyans. Most of these were armed with canes loaded with lead or billies, and a few had revolvers. Fists, canes, billies, cudgels, and booted feet were used vigorously and, often indiscriminately. The trio was standing on top of a flight of steps at the street's upper end but found this position no guarantee of safety. The tide of ruffians swept them off the steps.

Fogg used his fists to protect Aouda. A large muscular chap with a red face and an even

redder beard aimed a blow at Fogg. Fix
stepped in and took the fist. His knees gave
way, along with his silk hat. He staggered
back up onto his feet but with glazed eyes. He
was destined to carry a large lump on top of
his head for the next few days.

"Yankee!" Fogg said, looking contemptu-
ously at the red-bearded rogue.

"Englishman! We'll meet again!"

"When you please," Fogg said.

"What is your name, sirrah?" the American
said.

"Phileas Fogg. And yours?"

"Colonel Stamp Proctor."

The avalanche of bodies stormed by. Fogg
thanked the detective for his noble inter-
positioning. Neither was badly hurt, though
the clothes of both looked as if they had
jumped off a train going at sixty miles per
hour. Aouda was, if not untouched,
unbruised.

The three repaired to a tailor shop. One
hour later, they were back at the hotel in new
clothes. On the way, Fogg considered the
incident with the colonel. Perhaps he was only
a Frisco bully. But that name, Stamp Proctor!
Could he be the Capellean proctor, the
supervisor, the monitor, of the U.S.A. for the
enemy? Did the Stamp indicate that another
of his functions was the assassination, the
stamping out, of Eridaneans? Or was his
name only a coincidence? Nemo had said that
the Capelleans were abandoning the old
custom of using functional names. Nemo,

however, was a liar. And even if he were telling the truth, the reform might not yet have been put into effect.

He told himself that he should not have taken a tour but should have remained, as was his habit, in his room. And why had he broken this habit? He had wanted to show Aouda the city.

Fogg also thought about Fix. He had rushed in to take the blow meant for him. Why would he do this if he were a Capellean? Was it to convince Fogg that he was only an Englishman who would defend another Englishman in Yankeeland? This did not seem likely. If Proctor were a Capellean, he would not want his efforts frustrated. Fix, in fact, should have helped Proctor.

But he had not. On the contrary.

After dinner, Fogg said to Fix, "Have you seen this Proctor again?"

"No."

"I will return to America to find him," Fogg said calmly. "It would not be right for an Englishman to permit himself to be treated in that manner without retaliation."

Fix smiled but did not reply. Fogg wondered what he was thinking. As for his speech, it was true enough. After this was over, he would be back looking for the colonel. As an Englishman, he would have done it for the sake of honor. As an Eridanean, he would be doing it to eliminate a Capellean —if Proctor were such.

There were 3786 miles of railway to be

traversed from San Francisco to New York
City. Between the ocean and Omaha,
Nebraska, the railroad passed through a
rugged land dangerous with beasts and
wilder Indians. Part of the territory was
occupied by the Mormons, a comparatively
peaceful people, though regarded by most
Gentiles of that time as uncivilized. The train,
averaging only twenty miles per hour because
of the many stops, would take seven days for
the journey. That is, it would if buffalo,
savages, storms, floods, washouts,
breakdowns, and avalanches did not
interfere. If the schedule were met, however,
Fogg would arrive on the eleventh of
December to catch the steamer from New
York for Liverpool, England.

At eight o'clock, in the midst of falling
snow, the car in which Fogg and party rode
was converted into a dormitory. At noon of
the next day, the train stopped for a breakfast
break of twenty minutes at Reno, Nevada. At
twelve o'clock, the train was forced to stop
until nightfall to let a vast procession of
buffalo cross the tracks. At thirty minutes
after nine in the evening, the train crossed
into Utah.

On the night of the fifth of December, the
train was about a hundred miles from the
Great Salt Lake. Though Fogg was not aware
of it, this was the day that the brigantine *Dei
Gratia* discovered the *Mary Celeste* sailing
along without a soul aboard. If Head had
trusted to his luck, he would have been put

aboard the *Dei Gratia* and would, on the twelfth of December, have disembarked at Gibraltar. It is true that he would have been held up by a court of inquiry, but he could have escaped. Thus it would have added one more element of mystery to a case that has puzzled savants and the public and originated many false stories for a hundred years. Even the name of the ship is known to most people as the *Marie Celeste*. This error is no mystery, however. This derives from an incorrect notation in the New York City pilotage record of the seventh of November, 1872. The error was even perpetuated in the archives of the U.S. State Department, and the American newspapers continued to use the false name.

Perhaps the most influential in spreading this error was A. Conan Doyle, who refers to the ship as the *Marie Celeste* throughout his well-known story, *J. Habakuk Jephson's Statement.*

On the seventh of December, the train halted for fifteen minutes at the Green River Station in the Wyoming Territory. Several passengers got off to unlimber their legs. Aouda, looking through the window, became alarmed. She had seen Colonel Stamp Proctor on the platform.

Verne says that it was only chance which brought Proctor on the train, but we know better. Verne also says that Fix, Aouda, and Passepartout conspired to keep Fogg from learning that the colonel was a passenger on another car. This was one of Verne's

novelistic insertions. Aouda, in fact, woke Fogg up to tell him about Proctor.

Fogg merely asked if Aouda and Fix could play whist, and they were soon playing.

Aouda, using the cards as code transmitters, asked Fogg what he intended to do about Proctor. Fogg replied, "Nothing—for the moment."

"Why not, if I may ask?"

"The time and place are not appropriate."

The train soon bore them over the Rockies through snow. Some distance past Fort Halleck, the train unexpectedly stopped. The alarmed passengers, with the exception of Fogg, poured out. They discovered the engineer and conductor talking to a signalman. He had been sent from Medicine Bow, the next stopping place, to halt the train. A suspension bridge over some rapids was in too ruinous a condition for the train to chance crossing it.

An American, Forster, proposed that the train back up so it could get a running start. If it gained enough speed, it would practically jump over the bridge.

After some hesitation, the passengers, with one exception, agreed. Passepartout, using the logic that distinguishes the true Gaul, asked why the passengers did not walk over the bridge? Why ride on the train, which might be precipitated into the abyss?

He was overruled by all and so rode trembling while the train, going a hundred miles an hour, shot across the perilous

stretch. No sooner had the rear wheels of the
rear car passed onto land than the bridge,
with a great noise, fell into the chasm.

Passepartout, wiping his brow, thought that
there must be something in the air of this
continent that made all its inhabitants mad.

The whist game was resumed. When the
train was in Nebraska, a voice familiar to
three of the players spoke behind them.

"I should play a diamond!"

It was Proctor, who pretended that he had
not recognized the Englishman until that
moment.

"Ah, it's you, the limey? It's you who're
going to play a spade?"

"And who does play it," Fogg said, throwing
down the ten of spades.

"Well, it pleases me to have it be
diamonds," Proctor said. He reached out as if
to grab the card, saying, "You don't know anything about whist."

"Perhaps I do, as well as another," Fogg
said as he got to his feet.

Fix also rose. He said, "You forget that it is
I whom you have to deal with, sir. It is I whom
you not only insulted but struck."

Fogg understood what Stamp was doing. He
would try to kill Fogg openly in a duel of
honor. These were not uncommon in the terri-
tories, but Nebraska had been admitted as a
state on the first of March, 1867. Did the state
forbid duels and enforce the law with harsh
penalties? It did not matter. Proctor did not
seem to think that legal retribution would

follow. Indeed, he was doing exactly what Fogg had expected. That was why Fogg had endured Proctor's insults and had forced him to come to him. If Fogg won and was then arrested, he could plead that he was not the aggressor.

"Pardon me, Mr. Fix," Fogg said. "This is my affair alone."

The colonel said, indifferently, that the time, place, and weapons were up to Fogg.

Out on the platform, however, Fogg did try to talk Proctor into a delay. Proctor sneeringly refused and intimated that Fogg was a coward who, once safe in England, would never dare return. Seeing that the colonel was set on having the duel now, and that he had plenty of witnesses to prove that he had tried to put off the affair, Fogg agreed to exchange shots at the next stop. Unflustered, he returned to his car. Aouda tried to talk him out of it but without success. Fogg asked Fix if he would be his second. Fix replied that he would be honored. Passepartout understood that this request was one more test of the detective.

A little past eleven in the morning, the train stopped at Plum Creek. Fogg got off, only to be told that the train could not delay more than a minute. It was twenty minutes behind schedule, and the time must be made up. Fogg got back on. The conductor then approached the two participants with the suggestion that they fight in transit.

Fogg and the colonel agreed. The duelists,

their seconds, and the conductor walked to the rear car. There the conductor asked the dozen or so passengers if they would leave until the two gentlemen concluded their argument. They left, happy at some excitement relieving the tedium.

The car was fifty feet long. Fogg stood at one end; Proctor, at the other. Each held two six-shooter revolvers. The conductor left, and the two seconds closed the doors of the car. After the engineer blew the whistle of the locomotive, the two would advance toward each other, firing as they wished.

Before Fogg and Proctor could start shooting, the train was attacked by about a hundred mounted Sioux. The two duelists were the first to fire against the Indians; they agreed without a word spoken to each other to put off the duel until this peril was over. If they survived this attack, they could resume their quarrel.

As many may remember from Verne's account, some Sioux boarded the engine and stunned the engineer and fireman. The chief of the Indians, trying to stop the train, opened instead of closed the steam valve. The train was soon roaring along at one hundred miles per hour. This made it vital that the passengers somehow stop the train at Fort Kearney. If the train went on past it for any distance, the Sioux would have time to overwhelm the passengers. Many of the Indians were aboard it now, shooting and battling hand to hand with their enemies, who were indeed palefaces at this time.

Passepartout had been frightened at the illogic of the others when they rode the train across the ruined bridge. But when logic demanded action, he cast aside his fears. Logic now required that the train be stopped in time. Bravely and expertly, since he was an acrobat, he crawled under the cars on their chains and axles. He loosened the safety chains between the baggage car and the tender, and a violent jolt drew the yoking bar out. The locomotive and coal tender soon passed out of sight while the cars rolled to a stop. The troops from Fort Kearney attacked, and the Indians fled. Unfortunately, Passepartout was carried away on the tender.

Aouda, who had coolly shot a number of Sioux, was untouched. Fogg was also unwounded. Fix had a slight wound in his arm. Colonel Proctor had not been so lucky. He had received a ball in his groin which had not only incapacitated him but might result in his death. Through his pain, he glared at Fogg, who coolly stared and then turned away.

Verne assumed that it was a Sioux bullet which had struck Proctor. Fogg records that it was he who put the colonel out of action. As soon as he saw that they would be safe, he had shot the colonel. He would have put the bullet in the man's head if he had been absolutely certain that he was a Capellean. In any event, he wanted to make sure that he would not be delayed.

As it turned out, he was held up anyway. On

being informed that Passepartout and several
other passengers had been carried off, he
determined to go after them. This meant that
the train would leave without him and that he
would probably not catch his steamer at New
York. He did not hesitate. He could not desert
the brave Frenchman, knowing that he would
be horribly tortured by the savages. He
shamed the captain of the troopers into
getting thirty volunteers to accompany him
on a rescue expedition. That Fogg offered five
thousand dollars to be split among the
troopers may have had something to do with
their willingness to face the Sioux. And that
Passepartout was carrying the distorter may
have had something to do with Fogg's
insistence on going after him. However, in
view of his character, it would be well to dismiss this unworthy thought.

Fix, be it noted, stayed behind. He did not
believe that any of the party would return. He
would have liked to volunteer, because this
would have removed the last of Fogg's suspicions about him. But at the thought of what
the Indians did to their captives, he quailed.

Afterward, he cursed himself for a coward.
But what a brave fellow that Fogg was! Eridanean or not, he . . . But no! Such thoughts
were treasonable. He paced back and forth
before the station house. Should he enter and
make himself known to Proctor? Or was the
colonel even aware that he, Fix, was a Capellean? If so, he had made no recognition signal.
And if Proctor did not know, then Fix would

have a perfect excuse for his inaction. Nemo, who had stayed behind in San Francisco, had only instructed him to stick close to Fogg. He was to report on Fogg's activities when an agent made contact with him.

The train pulled out, leaving Fix and Aouda behind. Watching it dwindle on the vast prairie, Fix suddenly lost his sense of security at having at least followed Nemo's orders. He was not supposed to leave Fogg for any reason. And he had refused to go with him! What would Nemo say? He knew well what he would say. Unless Fogg did come back, Fix was lost. Nemo would say that Passepartout and Fogg might have used the distorter to get away from both Sioux and Capelleans. Fix would argue that this was not likely. To use the distorter, Fogg would have to rescue Passepartout first, and how could he do that? Besides, it was thought that the Eridaneans had only one distorter left. Where was the other one needed for their transmission?

Nemo would reply that it was uncertain that the enemy had only one device. Moreover, what was to prevent the wily Fogg from repeating the *Mary Celeste* incident with the distorter now carried by the Chinese agent? Indeed, the Chinese agent may have been killed by the Eridaneans, who would then be in possession of a second distorter.

And this had happened because Fix had not been able to help Nemo on the *General Grant*. And had Fix been as sick as he said he was? Perhaps he had been malingering. And so on.

A fatal so on.

Fix went into the station house. If he had no internal fire to warm him, he could at least get an external fire from the stove. But he went out again almost at once. He felt a need to be punished. He would sit out here and freeze until Fogg came back. At least, until the sun arose. The sun. It was said to be ninety-three million miles away. He had heard Earthlings exclaim with wonder at this inconceivable distance. He had always snickered inwardly when this happened. What did they know of the mindreeling stretch of interstellar space? His own homeland was forty-five light-years away. A man walking twenty miles a day would take four million and six hundred and fifty thousand days to travel to the sun. Almost thirteen thousand years. Yet that was a mere stroll to the corner green-grocer's for one who walked to Capella.

His homeland? Why did he call it that? In reality, he had never seen it nor had any of his ancestors. He and they were homebodies, Earthlings, in face. They had always been restricted to this tiny far-off planet. Only the Old Ones could call Capella home, and even those who had come from it were probably all dead.

The original settlers had stopped here because they had thought that it might make a site for another fort. Also, because they had to make scientific survey of this unknown planet. They had to ascertain, among other things, if it held sentients. And, if it did, if the sentients were dangerous to Capella. That had happened over two hundred years ago. The sentients then, and now, were a long way from interstellar, or even interplanetary, flight.

By the time they attained the latter, they would probably kill themselves, the whole planet, too, with nuclear wars or, even more probably, global pollution. It was doubtful that their technology, and its intelligent use, would ever match their ability to create social stupidities. If it did, it would be too late. Or so said the original Old Ones. The mystics among them claimed that man was descended from some type of now-extinct ape. The simian strain would never die out, no matter how far the physical appearance of the human species got from the simian. They were inherently committed to dirt and dissension.

But if they had proper guidance?

If the Old Ones had been able to land in force, instead of in a single scoutship, they could have conquered the sentients. These, guided by the Old One's superior wisdom and knowledge, could have been set on the right path. But the Old Ones had to hide while they observed. Otherwise, they would have been killed, no matter how many thousands they might have slaughtered.

The Old Ones were just completing their report on Earth when the Eridaneans landed. There had been war, and both spaceships had been damaged beyond repair. And so both forces had gone underground. With surgery, they had remodified their bodies to pass for

humans. After a while, because of their small
numbers, they had enlisted a few Earthlings
as allies. Through infant adoption, secret education, the bloodsharing ceremony, and,
strongest of all, the millennium medicine,
they had secured the loyalty of their allies.
There was also the Great Plan which would
make mankind long-lived and happy.

But first, the Eridaneans must be exterminated.

Fix shook with the cold. He was freezing to
the core of his brain. The fires were going out.
Still, there were enough to cast some
shadows. Now he could see, suddenly,
without the obstacle of the shadows. He must
be frozen through and through. Emotions
were dead; only logic could live in this extreme cold. If the Capelleans and Eridaneans
were so highly advanced, why had they ever
thought it necessary to make war on each
other? War was all right for the Earthlings,
since they were so retarded. They did not
know any better. They were still like baboons.
But why the two peoples from the stars?

The Old Ones had said—or so he had been
told—that the Eridaneans had started it all.
They were not quite as advanced as the Capelleans, not at least in social wisdom. They had
attacked the Capelleans somewhere on some
outpost planet many millennia ago. And the
Capelleans had been forced to fight or become
extinct.

The sun rose. Fix became a little warmer
though no less confused.

Shortly after seven, he heard a shot. He rushed out toward the sound with the soldiers and found Fogg, Passepartout, and two other passengers marching with the volunteer troopers. Aouda, too choked up to talk, could only hold Fogg's hand. Fix was happy yet ashamed. Passepartout was lamenting how much he had cost Fogg in money and time so far. Then he looked around for the train and became even more desolate on finding that it had gone on.

Phileas Fogg was twenty four hours behind schedule.

CHAPTER 17

Fix knew that Fogg had to be in New York City on the eleventh before nine o'clock in the evening. At that hour the steamer left for Liverpool and another would not be available until the next day. It seemed inevitable that Fogg would miss the steamer. But Fix came to the rescue this time. The evening before, he had been approached by a Mr. Mudge, who had offered to take Fix at once to Omaha, though by a rather unconventional conveyance. Fix had turned him down because he had to wait for Fogg. Now he informed Fogg that all was not yet lost. He could be transported on an ice-sled. This vehicle held five or six persons and was equipped with a mast which held a brig sail and afforded attachment for a jib sail. It was steered by a rudder which dug into the snow.

Would Fogg care to use this craft?

Mr. Fogg certainly would. Presently, the party was being driven by a west wind over the ice and snow of the prairie. The two hundred miles between Fort Kearney and Omaha were covered in five hours. Fix said nothing during the journey, but he was happy. His service in obtaining the ice-sled would be one more item in his favor to reduce Fogg's suspicions of him.

The sled arrived just before the Chicago and Rock Island train was to leave. Fogg and party boarded it and so arrived in Chicago at four in the afternoon of the next day. This city, partially destroyed in the Great Fire of the eighth and ninth of October, 1871, had been rebuilt with some attention to beauty. The party had no time to inspect the new constructions or to take a drive along the superb Lake Michigan. They had nine hundred miles to go and so departed at once on the Pittsburgh, Fort Wayne, and Chicago Railway. On the evening of the eleventh of December, at eleven o'clock, the train pulled into the New York station. This was near the pier of the Cunard line but, unfortunately, the *China* had left for Liverpool forty-five minutes ago.

Fogg seemed to be beaten. The Inman liner would not leave until the following day and was not fast enough to make up the lost time. The Hamburg ships went directly to Havre, France, which meant that the trip from Havre to Southhampton and thence to London would make him too late. A French liner did not depart until the fourteenth.

Mr. Fogg only said, "Tomorrow, we will consult about what is best. Come."

They took the Jersey City ferry over the Hudson and a carriage to the St. Nicholas Hotel on Broadway. The next morning, Mr.

Fogg went out alone (according to Verne). Actually, Passepartout trailed him by about sixty feet to detect any shadowers or intercept any Capellean assassins. If Proctor had been sent to kill Fogg, it seemed unlikely that another attempt would not be made in New York. Yet, nothing of this nature happened. Perhaps Proctor was after all only a Western ruffian. But why were the Capelleans leaving him alone? What was behind this? If one thing was sure, they had not given up on him.

Mr. Fogg inquired along the banks of the Hudson for any vessels that seemed about to depart. There were many of this kind, recalling Whitman's phrase of "many-masted Manhattan," but sailing ships would be too slow. At the end of his quest, Fogg saw, anchored at the Battery, a steam-driven freighter with the usual auxiliary sails. The puffs of smoke from its stack indicated that it would soon be leaving. Fogg hired a boat and was rowed to the *Henrietta.* It was bound for Bordeaux and was carrying only ballast for this trip. Its captain, Andrew Speedy (neither Capellean nor Eridanean despite his functional name), loathed passengers. He refused to take Fogg and party at any price nor would he think of going anywhere but to Bordeaux. However, at the offer of two thousand dollars for each passenger, Speedy relented. As Verne says, passengers at this price are no longer passengers but valuable merchandise.

Speedy gave Fogg an unalterable half hour

to get all aboard. Fogg hurried in a cab to the
hotel and returned with the others just in
time. (New York was having traffic problems
even in 1872, but the fact that Fogg was able
to make such speed shows that the problem
was not as bad as now. Or perhaps Fogg
ignored all traffic laws.) An hour later, the
Henrietta passed the lighthouse marking the
entrance to the Hudson, turned past Sandy
Hook, and was in the sea.

Passepartout, it can be presumed, regretted
not having been able to tour Manhattan. Due
largely to immigration from Europe, New
York City held a million people. It was,
generally, a dirty, drab, drunken, corruptly
governed city with many slums. Muggings,
killings, brawls, and mob violence were
common. The guidebooks warned newcomers
not to walk out at night except in better areas
well-lit by gas. Despite this, the visitor with
means might enjoy it. Passepartout would
have liked to drive through the recently
constructed Central Park, even if slums did
ring it. Trinity Church was the tallest
structure in town and, though it would be
nothing unusual in London, it was notable in
contrast with its surroundings. Passepartout
might also have wanted to view the new resi-
dential areas with their brownstone fronts
and the business sections with their cast-iron
facades. He could have compared the mass-
transportation problems vexing New York
City with those vexing London. If he had
talked to the Gothamites, he would have

heard rumors of gunrunning to Cuban revolutionaries and the seriousness of the epizootic disease which was killing horses. He would have noted that it was only because of this "horse influenza" that Manhattan's streets in summer were not as foul with manure and the air as thick with huge horseflies and a compound of dust, coal smoke, and manure particles as were London's.

All this was not to be. Passepartout also had more to think about than the rather sleazy exotica of Baghdad-on-the-Hudson. Mr. Fogg had locked Captain Speedy up in the master's own quarters.

Mr. Fogg, seeing that Speedy was adamant about not changing his course to Liverpool, had bribed the crew to cooperate with him. This was, as Speedy screamed behind his door, mutiny on the high seas and piracy, the penalty of which was hanging by the neck until dead. Fogg heard him with his customary serenity and continued to give orders from the bridge. It is here that Verne says (truly) that Fogg's management of the craft showed that he had once been a sailor.

As for Fix, he was fighting a tendency to admire Fogg more and more. He was also wondering why he had received no orders in New York concerning Fogg. Doubtless, Nemo had changed his plans, but it would be nice to know what was going on. Perhaps one of the crew was a fellow Capellean charged with killing the Eridaneans even if he had to blow up the vessel to do it. Fix did not like to contemplate this plan, since it would mean his own demise. And, to tell the truth, he admitted, he was getting more and more excited about the wager. Several times, he had to remind himself that he had no business rooting for the chap.

On the sixteenth of December, half the trip across the Atlantic was behind the *Henrietta*. She had passed safely through the Newfoundland fogs and a storm. But now the chief engineer informed Fogg that the fuel supply was running out. The ship did have enough coal to go on "short steam" at a reduced speed to Liverpool. The furnaces were still on "full steam."

Fogg, after some deliberation, told the engineer to keep the fires at maximum until the coal was all gone. On the eighteenth Fogg was told that the fuel would be exhausted sometime that day.

Near noon, Fogg sent for the captain. His face purple, Speedy bounded onto the bridge.

"Where are we?" he cried.

"Seven hundred and seven miles from Liverpool," Fogg said calmly.

"Pirate!"

"Sir, I have sent for you . . . "

"Pickaroon!"

" . . . . to ask you to sell me the ship."

"By all the devils, no!"

"Then I shall be forced to burn her."

"What, burn the *Henrietta!*"

"The upper part at least. The coal has run out."

"Burn my ship? A ship worth fifty thousand dollars!"

"Here are sixty thousand," Fogg said. He handed him the money.

Here Verne makes his classical remark: "An American can hardly remain unmoved at the sight of sixty thousand dollars."

True, but Verne's ethnicism is evident in this statement. Few of any nationality, then or today, would not be emotionally affected on being presented with this sum.

Speedy forgot his hate. Money, more than music, soothes the savage beast. He was getting by far the best of the bargain.

"I will still have the iron hull?" he said.

"The iron hull and the engine. I am only buying the wood and all other combustible substances. Is it agreed?"

Fogg then gave the order to strip off all the interior seats, bunks, frames and other furniture and to put them into the furnaces.

The next day, the nineteenth, the fires received the masts, spars, and rafts. On the twentieth, the railings, fittings, and most of the deck and upper sides followed. On this day, the hulk was within sight of the Irish coast and the Fastnet lighthouse. At ten that evening, Queenstown appeared. This was the Irish port where trans-Atlantic steamers put in to deliver the mail. From there express trains sped to Dublin, from which the mail was carried by fast boat to Liverpool. This route got the mail into London twelve hours ahead of the ships.

The *Henrietta* waited three hours for high tide, after which it steamed into the harbor and discharged the Fogg party. A little after one o'clock, the travelers stepped onto dry land. Since this was British soil, Fix was in a position to arrest Fogg and clap him into jail. Verne says that Fix was much tempted to do so. But Verne could only speculate on why he refrained.

"What struggle was going on inside him? Had he changed his mind about *his man?*"

No, Fix had not changed his mind. He just could not make it up. The long intimacy with his three enemies had forced him to acknowledge that Eridaneans could be, and were in this case, as humans as he. They were, even if the deadly antagonists of his own people, not evil incarnate. He admired Fogg for his undeviating courage, quick-wittedness, resourcefulness, loyalty, and generosity. He liked him. He liked the other two for similar reasons. He liked Fogg far more than he did Nemo, who, he admitted to himself, he hated, feared, and loathed. And he had not liked Stamp Proctor; he had been glad when the colonel's plan to kill Fogg had been spoiled by the Sioux.

Time and again, he told himself that he was thinking wrongly. No matter. He continued to think along the same lines. He could not sleep at night because of his conflicts, and his days were tearing-aparts. What was he to do?

At twenty minutes to high noon, the Fogg party got off the boat at Liverpool. Fogg had only a six-hour train ride to Charing Cross Station, London, and a brief carriage ride to the Reform Club.

Fix could no longer refuse to act. Both the English law and Capellean orders required him to proceed. He put his hand on Fogg's shoulder, a familiarity he would not have dared except in an official capacity. Verne says that he showed the warrant in the other hand, but Verne forgot that Fix had had no opportunity to get a warrant.

"You are really Phileas Fogg?" he said.

No doubt, a variation of Pilate's classical remark flashed through Fogg's mind. What is truth? What is reality? What or who is the real Fogg?

But he replied, "I am."

"I arrest you in the Queen's name!"

Fogg went quietly into custody in the Custom House. He would, he was informed, be transferred the next day to London.

Passepartout tried to attack Fix but was restrained by several policemen. Fix did not prefer charges against him, as he could have done for this attempted assault. One, he felt that the Frenchman was justified. Two, Passepartout was still carrying the distorter. If the Capellean chiefs still wished to get hold of it, which they surely must, they could do so much more easily if Passepartout were at large.

Aouda was paralyzed with astonishment. Contrary to what Verne said, Aouda understood what was happening. But, since Fix had

not tried to arrest Fogg in Ireland, the three
Eridaneans had assumed that he meant to
wait until they reached London. Just as they
had had plans to tie him up and leave him
behind in Ireland, so they had intended to
take care of him at London. They even thought
that he might mean to wait until after Fogg
had won the bet.

Evidently, Fogg had overlooked this
particular section of the foreseen.

That gentleman, calm as ever, sat in a
locked room in the Custom House and read
the London *Times*. Among other items
attracting his interest was a story about the
Mary Celeste. This had first been noted by the
Times of the sixteenth of December in its
Latest Shipping Intelligence section. The
derelict had been brought into Gibraltar by a
prize crew of three from the British brigantine *Dei Gratia*. Not many details were as yet
available, but the ship had a cargo of seventeen hundred barrels of alcohol and was seaworthy.

Verne says that, while in this room, Mr.
Fogg carefully put his watch on the table and
looked at its advancing hands. Verne wonders
what Fogg was thinking at this time.

This incident is a curious one. Except for
one previous occasion in Verne's book, Fogg
had no watch to consult. He had relied on
Passepartout's watch. Furthermore, if he had
had a watch, why would he have fallen into
the same error that Passepartout made about
the time zones? Fogg, according to Verne,
thought that that day was the twenty-first of

December. It was, in reality, the twentieth.
Would Fogg, who was a veteran sailor by
Verne's own admission, one who had been
everywhere and seen everything, who was
highly educated, have not known what
happened when the ship crossed the 180th
meridian? By no means. Verne must have
known this. But he was eager to provide
drama and suspense. He cannot be blamed for
using this little piece of trickery in his
narrative. After all, he got it from the public
report issued by Fogg himself. The Englishman had to create some excuse for the events
that were to follow his incarceration in
Liverpool. His fertile imagination supplied
one which Verne was eager to accept.

So, when Verne says that Fogg wrote in his
journal that day, "21st December, Saturday,
Liverpool, 80th day, 11:40 A.M.," he is
inserting his own fiction. Indeed, Verne adds
more imaginative detail by writing that Fogg
noticed that his watch was two hours fast. If
he took the express train at that very moment,
he would just make the quarter to nine
deadline.

It was at this time that Fix was told that the
real thief, a James Strand, had been arrested
three days ago. Fogg was in the clear.
Stammering, Fix related the news to Fogg.

Phileas Fogg walked up to Fix, gave him a
steady and cold look, and knocked him down
with one blow of his fist.

Fix, lying on the floor, felt that he still had
not been properly punished. But he at least
could salvage something from the incident.

Fogg evidently believed him to be nothing more than a meddling detective.

This incident shows that Fix was as ignorant of the real date as Passepartout. Otherwise, he would not have believed that Fogg had lost his bet because he had arrested him.

But if Fogg knew that he still had plenty of time, why did he hit Fix?

The answer is obvious. As Phileas Fogg, English gentleman, he could be expected to resent being arrested by a man whom he had so generously treated. He had to play out his role.

The party, minus Fix, took a cab and arrived at the station at twenty minutes before three. They were thirty-five minutes too late to catch the express.

Fogg ordered a special train but could not get one until three o'clock. He wondered if Nemo's hand was in this delay, if Nemo was planning to have unauthorized passengers on board. Before the train left at three, Fogg thoroughly searched the locomotive, tender, and his car. Satisfied that these hid no one, he signaled the train to depart. It soon roared along at a speed that should have brought them to London in five and a half hours. There were, however, unexpected delays.

When Fogg stepped from the car at Charing Cross, he was five minutes late. (Or would have been if this had been the twenty-first.)

All the clocks of London were striking ten minutes to nine.

CHAPTER 18

As noted, this remarkable phenomenon has been commented on by various critics and translators. The original French version contains no footnotes about this, so it may be presumed that Verne thought this singularity was unique to the clocks of the English, an eccentric people all told.

Fogg made no such mistake. He knew that, somewhere in London, a distorter was being used. As far as he knew, the Eridaneans had only one, so it must be a Capellean's. Probably, the man from China was using his to transmit himself to London, which meant that they had at least two now. Had the box with the distorter taped on its underside failed to be washed off the *Mary Celeste*? Had it been stolen by a Capellean sent to Gibraltar for that very purpose? Surely, that must be the explanation.

After leaving Charing Cross Station, Fogg ordered Passepartout to buy some food for their stay at No. 7, Savile Row, that night. Fogg and Aouda would proceed straight to his house for a night's rest. There was plenty of

time to win the bet. In fact, Fogg planned to
make his entrance into the Reform Club only
a few minutes before his time was up. Stuart
might be angry at this delay because he had
important information or orders for him. But
Fogg desperately needed that night. The
anxieties and terrors had been accumulating
in him to the bursting point. He had to discharge at least some to keep his psychic boiler
from exploding. About six hours of thera-
peutic emission of neural current would
restore him.

On the way, however, he changed his mind
about Stuart. He would have to tell him that
he was at No. 7. The Capelleans were up to
something; the clangings showed that. By
indulging himself, he might be ruining his
own people, not to mention himself.

As they passed a telegraph office, he
ordered the cab to stop. He took only a little
time to write the telegram since it consisted
of one codeword with his name in code.
Directing the clerk to send a messenger at
once if a reply came, he left the office. The cab
soon drew up before his house. Fogg did not
enter it for a few minutes. The front of the
house looked as he had left it. The light from
Passepartout's gas jet was shining through a
narrow opening between the blind and the
windowsill. Fogg led Aouda quietly into the
house. Both held revolvers. Fogg had
smuggled these into England, adding this
crime to piracy on the high seas. A thorough

search of each room revealed nothing untoward.

Presently Passepartout entered with the provisions. He deposited the bags in the pantry and hurried upstairs to his own room. The jet had not been turned off by Fogg, who thought, correctly, that this was his valet's duty. Passepartout reached out to extinguish the flame, then held his hand. Why turn it off now when he would be needing it?

He went downstairs and removed the mail from the letter box. On seeing the bill from the gas company, his eyes bugged. He would never be able to pay off his debt, not unless he worked for nothing for eighty days and then some. Fogg, being a stickler, even if a hero, would not bear the expense himself.

The night lurched, bumped, and groaned by. Aouda reached vainly for sleep in her room. Fogg sat in his chair in his room and delved into his own mind. He had to be as careful in his probing as an electrician without a schematic trying to find the cause of a malfunction in a tangled mass of high-voltage equipment. One mistake, and he could be severely injured or even killed. From time to time, a shudder passed through him. His pupils dilated or contracted. His nostrils flared. His ears and scalp twitched. His fingers fastened upon the arms of his chair as if he would tear the leather off. Sweat poured out all over him.

Now and then, he groaned. Pain, hate, loathing, contempt, and horror twisted his face in succession. He soundlessly mouthed words he should long ago have verbalized. Sometimes, his body became rigid and shook as if he were in a grand mal seizure. Sometimes, he was as limp as if he were newly dead.

Dawn came while Passepartout watched outside Fogg's door. If he heard sounds that seemed as if Fogg were hurting himself or even killing himself, he was to hasten in. But this had not occurred, though there were moments when he was about to interfere.

Shortly after dawn, Passepartout, looking through the keyhole, saw Fogg sleeping in bed. The crises were over, for that night at least. Fogg had told him that it would take at least three sessions to discharge most of the heavy stuff.

The Frenchman went to his own room then to perform some therapy on himself. Since he was much less self-controlled than Fogg (as who wasn't?), and had a temperament which naturally discharged anxieties more easily than Fogg's, his therapy was shorter and less dangerous. After an hour, he went to sleep.

Fogg, looking haggard and pale, rose late that morning. By noon he had regained his customary healthy appearance, though he acted as if he still had much energy bound up in him. Aouda came down for breakfast about twelve. She, too, was pale and had bags under her eyes.

At half-past seven that evening, the occupants of No. 7 heard the clanging of fire-

wagon bells. Looking out the windows, past
the curtains, they saw by the gaslights many
people, including their neighbors, hurrying
up Savile Row. The bells became louder, and
two firewagons, each drawn by a team of
horses, sped by. The bells had no sooner died
out than the boom of an explosion rattled the
windows. Passepartout, quivering with
curiosity, asked if he could not leave the
house to find out the source of all this excitement.

"No," Fogg said. "Someone might see you
and thus know that I am back. I prefer to keep
it secret until the last moment."

Passepartout thought that that was not
likely, since everybody, servants and masters,
seemed to have rushed off to the fire or whatever it was. They did not know what he looked
like, and he would take care to be back before
they returned to Savile Row. But he did not
argue. He could not, however, refrain from
looking between the curtains several times.
Just as he was about to turn away from his
latest peek, he saw a hansom cab stop two
houses from No. 7. The horse drawing it stood
for several seconds while the driver, perched
high on a seat at the rear of the two-wheeled
carriage, shouted at it. The passenger turned
around and in turn shouted at the driver
through the opening in the roof. The horse,
quivering, took several more steps forward.
The driver stood up to lash his whip at it. A
moment later, the horse suddenly collapsed,
causing the cab to tilt even more forward and

precipitating the driver off to one side and onto the street.

The occupant of the hansom must have been startled, since he did not open the door for at least a minute. Then he got out slowly on the other side, where he examined the driver, who had not moved after striking the street. Presently, he rose from the driver, looked around at the deserted street, and then headed for the nearest house across the street. He leaned on a heavy walking cane, dragging his right leg somewhat. He wore a long heavy cloak against the late December cold. On his head was a military cap, probably an officer's. He knocked on the door so hard that Passepartout could hear the banging. Receiving no answer, he turned and walked with awkward and slow three-legged gait to the next house. He must be some officer who had returned wounded from India or some far-off place, Passepartout thought. His bronzed skin indicated a long residence in the tropics.

Meanwhile, the driver had sat up and then fallen back again. The horse had not moved.

Passepartout did not go out to help the man, since he had been forbidden to leave. The officer, however, would soon work his way to No. 7. What should he do? Passepartout thought. The poor fellow on the street evidently needed help. Well, he would go ask Fogg for his orders.

The officer had just turned toward Fogg's house when Passepartout saw a man in the

uniform of a telegraph officer runner on the
opposite side of the street. Could he be
bringing a message to No. 7? Fogg had said
that he might be getting one. Yes, he was
crossing the street at an angle toward No. 7.
This relieved Passepartout's predicament. He
had orders to open the door only for a telegram. He could not help it that the officer
would arrive at the same time as the
messenger. Fogg could not reasonably refuse
help to the injured man; besides, it would look
suspicious if he did.

Though he kept on the latch chain, he
opened the door. Now he saw, coming up the
street, a chimney sweep. And, down the street,
on the other side, the door of a house opening.
A young man, bareheaded and in a dressing
gown, stepped out. Evidently, he had been
sleeping and had just awakened. Looking out,
perhaps wondering why the servants were
gone, he had seen the fallen man. This was
good. Passepartout could direct the officer to
him, telling the officer at the same time that
he was unauthorized to leave the house.

The officer reached the door first and
addressed him through the opening in a rich
baritone.

"There's been an accident, as you can see.
My driver seems to have broken his arm and
also suffered head injuries. I'm afraid that he
has been drinking. Could you run for the
nearest doctor?"

Now that the officer was closer,
Passepartout could see the cold blue eyes

under heavy lids. These, combined with the bushy eyebrows, the thin, projecting nose, heavy black moustache, heavy lips, and strong jaw, combined to form a ruthless yet sensual face. Passepartout did not care for him, but, after all, it was the driver who needed medical attention.

"There is a Doctor Caber several blocks from here, sir," the Frenchman said, remembering that Fogg had told him so before retiring. "I cannot leave the house, but you might send that sweep after him. Or perhaps the messenger would oblige you?"

The runner had drawn to within a few feet of them. He was an exceptionally broad-shouldered fellow with a bushy moustache and long hair, both streaked with gray. His bulbous red nose indicated his chief occupation when not on duty.

"Ah, perhaps I could, my good fellow!" the officer said. He pointed the cane through the opening at Passepartout. The Frenchman saw the round hole in its end.

"But I do not care to," the officer said. "And don't think about trying to leap away. This is an air gun disguised as a walking stick. It can, and will, drive a rifle bullet through you at this range. So open up for us or suffer the consequences."

The messenger must have had concealed a pair of bolt cutters under his cloak. Their ends appeared and closed on the latch chain, which fell apart. The door was pushed violently inward against Passepartout, and he

staggered backward. Despite the officer's
demand for silence, Passepartout gave one
loud cry. The officer, no longer crippled,
lifted the air gun and brought it down over
Passepartout's head. Passepartout ducked so
that he did not receive the full impact.
Stunned, he still had sense enough to throw
himself to one side. He had intended to
bounce up onto his feet but found that his legs
failed him. The officer ran at Passepartout
with the messenger close behind him. In a
flash, Passepartout recognized him, under the
dyed hair and the false nose, as Nemo. He
tried to get up again, but this time the stick
came down fully on his head.

A few minutes later, according to the clock
on the mantel of the fireplace, he awoke on
the floor. His head hurt. His hands were
bound behind him, and he was gagged. The
only other occupant of the room was the
hansom driver, recovered from his "broken
arm." He was a tall, very stooped man in his
early forties. He bore a resemblance to Nemo
but lacked the widely spaced eyes and was
much darker in eyes and skin. He held a
peculiar weapon in one hand. Passepartout
thought it must be an air gun. It was small
enough to be concealed under a cloak.

The minutes throbbed by, along with his
head, as the clock hands progressed. About
ten minutes later, Passepartout heard footsteps on the staircase. He twisted his neck,
not without pain to his head, to see who was
coming. He was shocked. This was a stranger.

How many others had invaded while he lay unconscious?

The newcomer also carried an air pistol. He was tall and looked as if he were in his late forties. He had bold aquiline features on which was an arrogant and predatory expression. His peculiar yellow-green eyes and sharp profile made him look like a hungry fish-eagle.

"They're still locked in his room," he said. "Nemo says there's no hurry to take them. We want as little noise as possible. The people are starting to come back from the fire. Moran is stationed in the back with his air rifle. If they try to get out of the third story window, he'll drop them. He won't miss, that one."

The other frowned and said, "Why don't we just break down the door and storm them? If they get off a few more shots, they're not likely to draw much attention. The sounds will be confined in their room. But if Fogg shoots out the window, the sound will carry a long distance."

"Your brother says no. Too many people returning. Evidently we didn't provide them with a large enough spectacle."

He laughed harshly and said, "We should have set the whole block ablaze."

"Nemo knows what he's doing," the tall dark man said. He looked at Passepartout. "While they're holed up, we can work on this frog. You should enjoy that. You've had so much practice."

"Excellent!" the man with yellow-green

eyes said. "But what is to keep the other two from killing themselves?"

"Nothing. But that's the way Nemo wants it. You ask too many questions."

The other looked as if he did not like that. Though he did not carry himself as if he were or had been a soldier, he radiated the air of one who had been in command of many and would like once more to be.

"Also," he added, "how do we know that Fogg doesn't have secret escape routes?"

"I presume that the house was examined while Fogg was gone," the tall dark man said. "Why don't you ask Nemo?"

"We're always left in the dark," the predatory-looking man said.

The tall dark man shrugged and then walked over to Passepartout. He looked at him.

"I wonder if he knows anything we don't."

"The code?"

"It's been changed since he started on his trip, and we know the old one now. But he'll have some items of interest for us, I'm sure."

"We'll have to keep the gag on, since we wouldn't want the neighbors to hear his screams. So we'll leave the right hand untouched. He has to be able to write out the information."

"What if he uses his left hand to write with?"

"We'll find out."

The tall dark man said, "Before the entertainment begins, I have to revive the horse and get the cab out of the way. It's a wonder that someone hasn't noticed the beast. Where's the kitchen? A pailful should do it."

He left the room, and the yellow-green-eyed man sat down. He seemed disgruntled.

Jealousy, Passepartout thought. He was jealous of Nemo's authority. If only he could work on that. But that was a forlorn hope even if Passepartout could talk. And he couldn't talk.

A familiar voice came from the head of the stairs. Yellow-green eyes rose and walked to its foot.

"Yes?"

"Yes what, Vandeleur?"

"Yes, sir."

"Hold the colonel for a minute. I have another idea."

"Yes, sir."

Vandeleur? Passepartout thought. Where had he heard that name before?

The colonel's footsteps sounded, and he entered holding a large pail from which water sloshed.

"This should be enough to get the beast back onto its legs," he said, chuckling. "We must thank Moran sometime for discovering this rare Oriental drug. One pill, and the beast drops seemingly dead at a precisely calculated moment. One pailful of water, and it is resuscitated in a minute."

"I know that," Vandeleur said.

Now Passepartout remembered where he had heard Vandeleur's name before. He must

be the notorious Englishman whose duel with
the Duc de Val d'Orge, one of the best swords-
men of the world, had been in all the French
newspapers. The Duc had lost a hand during
the encounter and his wife afterward, since
she had run off with Vandeleur. A few years
later, Vandeleur had become, for a brief time,
the dictator of Paraguay. He had eventually
been forced to flee because of a rebellion
caused by his atrocities. The Duchess had
died during his flight, some said under circumstances which did not reflect credit upon
Vandeleur. He had also, it was said, been of
service to the British government during the
Indian mutiny, but his exploits were such that
the government did not dare acknowledge
them. There was also a story afloat that he
had never backed away from a duel with any
man, except one, the equally notorious
Captain Richard Francis Burton. Vandeleur's
admirers, however, claimed that the government had interfered because Vandeleur was
then engaged in the delicate and extremely
important task of recovering the jewels of the
baronet, Sir Samuel Levy. The duel would be
resumed whenever Vandeleur and Burton
happened to meet again, which was not likely,
since both were seldom in England.

Passepartout shivered. With such men
holding them prisoner, what chance had they?

Vandeleur said, "Your brother wants you,
Colonel."

The tall dark man set the pail down and
called up the stairs, "Shall I come up?"

"No," Nemo said. "Don't forget to stay out of the way of the horse when he first revives. The drug sometimes causes the beast to go into a frenzy. Hang onto his head for a minute, keeping out of the way of his hooves, and he'll soon be quiet."

"I haven't forgotten," the colonel said. "I'm no green recruit."

"Also," Nemo said, "I want you to take a message to Nesse I. Tell him to listen for our signals. We may use the distorter after all. There's too much chance of the police or the neighbors getting curious. Those Reform Club swine may send somebody over to ascertain if Fogg has at least gotten home even if he hasn't shown up there. And Fogg's colleagues may try a rescue attempt. He surely must have notified them that he was back."

"Why didn't you think of that before we came here?" the colonel said somewhat sulkily.

"Because, my dear brother, I had expected to overpower these Eridaneans at once. I didn't know how inept my help was."

"You were with us," the colonel said.

"Yes, and I should have handled the Frenchman myself. He would never have been able to get that shout out, and we would not now have Fogg and the woman giving us a problem. And pray shut up, brother, while I tell you what else you must do."

"All right," the colonel muttered.

"After you've delivered my message, stay at Nesse I. We don't want too many coming and going here. Remember, Fogg's a celebrated man, and if we hadn't lured his neighbors away, they'd be down around our ears by now."

"I'll miss all the fun. Can't Vandeleur go instead?"

"Do I have to repeat everything?" Nemo said in an exasperated tone. "You are dressed like a cabbie. What if someone should see a gentleman drive off a hansom?"

"Very well," the colonel said reluctantly. He turned and went to the pail.

Nemo's voice came sharply. "Can't you wait until I'm through? You will take one of the distorters with you. Nesse doesn't have any, and I think it'd be better that we be transmitted there than to the other place, which is too close to the heart of London."

"Which one?" the colonel said. "Passepartout's or the one you made?"

The one you made! Passepartout thought. Then that was why Nemo stayed behind in San Francisco! And it was his arrival via the distorter that caused the clangings. That was sorry news indeed! Nemo could *manufacture* distorters! But how had he been able to accomplish something that both Eridaneans and Capelleans had been trying to do without success for two hundred years? The original Old Ones had brought some distorters with them, those still in use, but they had lacked the knowledge to make new ones. And their desire to take some apart for analysis had been unfulfilled because opening them would cause them to blow up.

The distorter which Head had carried! Was that one which had been recently manufactured? Had he taken passage as a mere cook-steward on a small merchant sailing vessel to avoid the Eridaneans covering the liners? Had he done this because the chief of the Eridaneans knew that he was coming to Europe with the distorter?

Where then had Nemo gotten the knowledge to make a new distorter? Surely, from schematics. Where had he gotten them? From Head? But Fogg had examined Head's clothing and body, and Nemo had been examined by both Passepartout and Fogg. Still, Nemo had not been frisked again after returning to the *General Grant.*

Could Nemo have removed the schematics from Head's body during the disarming and the cleaning up of the *Mary Celeste?* The only time he had been close to Head after he had been searched was when he had helped Fogg throw the corpse overboard.

Somehow, he had gotten hold of the schematics. And he had made two new ones in San Francisco while Fogg's party was traveling east. One of the new distorters would have to be left behind. He had brought with him the other distorter when he was transmitted, undoubtedly by the device brought to London by the man from China.

And he had carried the new distorter with him to Fogg's house just in case he would not be able to get hold of Passepartout's.

The colonel went up the steps and returned a minute later. He left the house with a hard slam of the door. Nemo called out, "The fool! Will he never go quietly?"

Valdeleur got up to look through the window. He gave a cry and clutched the curtains. Then he said, "The idiot!"

He whirled and ran to the foot of the staircase and called up, "Your brother's in trouble!"

Passepartout could hear the heavy footsteps of Nemo as he ran to the room overlooking the street. A moment later, his boots sounded on the floor as he returned and on the steps as he descended. He strode to the curtains, pulled Vandeleur roughly aside, and looked out.

He swore and said, "I told him! He was to keep his body away!"

He swore again, ran to the door, opened it, and then closed it again.

Passepartout heard a shrill whinnying, the clatter of hooves, and a scream. Shouts from down the street came faintly.

Vandeleur swore also.

"The beast knocked him down and the hansom rode over him!"

He turned to Nemo.

"What do we do now?"

Nemo said, "Oh, the fool! He'll pay for this!"

"In more ways than one," Vandeleur said. "He's unconscious, the bloody blighter!"

"How he ever got to be a colonel is understandable only if you know the general level of intelligence of Her Majesty's officers," Nemo said. "But how I could be brother to him and that other idiot is explainable only by the fact that we had different mothers!"

"I didn't know that," Vandeleur muttered. "That explains why your brother's named James, too."

"And a fine lot of confusion that resulted in, too!" Nemo said. "She would insist on naming him after her father, even if my father objected!"

His expression became even harder. He said, "That's neither here nor there."

He went back up the stairs. Presumably, he was notifying whoever was stationed at the door of Fogg's bedroom of the situation.

Passepartout groaned behind the gag. If only Mr. Fogg and Aouda had known about this, they could have made a break. With only one man at their door, they might have gotten loose.

CHAPTER 19

Aouda was in her room and wondering if
Phileas Fogg would ever ask her to marry
him.

If she were called away on another mission,
she might never see him again. If he did not
ask her soon, he might not get a chance even if
he wished to do so. Perhaps he was hesitating
now only because she was a Parsi. Still, she
could pass for a European, and their children
would be even more European-looking than
she.

But she doubted that her Oriental origin
had anything to do with his failure to speak
up. What did Fogg care about the opinions of
others? No, his difficulty was his inability to
express his deepest feelings. He had too much
self-control, which meant, in effect, that in
many things he could not control his true self.

Fogg, in his room, was thinking about
asking Aouda to marry him. But what kind of
life could he offer her? It was true that, once
she started having children, she would be
exempt from missions. Yet, she would know
no ease of mind. He would be gone for long

periods, in peril most of the time, and could
be expected to be killed at any time. Moreover, if the Capelleans found out where she
lived, they would kill her and perhaps the
children, too.

At that moment, both Fogg and Aouda
heard Passepartout's cry.

Fogg ran out into the hall with a revolver in
his hand. A few seconds later, Aouda came out
of her room. She was holding a Colt six-
shooter.

Fogg gestured for her to go to the other end
of the hall so she could command the
approach up the servants' staircase. He
hurried to the landing off the big central staircase. As he did so, he heard bootsteps clatter-
ing on the stairs. He got to the landing just in
time. Three men were running up the second-
story stairs, and all were armed with weapons
which he instantly recognized as air pistols.
He also recognized two of the men. One was a
neighbor, the dissolute wenching young
baronet, Sir Hector Osbaldistone. The other
was Nemo. He had torn off the eye-mask
which half-blinded him and the putty nose
and false moustache.

Fogg's shot and Nemo's went off almost at
the same time and both missed. The three
men retreated down the stairs.

A shot sounded behind him. He whirled and
saw smoke curling from Aouda's pistol, and
then he saw Aouda stagger back until she hit
the wall. She slid down, dropping the pistol
and clutching her right shoulder. Blood

welled out from between the fingers of her
left hand.

Fogg, crying, "Aouda, Aouda," ran down the
hall to her. She was pale, and her eyes looked
strange, but she was able to murmur, "The
bullet only creased me."

He removed her hand and saw that it had
done more than just burn the skin or break it.
It had skimmed the upper part of her right
breast but had gone into her flesh just below
the collarbone. It seemed to have emerged
without striking the shoulder bone, though he
could not be sure. She was bleeding from both
wounds profusely and would soon be in
deeper shock, or even dead, if the bleeding
were not stopped.

But if he attended to her, the staircase
would be left open to the enemy.

She could not continue to man her post
here, and he could not defend both positions.
There was only one thing to do.

He lifted her and carried her down the hall
and into his bedroom. Blood dripped from her
and left a trail. Again, that could not be
helped.

In the bedroom, he placed her on his bed
and then locked the door. From the medicine
chest in the bathroom he got dressings and
bandages, which he applied in a feverish
haste. For once, he was not serene.

Aouda stared at him and muttered something. He said, "Shh, dear!" and put a finger
lightly over her lips. A few minutes later, he
completed the bandaging. Some of her color

seemed to be returning, though he was not sure that his hopes were not supplying it for his eyes. He started to move a heavy bureau toward the door when he heard a door slam down the hall. They were now on this floor and, though they had the trail of blood to follow, were searching the other rooms anyway.

Presently, the knob turned on his door. He fired his revolver at a point just above the knob. If he hit anybody he could not hear anything to indicate so.

A moment later Nemo's voice came to him. "We have you, Fogg. There's a man out in the garden with an air rifle. He'll drop you without fail if you so much as even show yourself at the windows. He's the best shot in the East and perhaps in the West, too. We have the Frenchman and his distorter, and we can shoot our way in at any time."

"Not without loss," Fogg said calmly.

Nemo said something Fogg could not hear distinctly. Footsteps sounded as a man walked heavily away. Fogg shoved the bureau toward the door but decided not to bring it against the door. He would leave it several feet away and would place burning oil lamps on its top and at its bottom. If they did try to storm him, he would shoot both lamps. The paraffin oil (called kerosene by the Americans) would form an impenetrable barrier, and some of it might even splash on the invaders and set them afire. The dangerous disadvantage of this was that he

and Aouda would have to get out of the room
to escape being burned alive. Aouda might be
incapable of getting out by herself, in which
case he would have to lower her on the rope
made out of bedsheets. This would make both
of them somewhat easy targets for the rifleman in the garden.

That would have to be taken care of when it
occurred. Fogg would throw out his last lamp
and hope that its burning would illuminate
the garden enough for him to see the rifleman.
Also, the fire might be seen by the neighbors
behind him, and an alarm would, he hoped,
force the Capelleans to run. He could, of
course, shoot out the window now and try to
attract the attention of the neighborhood. But
he had heard the fire wagons and the
explosion and had comprehended that the
explosion was a trick to draw his neighbors
away for the time being.

He set the third lamp, as yet unlit, by the
window, peered between the curtains, and
then turned away. The sky was overcast; the
garden was in an impenetrable darkness. If
only there were snow there, he might be able
to see better what the garden held.

After turning off the jet light, he got some
brandy for Aouda and lifted her head so she
could drink. Some blood had spread beyond
her bandages, but the flow seemed to have
stopped.

"Did you hear all that?" he whispered.

"Yes," she said.

"He hasn't much time to do whatever he is

going to do," he said. "And the neighbors will
surely be back soon. At least, some of the
servants will have to return; they won't want
to take the chance of displeasing their
masters by staying away too long. And our
chief is sure to reply to my telegram. Perhaps
even now the house is under surveillance by
our people."

"I trust you to see us all through," Aouda
said weakly.

"One way or the other," Mr. Fogg said.

"Did I hear you call me *Aouda dear?*"

"You were not mistaken," he said.

"Would that mean . . . ?"

"It would."

She smiled slightly, and her eyes looked
brighter.

"I have been waiting to hear you say that,"
she said. "And then . . . "

"And then . . . ?"

"And then kiss me."

Fogg stooped over and kissed her lightly.
Straightening, he said, "I dare not press my
ardor, Aouda, since you are in no condition to
receive anything but a tender nursing. But
would you marry me?"

"If we had a minister, immediately," she
said.

Passepartout, meanwhile, watched Nemo
and Vandeleur as they watched the scene on
the street. According to their comments,
which were frequently asterisked by oaths,
the plight of the colonel had attracted a
number of people returning from the excite-

ment. From Vandeleur's exclamations, the
first to reach the colonel was a street boy, a
ragged and dirty urchin. "He's not helping
him!" Vandeleur said. "He's robbing him!"

"What?" Nemo said, and he opened the curtains a trifle more.

"He's taking the distorter!" he said. "He's
running away with his wallet and the watch!"

Vandeleur turned to his chief for orders
and saw then that he was in no condition to
give them. He had been seized with a fit of
shaking.

Vandeleur said, "By God, you aren't fit to
command us!" He started to open the door,
but Nemo, by a great effort of will, overcame
the shaking. He bounded forward and struck
Vandeleur on the back of his neck with the
barrel of the air pistol. Vandeleur crumpled.
Nemo shut the door.

Though his body had quit shuddering,
Nemo's head still oscillated. And when he
spat out his recriminations at Vandeleur, he
seemed to Passepartout to resemble a giant
snake even more.

"Did you think you could really catch that
guttersnipe? What did you think would
happen when you dashed out of a house
supposedly uninhabited? And so you think
that I am not fit to command?"

Vandeleur did not answer. Nemo kicked
him heavily in the ribs and snarled, "Get up!"

Vandeleur groaned but made no effort to
rise.

Nemo placed the flats of his palms against

the door and leaned against it for a moment. When he pushed himself away a moment later, the oscillations had ceased. He started to turn away, and his composure, only just regained, was immediately lost.

Passepartout, with his acrobat's skill and agility, had gotten to his feet though his ankles were bound together. He had advanced across the room in a series of very small hops. Any small noise he might have made was drowned out by the exclamations of the two Capelleans. When he had seen Nemo starting to run toward him, he had crouched low, leaped high into the air, and kicked out in a double-sabot.

The heels of his boots caught Nemo on the side of his jaw. Nemo crashed sideways into the door and slumped to the floor. Passepartout fell heavily on his back, hurting the arms tied behind his back and knocking the wind out of him. For a moment he writhed in agony. Vandeleur groaned again and rolled over onto his side. Nemo, sitting with one side against the door, his head on his chest, seemed completely unconscious.

Passepartout, his breath regained, got to his knees with a jerk of his body. With another violent contortion, he got to his feet.

Vandeleur managed to struggle to all fours. He shook his head, an action which must have pained his injured neck, because he groaned.

There was a slight cracking sound as the Frenchman disjointed his arms. He brought them up and over his head and now had his arms in front of him. If Nemo had been able to see him, he would have understood how the three Eridaneans had managed to get free of their bonds in the cabin of the *General Grant*.

It was at this moment that someone banged on the front door and that he heard a voice raised in some room in the back of the house.

Passepartout fumbled desperately in Nemo's clothes for a knife. The banging on the door continued, and now he recognized Moran's voice as the captain approached. He was asking why in blue hazes someone had not brought the promised hot coffee and brandy? Post or no post, he was coming in for a moment. His hands were so cold that he couldn't even handle the air gun properly.

Passepartout brought a knife out of one of Nemo's boots and slashed at the ropes binding his ankles. Moran's footsteps became louder; he was just about to enter the room.

Vandeleur got onto his feet and lurched toward the Frenchman. Passepartout turned and slashed at him, gashing him on the left side of his face. Vandeleur screamed and stumbled back with one hand held over the wound. Blood spread out between his fingers and ran down his neck.

Still holding the knife, Passepartout ran across the room and raced up the steps. Just as he was about six steps from the first landing, he heard a shout behind and below him. He cleared the six steps and dived forward. He slid forward, stopped, rolled over, and saw a hole in the ceiling just above the landing where the missile from the captain's air rifle had struck. He got onto his feet and sped down the hallway. At its far end was the staircase used by the servants. If he could get to that and then back down, he might escape from the house. But it was a long way to go, and Moran was not far behind him, and if he caught him while he was still in the hall, he would probably not miss.

He dared a glance behind him. The captain had halted a few steps past the end of the hall and was bringing up his weapon to his shoulder.

Passepartout threw himself to one side so hard that he rebounded from a door. The door opposite was part way open, offering an opportunity which he could not afford to dismiss. He staggered sidewise into it and fell through. He was up quickly and locked the door. He stuck the hilt of the knife between his teeth and sawed at the rope around his wrists. The knob rattled; the door crashed as Moran vainly hurled his body against it. Passepartout cut the last fibers and stood up, his hands free.

Moran's voice shouted down the hall; somebody shouted back. Evidently Moran would be telling them to guard the door while he returned to the garden. Passepartout quickly pulled back the curtains and opened the window. He could drop one story to the walk below and dash across the garden. But Moran would be out almost as quickly, and he would have too much time to aim while Passepartout tried to scramble up over the eight-foot-high wall. No, that was out.

He swore a few Gallic oaths. He had hoped to go through the door from which he had rebounded and so have access to a street window. There he could have shouted to the people in the street or even have dived through a window. But now he was in the same situation as Fogg and Aouda.

Nemo, on coming to his senses, may or may not have had another seizure. It is safe to assume that his jaw, head, and side hurt and that he raved at his aides and threatened horrible punishments. Then he turned his attention to the banging on the door. He opened it a crack. By the illumination of the nearby gaslight, he saw Fix. Fix was dressed in a messenger's uniform.

Beyond, two men were carrying off the still form of the colonel on a stretcher. Leading them was a man carrying a leather bag. Doubtless, this was the Doctor Caber who lived near Fogg. He was bringing the colonel to his house to wait for the ambulance.

"Go away!" Nemo said through the crack. "Go away, you fool! The situation has changed!"

"What?" Fix said, and then, hesitatingly, "But you must read this telegram!"

Nemo could see that everybody in the crowd was turned to watch the colonel being carried off. He opened the door, reached out, grabbed Fix by his coatfront, and yanked him inside. He shut the door and said, "I must, must I?"

"Yes," Fix said. He looked curiously around in the light afforded by the single gas jet. "What's happened?"

"Never mind that," Nemo said. He tore the envelope from Fix's grasp. It had been opened, so obviously Fix had read it.

"Just as you told me, sir," Fix said. "I stopped the real messenger, and I showed him that I was a detective. I told him that I had to have the telegram because it was evidence in a criminal case. I gave him two shillings to assure his cooperation, then read the message and hurried here as swiftly as I could."

"Shut up!" Nemo said. He walked over to the gas jet and read the telegram silently the first time and loudly the second time. It was evident that he did not like what he read either time.

RELEASE THE THREE UNDAMAGED BY 8:30, AND YOU MAY GO UNTOUCHED. WE HAVE NESSE I. THE OLD ONE IS NO MORE. CONGRATULATIONS. YOU ARE NOW THE CHIEF. CONSIDER THE CONSEQUENCES.

                                  CHIEF OF ERID

Fix put his hands in his pockets to conceal their trembling. He said, "What does all that mean?"

"It's obvious," Nemo said scornfully. "They managed to located Nesse I when I arrived because of the noise made by the distorter. It took them some time, which is why I got away before they found it. They've killed our chief, the last . . . "

He paused, thinking of the effect on their morale if they knew that the last of the Old Capelleans was dead. He was too late. The others understood what he meant.

"The Old One is dead!" Fix said, almost wailing.

"Perhaps," Nemo said. "The Eridanean may be lying, you know, and probably is. But he's not lying about his knowledge of the situation here. So he's giving us until eight-thirty to produce Fogg, the Frenchman, and Jejeebhoy unharmed. If we don't, we'll probably be invaded, no matter how many Earthlings are attracted by the battle."

Fix started to the curtain as if he meant to look outside.

Nemo said, "Belay that! They're out there somewhere."

He stood for a moment in thought, softly rubbing his jaw, on which a swelling had appeared.

"Get Osbaldistone and Vandeleur back down here."

"And what about . . . ?"

"The others? They won't know they've been left unguarded. They won't open the door for fear they'll get a ball in the head. I want everybody to be acquainted with this new situation. Moran can be told later; if they saw him coming back into the house, they might try to leave by the windows. Hurry!"

Fix went upstairs and quietly got Vandeleur and Osbaldistone away from their posts. On the way down from the second floor, he whispered the news to them. Vandeleur said nothing. The baronet went gray. "The last of the Old Ones is dead," he murmured. "What do we do now?"

"Nemo says that the Eridaneans may be lying about that," Fix said. "But I doubt it. They must have taken Nesse I; otherwise, how would they have even known that that is what we call the prime headquarters? But Nemo is the first chief now."

Nemo affirmed everything that Fix had said. "But don't feel that the Eridaneans have any advantage over us because they might still have an Old One to lead them. For all we know, they don't have any either. Even if they do, what about it? The Old Ones were no more intelligent than we. In fact, their very alienness has handicapped us, in my opinion. It takes a genuine human being to know how to fight human beings, and now we Capelleans have one—myself—to lead them! Now we can conduct our war as we please and with a more realistic goal."

Fix wondered what Nemo meant by *more realistic*. Was he intending to abandon the Grand Plan, to use the Race for private gain only, mainly his own private gain?

Osbaldistone said, "But what about the sharing of the Blood? There is no more Blood from the Stars to mingle in our veins at the puberty ceremonies."

"So what?" Nemo said, glaring. "The Blood itself has no intrinsic value. Its only value is symbolic. From now on the blood of the human chief will be used in the ceremonies. Capelleanism is an ideal; its goal is the conquest of Earth for the good of the Earthlings. The Earthlings must be saved from themselves."

"But the way things are going, the Eridaneans might win!"

"That's close to treason," Nemo said. "It is true that the end is near, since neither we nor the enemy probably number more than a hundred each, if that. But I have a plan. We'll conduct a campaign such as the Old Ones were too inflexible, too unintelligent to conceive. We'll concentrate, bring in our people, who are scattered all over the globe, reorganize, and launch a hunt which will not stop until we have run every Eridanean to the ground and killed him. And . . . "

"Only a hundred each!" Fix said.

Nemo looked as if he wished he had not said so much. Then he said, "Enough of the future. The present is what counts, and, for the present, we must retreat. The enemy has won this round, but it'll be the last he'll win."

He took Passepartout's watch from his coat pocket and snapped the lid on its back open.

"We'll retreat, but only after Fogg and company have been eliminated," he said. "Then we use the distorter to get to Nesse II. Vandeleur, you're carrying the tape for . . . "

He stopped, his mouth hanging open. First, he paled. Then he became red.

"This isn't the Frenchman's watch!" he cried. "This doesn't have any controls! It's just a watch, that's all, just a watch!"

Fix became numb.

Vandeleur said, "What do you mean?"

"I mean those swine have tricked us!" Nemo said. "That Fogg! He must have taken the distorter and given the Frenchman a watch to carry so we'd think . . . he . . . he . . . Fogg . . . has the watch with the distorter!"

Fix said, "Then we're trapped! We can't get out!"

"No, by all the furies!" Nemo said. "We'll get it from Fogg!"

"Sir," Fix said, "why don't we just accept their terms and leave quietly?"

Fix, half-stunned, lay on the floor. He tried to rise, but, seeing that Nemo was about to hit him again, decided to stay where he was.

"Do you think for a moment they'd keep their word any more than we would ours?"

He turned away, and Fix thought it safe to get up. He was scared to speak up, but he felt that he must. Their salvation depended upon it.

"Sir," he said, "if Fogg gave his word, we'd be safe. He wouldn't go back on his word."

Nemo swung back to face him. "What, an Eridanean's word is good?"

"Eridanean or not, Fogg would not betray us because then he'd be betraying himself," Fix said. "I know the man well."

"Perhaps you know him too well!" Nemo said. "Perhaps he has seduced you into turning traitor?"

"Exactly my thinking," Vandeleur said.

Fix trembled, but he said, "Not at all. But I do know that Fogg, whatever else he may be, is a true man. He would not break his oath, not even to us."

"Not *even* to *us!*" Nemo said. "Just what do you mean by that?"

He threw the watch against the fireplace so hard that the works burst out.

"Fix, I've had my doubts about you for a long time. There is only one way you can convince me you're not a traitor; only one way you can keep from dying as a traitor."

"Yes, sir," Fix said. He tried to keep his face from twitching.

"We must have that distorter and have it quickly. There is no time for subtlety now; we must storm Fogg's room. You will lead us into it."

And so he would die, Fix thought. Fogg wouldn't miss the first man who entered. Fix would be the sacrifice, and Nemo would, in effect, have executed him. And why? Because Nemo thought Fix to be a traitor.

"Well, Fix?" Nemo said.

"If that's the way it has to be," Fix said.

"That is the way it has to be."

"Will you see that my family is taken care of?" Fix said.

"Take care of a traitor's . . . ?" Vandeleur

said, but Nemo interrupted him with a, "Quiet!"

Fix said, "I am no traitor."

Nemo's voice became softer. "Vandeleur is too hotheaded. We're all disturbed by this, but now is no time to get panicky. Yes, Fix, I promise you that if something should happen to you, your family will not have to suffer."

And what did that mean? Fix thought. That they would be killed quickly?

"We'll get the Frenchie first," Nemo said. "Sir Hector, you'll resume your post at Fogg's door. It's not likely that he'll hear us attacking the Frenchie, but if he did he might deduce that there couldn't be many of us at his door, and he might try to break out. Station yourself to one side, along the wall, so that if he does run out, you'll get the first shot."

Osbaldistone left. Nemo said, "Vandeleur, you'll have a chance to avenge the wound the Frenchie gave you. You will lead the attack."

"Excellent!" Vandeleur said. "But I'd like to carve his face before he dies."

"We don't have time for that," Nemo said. "He must be killed immediately and as silently as possible.

"Now, whatever our losses, we must get into Fogg's room and get it over with at once. That trail of blood indicates that the woman was badly wounded. She is either dead or too hurt to help Fogg, and a good thing, too, since she is an excellent shot. Fogg must be killed at once, otherwise he may open the distorter and so blow himself, and possibly all of us, to

kingdom come. I don't think he will do that
except as a last resort, so it is up to us to see
that he has no time for a last resort.

"I imagine that he has placed some
furniture before the door as a barricade. We
will remove the hinges of the door. At my
signal, Vandeleur will shoot the door lock off.
The door will be pulled away by Osbaldistone
and myself. You, Fix, will take a running jump
across the hall and dive over the barricade.
Fogg will have his room dark, but we'll turn
off the lights in the hall beforehand so our
eyes can be adjusted to a lack of light. This
will also make it difficult for Fogg to see
clearly. As you go over the barricade, Fix, fire
once to draw his fire. Then worry about how
you are going to land. We'll see the flame
from his revolver and know where to shoot
then."

Fix knew he couldn't clear that furniture in
one dive. And if Fogg had the furniture piled
all the way up to the ceiling, he'd be hanging
there a helpless target. No doubt, Nemo and
Vandeleur would be able to shoot Fogg once
they had seen his fire. But Fix wouldn't be
able to see that. He'd be dead. And for what?
For a man who had used him, not to advance
the interests of all Capelleans but only to
advance his own.

Nevertheless, he said nothing. Words would
be useless. He took his Webley from his
pocket and followed Nemo to the door behind
which Passepartout waited. Nemo used his
air pistol to shoot out the lock mechanism.

Fix opened the door, and Vandeleur rushed in with an air pistol in one hand and a knife in the other. The room was dark, but Fix carried an oil lamp which lit up enough for them to see that the Frenchman was not in the room. Nor was he hiding in the bathroom or the wardrobe or beneath the bed or behind the curtains. The windows were still locked.

"You said he wouldn't dare open his door and look out!" Vandeleur said.

"He's even more foolish than I thought," Nemo said. "I gave him too much credit for intelligence. Fix, run down and see if he's outside! He may have used the servants' staircase while we were coming up the main one!"

"Yes, sir," Fix said, "but I don't think so."

He started to run off, but Nemo called him back.

"What did you mean by that?"

"He wouldn't desert Fogg and the woman," Fix said.

"You do know these Eridaneans well, don't you?" Nemo said slowly. "Well, run on down and make sure. Then report to me on the third floor."

Fix was back a few minutes later. He found the others trying to revive a stunned Osbaldistone. The door to Fogg's room was open.

"You were right, Fix," Nemo said. "He came up here, hit Osbaldistone on the back of the head, and the three went . . . someplace. They could not have come downstairs, however. I went up the main staircase and Vandeleur went up the other. Osbaldistone just went up, so they have not had time to get far. I doubt they'd stay on this floor; they probably went on up. However, Fogg is so tricky, he may be in a room on this floor."

What a mess! Fix thought. Nemo might be a great brain, a genius at mathematics and engineering, but when it came to affairs in which lightning thought was needed, not a gigantic ratiocination, he did not do so well. He was also too arrogant, too egotistical. He underestimated everybody else. Perhaps he would learn a lesson from this and use his genius in a more appropriate manner. But what did Fix care about him? Nemo thought Fix was a traitor, and he'd see Fix die.

Well, he was a traitor, if thoughts made a man a traitor.

Nemo lifted Osbaldistone with one arm and carried the dangling body to the landing off the main staircase. He dropped the baronet, who groaned once but did not recover consciousness.

Nemo said, "Fix, you will pile furniture, curtains, anything flammable, on the landing and the steps of the servants' staircase. Vandeleur, you'll do the same for the main staircase. After the piles are completed, soak them with paraffin oil. We're going to burn down the house and with it Fogg, the Frenchman, the woman, and the distorter. The fire will bring a large crowd, into which we'll disappear. We'll meet at Nesse III."

He looked at his watch. "A quarter after eight. Fogg has thirty minutes to get to the

Reform Club. He is going to lose that bet, since he will be in Hell before then."

Fix shuddered at the image of Fogg and Passepartout and the beautiful and gentle Aouda screaming in the flames.

It took about ten minutes for the two to carry out wooden tables and chairs, curtains, bedsheets, and feather pillows and stack them on the stairs and the landings. Vandeleur and Nemo then began bringing out lamps, but not enough of these were filled with oil to satisfy Nemo.

"We'll turn on the gas jets, too," he said, "but I want to get a fire going that will absolutely prevent those three from getting over the piles. Fix, you go into the cellar and see if there are extra cans of oil. On the way back, notify the captain of what we are doing. Tell him to return to his post then and to wait until we leave before he goes over the wall. Determine that he has ladders or some means of getting over the back wall, since it will be dangerous to go through the house once the fires have thoroughly started. The jets won't be turned on until just as we leave, but the chances of an explosion will be high. Have you got that straight?"

Fix said, "Yes, sir," and he hurried off. He went into the deep and gloomy cellar, which was not as deep or as gloomy as his thoughts. A few minutes later, he emerged with two large cans of oil. There were several step ladders against the cellar wall which Moran could use. In the front room, he put the cans

down and went to a sideboard from which he
decanted a half-tumbler of brandy. He poured
this down, stopping only when he coughed.
Tears running down his cheeks, he put the
tumbler down. Then, not so pale and shaky, he
walked toward the rear of the house. On
reaching the main rear door, he looked out
into the darkness. Moran was a darker shape
among the shadows, crouched by the side of a
huge stone urn. Fix opened the door and said,
"Captain, come here quickly! I have a
message for you."

Nemo looked at his watch again. Soon, the
gentlemen in the Reform Club and the great
crowd outside would see the flames rising
and would wonder whose house was burning.

Hearing footsteps coming up the staircase,
he turned. Fix, a few seconds later, climbed
up over the pile with a big can in each hand.

"Put one down there and take the other to
Vandeleur's pile," Nemo said. "We'll set his
afire first."

Fix set one of the containers on the floor
and walked toward Nemo. Nemo turned away
to watch Vandeleur, who was bringing a
bundle of curtains to add to the large pile. Fix
reached into his coat and brought out his
revolver. He held it by the barrel.

Fogg, Aouda, and Passepartout were at a
window in a front room on the fourth story.
The gaslights below showed an almost
deserted street. Four gentlemen were standing talking across the street near the corner
light.

"They must be the men Nemo's stationed to intercept us if we should escape," Fogg said. "There's no way of getting away from them. As soon as they see us coming down on this bedsheet rope, they'll come running. We must drop fast and start shooting as soon as we reach the ground."

Aouda, sitting in a chair, said, "I still think I should stay here. I can use only one hand, and I'm not strong enough to hang on with it."

"Nonsense, my dear," Fogg said. "I told you that we will go down together and that I will have one arm around you. Our gloves will keep us from burning our hands."

"But . . ."

Aouda stopped. Fix's voice was coming from the end of the hall.

"Mr. Fogg! Believe me, this is no trap! I have knocked out Nemo and the others! I could not let them burn you alive. Please believe me, Mr. Fogg, and come quickly!"

"It might well be a trick to locate us," Fogg said.

"Mr. Fogg! Nemo said I might be a traitor, and I'm sure he was going to see that I was killed. And God knows what he meant to do to my family. Please believe me. I have a pistol, but it is in my coat, and my hands are in the air. See for yourself. But quickly!"

"It could be true. It's not entirely unforeseen," Fogg said. He walked to the door, unlocked it, and opened it a crack. There was Fix, slowly walking down the hall, his hands held high.

Fogg opened the door a little more, stuck the end of his revolver out, and said, "Come on in, Mr. Fix."

Fix entered. Fogg shut the door and said, "Where are your colleagues?"

"All unconscious, perhaps dead," Fix said. "I called Moran in and hit him over the head with the butt of my gun. Then I went upstairs and hit Nemo when his back was turned. Osbaldistone was still senseless, so I only had to make Vandeleur stand with his face to the wall and then hit him, too."

"And you did this for the reasons you stated?"

"Yes, but you'll have to protect me and my family from now on. You will, won't you?"

"Consider it done," Mr. Fogg said.

With Fix ahead of them, for Fogg was not sure that it was not a trap, they went down to the landing. All three of the Capelleans were still unconscious.

"Are you going to kill them?" Fix said.

"Would you want me to do so, Mr. Fix?" Fogg said.

"No. I do not like them, and Nemo would have killed me without mercy," Fix said. "But to slay them in cold blood . . ."

Fogg did not reply. He was searching Nemo's clothing. Within a few seconds, he pulled a small flat leather case from a pocket and took out of it small oblong papers covered with writing and diagrams that could only be seen plainly under a magnifying glass.

He said, "I was hoping he'd still be carrying these."

"What are they?" Aouda said.

"The schematics for the distorter. But how did Nemo get them from Head's body?"

"Head had them stored inside his glass eye," Fix said. "Nemo removed it when he helped you throw Head's body overboard."

"I should have raised Head's eyelids and looked at his eyes," Fogg said. "But where did Head get the schematics?"

"It was an American Eridanean who found out how to manufacture distorters," Fix said. "Head discovered that he had done so—how, I don't know—and killed him, burned down his laboratory, and fled with the schematics and the distorter which the American had made. Your chief must have found out about this at once, which is why Head took passage on the *Mary Celeste* to avoid the Eridaneans looking for him on the liners."

Fogg put the schematics in his pocket, looked at Passepartout's watch, and said, "And those men outside?"

"They are either loungers or Eridaneans waiting to see if Nemo will surrender you to them." He told Fogg about the telegram from the Eridanean chief.

Fogg looked at his watch again. "Let's go," he said.

"Where?" Aouda said.

"To the Reform Club. We have exactly ten minutes to get there if I am to win the bet."

Verne says that Passepartout dragged Fogg

outside by the collar, hailed a cab, and the two drove off at a reckless speed, running over two dogs and overturning five carriages. This is true, except for the dragging by the collar. But Aouda and Fix followed in another carriage at a somewhat slower pace. Aouda's wound did not permit her to be jostled much, and, moreover, she stopped long enough to inform the gentlemen on the corner, who were indeed Eridaneans, that they were safe and that Fix was now one of them. She also told the gentlemen to pick up the Capelleans in Fogg's house.

These hastened to do so, but, alas, they were too late to catch Vandeleur, Moran, and Nemo. These had recovered and fled, leaving Sir Hector behind. As the Eridaneans entered the front door, the trio went over the back wall of the garden.

Osbaldistone was carried out as if he were drunk and driven off in a cab. What happened to him thereafter, no one knows.

As everybody does know, Phileas appeared three seconds before his time was up. He collected twenty thousand pounds, though he had spent nineteen thousand during the journey, his last expenditure being a hundred pounds to the cabman who drove to the Reform. The remaining thousand pounds, he split between Fix and Passepartout. Within two days, Fogg and Aouda were married, and Verne ends his narrative on a happy note.

But what of the story behind Verne's? The other log of Fogg ends on the day he took

Aouda as his bride. No other literature on this subject has ever been turned up, so we must reconstruct the postlude. Fortunately, we have common sense and some narratives of a few other authors about some of the people Fogg met to help us build a reasonable sequel.

The Eridaneans and Capelleans, with Nemo out of the way, and through Fix's offices, must have made a truce or perhaps even an alliance. Many on both sides felt, as Fix did, that there was no sense in continuing this secret and gory war which could end only in extermination for one side and near-extermination for the other. Besides, life as a mere Earthling was hard enough without adding to it the perils of Capelleanism and Eridaneanism.

Moran, we know from the writings of a certain Dr. John Watson, went back to India and stayed there for years. After retiring as a colonel, he rejoined his chief in London.

The chief, whom Watson called Professor James Moriarty, seems to have abstained from a criminal career for some years. Probably, the shock of being outwitted by Fogg and of losing the chieftainship of the Capelleans accelerated his illness. Nemo became a teacher for a while, but, after recovering much of his health, went back into business. He formed a vast criminal ring, though he succeeded in keeping his part in it unknown for a long time. Eventually, he experienced a bad fall—and falls—near the little Swiss village of Meiringen. It was symbolically and esthetically appropriate that a man who started his career in the water should end there.

Nemo's brother, the colonel, had been so injured by the frenzied horse that he retired from the army. However, he did go back to his evil ways when older, though not as his brother's partner. He appears briefly in a semifictional book by Robert Louis Stevenson, *The New Arabian Nights*.

Vandeleur plays a more important role in the same book.

Fogg retired to Fogg Shaw in rural Derbyshire, where he tinkered around in his laboratory and raised a number of children, all as handsome as he or as beautiful as their mother.

Fix continued to be a detective, though he now served only one master, or mistress in this case, Her Majesty.

Passepartout settled down as manager of Fogg's estate and married a local girl.

And what of the Grand Plan?

From the situation of the world today, we may assume that it was abandoned.

What about the distorters?

Did the Eridaneans and Capelleans decide to throw the few remaining devices, along with the schematics, into the ocean? Or did some greedy person steal them? That we hear no more of the nine great clangings means nothing. It may be that someone, perhaps Fogg, invented a means for suppressing or canceling these noises. In which case, some of the many mysterious and seemingly impossible disappearances of things and people in this world may be explained.

Whatever happened to the distorters, the important thing is that Fogg and Aouda and Passepartout and Fix lived happily for many years. They may still be living for all anybody knows.

Fogg may even have thought that, after a hundred years, the public could be informed of the true story.

That Phileas Fogg's initials and your editor's are the same is, I assure you, only a coincidence.

ADDENDUM

The following article appeared in *Leaves from The Copper Beeches*, published for The Sons of the Copper Beeches Scion Society of the Baker Street Irregulars by the Livingston Publishing Co., Narberth, Pa., 1959

A SUBMERSIBLE SUBTERFUGE
OR PROOF IMPOSITIVE
By H. W. Starr

A familiar literary phenomenon is the novel which is actually autobiography, biography, or factual narration disguised as fiction. We see it in the work of Thomas Wolfe, Dickens, Watson, and a score of other writers; and perhaps we may find it also in two novels that we have all read as children: Jules Verne's *Twenty Thousand Leagues under the Sea* and *The Mysterious Island*. The popular impression of the most interesting character of this saga, an individual using the alias Captain Nemo, is that of an Indian prince, a disillusioned and embittered idealist, sickened

by civilization, who gathered a little band of
kindred spirits, devoted to him and tenderly
cared for by him, and vanished forever into
the depths of the sea in a marvellous submarine which he had secretly assembled. Yet
if we examine these tales we find certain inexplicable and absolutely irreconcilable inconsistencies appearing in them—for
example the dates. According to *Twenty
Thousand Leagues*, the *Nautilus* is recorded
as first being observed by seafarers in 1866
and vanishing in the Maelstrom in 1868,[1] at
which time Professor Aronnax and his companions escaped from the vessel. Yet we are
surprised at the beginning of *The Mysterious
Island*,[2] when Captain Nemo is a silvery-
haired old ruin, the last survivor of a
company of at least twenty-four sailors and
two officers, living in solitude on Lincoln
Island, that the date is given as 1865![3]

---

[1] Jules Verne, *Twenty Thousand Leagues under the Sea*, transl.
P.S. Allen (Chicago: McNally, 1922), pp. 3, 471.

[2] Jules Verne, *The Mysterious Island* (New York: Scribner's,
1924).

[3] Discrepancies of this sort are innumerable: the Captain must
have had time to design and build the submarine, collect a
large crew, wait for the crew to die off one by one, age from a
vigorous man apparently in his thirties or forties (the period of
Twenty Thousand) to sixty years of age (*Mys. Is.*, p. 458), and
retire to Lincoln Island—a sequence of events that would seem
to require about twenty years. Yet, according to the data in
Mys. Is., all this occurred between 1858, the date of the
suppression of the Sepoy Rebellion, and 1865, a bare seven
years. The reference to the Sepoy Mutiny in the *Mys. Is.* (p. 456)
cannot be an error—it is lengthy and explicit—nor may we
simply assume another and much earlier rebellion is meant,
for the detailed description of the *Nautilus* shows that much of

There are other inconsistencies. According
to the *The Mysterious Island*, Nemo is an
Indian Prince Dakkar, and presumably at
least some of such a man's followers would be
Indians. This could hardly havé escaped the
observation of Professor Aronnax, who for
months watched them fishing and working
about the *Nautilus*. Yet never does it seem to
occur to him that any are Orientals. Instead,

---

its construction was based on improvements made on
scientific discoveries of the 1850's or later (the work of
Ruhmkorff and Bunsen, for example, *Twenty*, pp. 98, 125).
Even more significant is the reference by Captain Nemo
(*Twenty*, p. 105) to fishing experiments at great depths made
in 1864, experiments that he could not possibly have known of
after he was cut off from society and which he clearly considered when designing the *Nautilus*. In other words, the vessel
was not launched until 1864 or 5—if not later. To add to this
total confusion, in the *Mys. Is.* (p. 457) the date of the
professor's escape from the *Nautilus* is given as June 22, 1867
(in *Twenty Thousand* it is 1868—see p. 471), but Captain Nemo
dies on October 15, 1868, a much older man than a few months
or a year could account for (*Mys. Is.*, p. 468). Furthermore, the
colonists of Lincoln Island, totally cut off from civilization
from 1865 to 1869, have heard, *before* their arrival in 1865, of
Aronnax's adventure, which could not, of course, have been
made public until 1867 or 8. On p. 454 of *Mys. Is.* (Oct. 15, 1868)
Captain Nemo says he has passed "three long years in the
depths of the sea" cut off from any communication with civilization—a statement which is in conflict with practically every
other date in both books! Some vague notion of a certain
inconsistency in dates seems to have worked its way into M.
Verne's consciousness, for in two notes (*Mys. Is.*, pp. 306, 455)
he remarks that his readers may observe "some discrepancy in
the dates; but later again, they will understand why the real
dates were not given at first." Unfortunately, there is
absolutely nothing in the book which would lead the readers to
such an understanding.

he says that all are Europeans.[4] No matter how dubious in the eyes of modern science identification of nationality from appearance may be, it is unlikely that a veteran biologist would mistake, after close and repeated observations, some two dozen Hindus for Europeans—especially Irishmen! Furthermore, in *The Mysterious Island* (p. 460) Captain Nemo defends the sinking of the hostile warship witnessed by Professor Aronnax on the grounds that he "was in a narrow and shallow bay—the frigate barred my way." Yet the Professor's account *(Twenty Thousand*, pp. 473-82) unquestionably proves that for over twenty-four hours Captain Nemo deliberately lured the frigate to follow him until it suited his whim to turn and sink her.

Many more such instances may be piled up, but I think the conclusion is too obvious for us to cite them. *The Mysterious Island* is a work of fiction turned out by a professional novelist who, after some editing of the manuscript of Professor Aronnax to ensure its popular sale, decided to capitalize on its success by writing an entirely imaginary sequel and, in doing so, to rehabilitate a rather brutal man by painting him as a Byronic hero with a heart of gold—a procedure thoroughly compatible with the literary fashion of the day. We must dismiss it, and with this dismissal must also vanish

[4] See p. 148, where the professor is sure some of them are Irish, French, Slavs, Greeks, or Candiotes, but "the European type was discernible in each one of them."

any and all reliance upon this later volume's account of Captain Nemo's character, moral values, and life as "Prince Dakkar."

Having disposed of *The Mysterious Island* as a source of information, let us now turn our attention to *Twenty Thousand Leagues*. Since this volume appears to be a novelist's rewriting or editing of Professor Aronnax's memoirs, we may put some faith in matters of fact observed by the professor. However, we should be more cautious in acceptance of matters of interpretation, for here the romantic Byronic aura which Aronnax and Verne saw surrounding the captain may mislead us. Consider the concept of Captain Nemo as the half-noble, half-ruthless, golden-hearted, disillusioned idealist, who loves the oppressed in general, his crew in particular, and who has provided an "Ark of Refuge" for a selected few to whom he is bound by ties of mutual devotion. Just how does the man Nemo really treat this crew of his? First of all, we should estimate how many men are on the *Nautilus*. From various bits of information it is clear that he cannot have had fewer than twenty-four crewmen in the original group and he may have had thirty or more.[5] The living quarters provided for these men are

---

[5] When the *Nautilus* is imprisoned by an iceberg in South Polar waters it is necessary for the crew, working in two shifts which must have been of approximately equal numbers, to dig it out. In the first shift, "a dozen of the crew . . . and in their midst" Ned Land and the captain get to work (*Twenty*, p. 414). Even if we count Ned and the captain as part of this "dozen," we find ten men in each shift, a total of 20. A more normal reading of

very interesting. The description of the berth-
room in which they seem to have spent practically all of their existence when not engaged
in their duties indicates that the room could
not have measured more than 22 feet by 16
feet.[6] If we line this room with tripledecker
berths, we can just fit twenty-four men[7] (the
smallest possible number) into these
quarters, generously leaving clear in the
center a floor space of 10 feet by 16 feet, in

---

the text would give 12 to a shift, totalling 24. To this figure we
must add the man previously killed by an accident in the
engine room and the tenants of the coral cemetery (pp. 210-30
passim). The number of graves is not stated, but the plural is
repeatedly used and the specific number *two* is not employed.
Hence we may assume a minimum of three men were buried
there. Consequently, the original complement of the *Nautilus*
must have consisted of Captain Nemo, one officer (or originally
more), and at least 24 crewmen—probably 28 sailors or even
over 30. One might argue that there cannot have been many
more since only about ten (p. 448) accompanied Captain Nemo
and his three prisoners in their poulp chopping activities, a
situation that certainly seems to require the full strength of the
ship's company. On the other hand, the very limited deck space
of the *Nautilus* might have made a larger number than fourteen
axe swinging enthusiasts more of a menace than a help.
[6] The length given by the professor is 16. The maximum exterior width of the *Nautilus* was 26 feet. If we subtract two feet
for the thickness of the remarkably strong hull and two more
for the passageway down which the professor walked (he went
from one end of the ship to the other, passing the closed door of
the crewroom [p. 98], the interior of which he never saw; hence
we must admit the existence of this passage), we reach the
figure 22. Since we have no assurance the room was halfway
from the bow of this tapering vessel, the correct figure may be
only 18 or 20 feet.
[7] We assume that somewhere in the vessel was a cubbyhole
where the lieutenant could swing his hammock in solitary
grandeur.

which they may dress, store their clothes, eat,
lounge, and otherwise amuse themselves.[8]
These are slum conditions of the foulest sort.
But perhaps Captain Nemo, whose bedroom
is described as "severe almost . . . monkish,"[9]
lived under equally Spartan conditions? Well,
his private[10] suite, into which the crew never
intruded, consisted of the following
apartments in addition to his fifteen foot bedroom; a dining room (15 feet long) equipped,
among other articles, with "exquisite
paintings" and with oak and ebony
sideboards bearing "china, porcelain, and

[8] There is no reference to any mess or recreation room for
them, nor is it easy to see from the description of the vessel (pp.
81-108 *passim*) where any such cabin could have been located
unless the extremely bare room by the stair well (containing
one table and five chairs, p. 63) was occasionally used as a
mess. However the paucity of its furnishings and the fact that
the professor and his friends were incarcerated there
whenever the captain wanted them out of the way suggests that
this was the brig. Question: If a hoosegow of this size (20' x 10',
p. 62)—and space is at a premium on a submarine—was needed
on the *Nautilus*, does it not indicate that Captain Nemo
expected (and perhaps had) either a good deal of trouble from
his devoted crew or a considerable body of other prisoners at
one time or another?

[9] Apart from the nautical instruments on the walls, a few toilet
articles, and some large paintings (p. 483) on the wall which the
professor rather inexplicably failed to see for the first nine or
ten months, it contained only "a small iron bedstead, a table,"
and a chair or two. See pp. 91-92.

[10] And private it was, by gum! With the exception of the
steward who served the meals and was so severely disciplined
that he didn't dare show even a flicker of resentment after Ned
Land had half choked him to death (p. 74) and the mate, who
appeared only to mark the submarine's position on the chart,
no member of the ship's company is ever recorded as entering
the entire forward part of the *Nautilus*.

crystal glass of inestimable value" (p. 81); a library (also 15 feet in length and running like the former room, the width of the ship) containing overstuffed divans upholstered in brown Morocco, movable desks, a huge table for periodicals, cigars, a bronze brazier for a cigar lighter, and a private collection of 12,000 books (pp. 85-87); a magnificent museum-drawing room (30 feet by 18 feet) provided with an arabesques ceiling, pictures "of great value" by Raphael, Leonardo, Titian, Rubens, etc. ("the greater part of which" Professor Aronnax "had admired in the galleries of Europe"), statues of bronze and marble, a large piano-organ, an invaluable collection of marine life in "splendid glass cases," and pearls some of which were "larger than a pigeon's egg" and which surpassed the most valuable pearl hitherto known.[11] With this[12] at his disposal, I think that one can see how Captain Nemo managed to survive the hardships of that severe, almost monkish bedroom.

In any event, the account does not fit the concept of a loving master served by an admiring group of acolytes. It does, however, fit the picture of the sybaritic commander of an old-fashioned warship living in luxurious quarters and ruling with an iron hand a crew of tough fighting men whose fear of their captain and expectation of high financial gain

[11] That of the Imaum of Muscat (pp. 88-90).
[12] Thus out of a total length of 232 feet (65 feet of which was the engine room) 75 feet of the *Nautilus* had been set aside for the exclusive use of the captain.

may make them willing to put up with physical discomfort.

One or two puzzling events are reported by the professor. The events we can accept, but his interpretation is less reliable. On a very rough day when the captain, the mate, and the professor are on deck, the two officers observe through a telescope an object so distant that the professor (whose vision seems normal) is unable to see even a speck with his naked eye. The officers are greatly excited, the professor and company are heaved into the brig again, doped, and a ship is sunk by the *Nautilus* (pp. 216-220). These are the facts; the interpretations that we are given is this: Captain Nemo on first sighting the ship immediately recognized it—necessarily by its flag—as belonging to that unidentified nation which he so loathed, and consequently rammed it with the ship spur mounted on the bow of his submarine. Yet a little thought shows us that this cannot be entirely correct: if the ship was so far away that Professor Aronnax was unable to distinguish it at all with the naked eye, how could the man Nemo even with a telescope possibly recognize its colors?[13] The conclusion, therefore, is that

[13] Should it be argued that the telescope was tremendously powerful—let us say 20, 30 power, or more—anyone who has tried to use such an optical instrument will reply that without placing it on a tripod mounted on a firm foundation one will find it almost impossible to see anything whatsoever. I doubt that on a pitching deck any instrument of much more than 10 or 15 power could be used effectively—and that would be utterly inadequate in this situation.

the one way Nemo could know that here was
the ship upon which he had designs was by
being given information that at this date and
in this location, just one particular vessel
could be expected. Yet our saline recluse
could possess up-to-date information concerning shipping only from some source
external to the *Nautilus*. And of this
supposition we have confirmation. He
appears to have devoted considerable effort
to scooping up the treasure from the sunken
ships in the Bay of Vigo. About a million
dollars in gold (pp. 300-01) he sent ashore in
the pinnace after his intermediary, one
Nicholas Pesca (an amphibious individual
who appears to have devoted most of his time
to swimming from one island of the Cyclades
to another), had, during an evening dip, swum
out to the *Nautilus* (p. 299). The interpretation
which Captain Nemo skillfully plants in the
professor's mind (pp. 326-27) is that he, as a
friend to all oppressed groups, has devoted
his wealth to the Cretans, who at this time
were in revolt against Turkish rule. The facts
are that he is in the habit of sending part of
his takings ashore and that he does have
certain connections with civilization which
might supply him with data concerning shipping and cargo schedules.

Now, following Watson's method (since we
dare not arrogate to ourselves the techniques
of the Master), let us see what conclusions we
can come to concerning the puzzling
character of the man Nemo:

1. He had a wide educational background—especially in biology, music, sculpture, painting, and history.

2. He must have been a genius of breathtaking stature in the fields of mathematics, physics, and theoretical engineering[14] to have designed such a submersible as the *Nautilus*.

3. Yet, strange to say, although Nemo surely had a reasonable acquaintance with the handling of ships by the time Professor Aronnax met him, we cannot be quite so certain that his practical maritime experience is very extensive. There seem to be curious lapses here. As a sailor the worthy captain is constantly—and accidentally—bumping into things: three passenger ships (not to be confused with the deliberate rammings), one iceberg, the Maelstrom, and the island of Gilboa. Furthermore, wonderful though the design of the vessel is, it has features which an experienced marine engineer would hardly

[14] The engines of the *Nautilus* are described as run by electricity alone (a modern submarine usually has two sets, one electrical and one diesel), but their tremendous power and their speed of 50 m.p.h. lead one to the strong suspicion that they were really atomic engines. Furthermore, the incredible strength of the vessel far surpasses that of any submarine of today. The *Nautilus* survived a descent to a depth of *48,000* feet (p. 357)—more than ten times the level reached by a bathyspheric descent of 1949, which in its turn attained a depth far greater than any twentieth-century submarine can reach. The mathematical genius required for this engineering feat is vastly beyond our own day, for it almost seems that such construction could be achieved by only someone capable of putting into practice the principle of molecular adaptation. This, however, must remain speculative.

incorporate into its design. For example, quite unlike almost all large vessels of the last thousand years or more—submarine or surface—it has no cutwater unless the very slight elevation of the deck provided a most inadequate one, for the bow is completely conical as it tapers to a sharply pointed spur. Since the deck elevation is only about a yard above water level, this means that in anything but a dead calm at any speed above the barest crawl tons of water would be constantly deluging the pilot's cage whenever the *Nautilus* traveled on the surface.[15] Walking on deck when the vessel was under way must have been a singularly damp—not to say hazardous—procedure. Indeed, the design of the *Nautilus* is amazing in its total subordination of the everyday needs of navigation to sheer military utility. It is an armored ram, but such a ram as could never be found in any classical trireme, Venetian war gallery, or nineteenth-century ram. It is a cigar shaped cylinder with pointed ends, one surmounted with a spur, retractable pilot and lantern cages, and collapsible railing—streamlined, in fact, so that the entire submarine may pass completely in needlelike fashion through a hostile vessel. So extreme a design is hardly necessary merely to sink a ship, and it reveals an appalling savagery of purpose in the

---

[15] The fact that the pilot could seldom see where he was going may have had something to do with the perpetual collisions which dot the *Nautilus*'s career.

designer which ill consorts with a bitter and disillusioned yet golden-hearted friend to the oppressed.

4. He is clearly a man of commanding and domineering personality, a man who rigidly draws the caste line.[16] This combination of an arrogant personality and a marked distinction between groups is of course to be observed in many walks of life, but it is particularly noticeable in those who follow two professions: officers in military organizations and teachers. Nemo, however, repeatedly shows an extreme aversion to the human race in general, a quality not exceptionally common in military men, but one which is frequently to be found in members of the pedagogical profession after several years spent in the refreshing experience of purveying sweetness and light to large quantities of Youth.

5. Finally, the captain is definitely a man of somewhat dubious ethics. No matter how romantic a light is cast over his activities, he is guilty of destruction of shipping, murder, and possibly theft. To put it bluntly, he is simply a pirate, a pirate who has turned to financial advantage his extraordinary scientific skill and who maintains on land

[16] Note that, as has already been observed, the sailors are not admitted to his quarters nor is even the mate allowed there save in performance of his duties. Furthermore, his treatment of the three prisoners shows that he accepts the professor as more or less his social equal and very decidedly does not accept Ned Land or the well educated servant Conseil.

perhaps a small[17] but necessarily a widely distributed network of secret agents, who at pre-arranged meetings provide him with essential information concerning the shipment of valuable cargoes.

On the basis of these conclusions I think that we can now advance the hypothesis which has already occurred to the reader: It is not likely that the portrait of Captain Nemo in *Twenty Thousand Leagues under the Sea* is a portrayal of a sinister figure well known to us —Professor James Moriarty? Let us examine some of the resemblances—or apparent lack of resemblances:

(a) Physical appearance: At first glance Nemo and Moriarty seem to have little in common save their high foreheads and stature, but consideration of their respective ages will modify this assumption. When first encountered in 1867 Captain Nemo is described as between thirty-five and fifty years of age, but when one realizes his strength, endurance, and agility, it is evident that between thirty-five and forty would be a

---

[17] No very elaborate organization would be needed, since most of the information could be picked up from the daily newspapers. Incidentally, the reader should note (pp. 299-300, 325) that *after* the professor has blundered into the saloon and witnessed frogman Nicky Pesca and his cohorts collecting their cut, the captain tells him that the gold ingots came from the sunken galleons in Vigo Bay. He had to make up some story to account for what the professor had witnessed. If this one happened to be the truth, very well—but, as far as we can tell, the gold delivered on Feb. 14 (p. 297) may have been looted from the ship we know the captain sank on Jan. 18 (pp. 214-15).

much more accurate estimate.[18] There seem to be no differences[19] that the passage of twenty-five years will not account for. (In passing we may note that the Nemo-Moriarty identification here solves a problem which must have puzzled many Sherlockians: no matter how enraged Moriarty was, how willing to die, and how tricky the footing at Reichenbach may have been, he never would have hoped that a stooped, sedentary, elderly ex-mathematics professor could succeed, without even employing the element of surprise, in a physical assault upon a thirty-eight year old, six-foot athlete well known for his boxing, wrestling, and single-stick ability. Those of us in the teaching profession have often eyed the athletes infesting the rear row

[18] He takes a tremendous undersea hikes which exhaust the others, attacks a huge shark with a hunting knife, hacks up giant cuttlefish with an axe, and floors the Herculean Ned Land with one punch.

[19] Here one slight hitch regrettably manifests itself: Nemo's eyes are described as black (p. 64); Moriarty's were gray ("Empty House," p. 563). Professor Aronnax makes his observation on the day after the collision of the *Nautilus* and the *Abraham Lincoln*, and it is possible that the phrase "black eyes" may refer to the ocular disfigurement likely to occur under such conditions: Appealing though this explanation may be, there is a more plausible one. We may be sure that M. Verne edited and polished the Aronnax manuscript for publication. Had the professor omitted to mention the color of Nemo's penetrating eyes, Verne would have been sure to supply it and, being a confirmed Gallic romanticist, would have made them the black eyes of the Byronic hero-villains of the exotic Gothic novel tradition—not to be confused with the superior Anglo-American literary code which requires all heroes to have steely gray eyes.

with thoughts of homicide drifting through our minds; yet we would only dream of a bare handed assault. If Moriarty were Nemo, though, the picture changes: a former athlete at the age of sixty or so may still possess great physical strength, and the consciousness of his youthful prowess and experience in violent conflict gives him the mental attitude which in a moment of desperation would make such an attack possible.[20])

Captain Nemo could hardly have been born later than 1831; Mr. Edgar Smith[21] has speculated that Moriarty was born about 1846, but so late a date seems improbable. It would make Moriarty about forty-six years old at the time of his death; yet the descriptions of his physical appearance in the "Final Problem" (pp. 544-45) and the *Valley of Fear* (p. 910) are more appropriate to a man in the sixties or even in the seventies than to a man in the forties. If we placed his birth about 1830 he would be around sixty-two at the time of his death, an age which agrees with the physical descriptions and with the approximate birth-date of Nemo.

(b) Educational level: Mr. Smith indicates that Moriarty came from a cultured background, as Nemo did. Both men were fond of

[20] Holmes seems to be aware of Moriarty's physical prowess: "There cannot be the least doubt that he would have made a murderous attack on me." ("Final Problem," p. 551).

[21] "The Napoleon of Crime," *Baker Street and Beyond* (Morristown, N.J.: Baker Street Irregulars, 1957).

art. Nemo had thirty old masters[22] and Moriarty kept, at considerable risk, a very expensive Greuze in his study *(Valley of Fear,* pp. 910-11).

(c) Manner: Moriarty was a teacher, a member of a family with some military tradition (his brother, we know, was a colonel), and of so forceful and dominant a personality that the unhappy Porlock wobbled in his dishonest boots at a mere glance from the Napoleon of Crime. He obviously had little devotion to humanity in general. All are traits we have noted in Nemo.

(d) Biographical data: We know surprisingly little about Moriarty's life.[23] Certainly it would have been possible for him to drop out of sight for three or four years[24]

---

[22] The one picture that seems to have had personal significance for Nemo was a portrait of a young woman and two children hanging on his bedroom wall (p. 483). This is taken by the casual reader to represent Nemo's presumably defunct spouse and offspring; but is it not more probable that on this occasion, having just completed a particularly juicy mass murder, the youthful Moriarty, who so early in his career might well suffer from a pang or two of conscience, was stretching out his arms to the portrait of his mother and her two wee bairns, James Moriarty and James Moriarty?

[23] See Smith, *op. cit.* Moriarty wrote his treatise on the binomial theorem when only twenty-one, got a mathematical chair on the strength of it, acquired a dubious reputation, left the university, set up in London as an army coach (military tradition again), and formed a vast criminal organization. We do not know any of the pertinent dates.

[24] No more time would be needed. The *Nautilus* was first observed in 1866, and M. Aronnax implies that there were no further sightings of it by ships after 1868. Moriarty would have realized that the game was definitely up after Aronnax's escape and that it would be far too risky to continue his venture once the *Nautilus* was generally known to be a piratical submersible. He got out while the getting was good.

during his thirties without Holmes's taking
any particular notice of it. So brilliant a
criminal could have buried all tracks so
effectively that even the master could not uncover the Nemo episode after a quarter of a
century.[25]

(e) Mathematical and scientific genius: This
has been amply demonstrated for both men.[26]

(f) Another curious point of resemblance is
to be found in Nemo's interest in scientific
men. Clearly the only sensible thing for a
pirate captain to do when he found Aronnax,
Land, and the valet squatting on top of the
Nautilus was to attach a few heavy weights
and drop them overboard. A man who
practiced wholesale murder could have had
no moral scruples about so trifling a gesture,
but Nemo, a proficient amateur biologist, had
discovered that one of these men was an inter-
nationally famous zoologist whose works
were in his own library—and by this time the
captain, whose only associates were a crew of
hardbitten buccaneers, must have been desperately lonely for intellectual companionship. Consequently he saved Aronnax. (Incidentally, observe the smug satisfaction with

[25] Yet it is odd to note in W. Baring-Gould's *Chronological
Holmes*, pp. 157-77 *passim*, that out of the ten or so Holmes
cases involving maritime matters, eight occurred during
Moriarty's lifetime.
[26] It seems clear from the studies of Mr. A. C. Simpson, "The
Curious Incident of the Missing Corpse," *BSJ*, n.s. IV (1954),
23-24, and Mr. Smith that Moriarty had done very advanced
work in atomic theory, and the obviously atomic engines of the
Nautilus have been noted above (n. 14).

which Nemo-Moriarty impresses his superiority upon a professional colleague such as M. Aronnax. There can be no doubt that this man was a college teacher.)

(g) A young mathematical genius of criminal tendencies is very likely to start his illegal career[27] by engaging in some activity in which he can exploit his special talents. Only later, when Moriarty had the time, the capital, and the foundation provided by his information service for the *Nautilus*, would he develop a vast organization of pickpockets, burglars, thugs, and gunmen. Members of these particular criminal strata are not found on the campus in very great numbers.

It is, therefore, difficult indeed for the writer to resist the identification of Professor Moriarty and Captain Nemo and to refrain from suggesting that here we have the first major step up in a spectacular criminal career whose final step down was a long one to the bottom of Reichenbach Falls.

[27] Outfitting the *Nautilus*, Captain Nemo *said*, cost about $1,737,000 (*Twenty*, p. 108), a sum which it does not seem likely the *young* Moriarty would have on hand. However, there is such a thing as credit, and since his orders were placed with dozens of different firms, the man whose *Dynamics of an Asteroid* dropped the scientific press cold in its tracks would surely have the timing and mathematical ingenuity for the necessary juggling. One fears that Messrs. Creusot, Penn, Laird, Scott, Cail, Krupp, Hart, *et al.* had a long wait before their bills were paid.